THE
CHILDREN'S
TREASURY

THE CHILDREN'S TREASURY

BEST-LOVED STORIES AND POEMS
FROM AROUND THE WORLD

Edited by Paula S. Goepfert

DISCOVERY BOOKS

Published in Canada
by Discovery Books
Key Porter Books Limited
70 The Esplanade
Toronto, Ontario
Canada, M5E 1R2

ISBN 1-55013-019-6

Design: Don Fernley
Jacket Design: Marie Bartholomew
Typesetting: Compeer Typographic Services Ltd.
Printed and bound in Italy

87 88 89 90   6 5 4 3 2 1

Contents

To the Reader

ADULTS will tell you that the book you are holding is an *anthology*, or a collection, of classic children's literature. As they look over the contents, they will recognize the names of stories they have loved. Perhaps they will be especially happy to see "Aladdin and the Wonderful Lamp" and "Rapunzel," or chapters from *Treasure Island*, *Anne of Green Gables*, *The Adventures of Tom Sawyer*, and *The Wind in the Willows*—or poems by Edward Lear, Elizabeth Coatsworth, Robert Frost, and Dennis Lee. Perhaps someone has made a gift of this book to you because he or she rightly saw all the treasures that it holds.

Now I want to tell you what I have felt as I have worked on *The Children's Treasury*. I would not try to tell you that you are not holding a book—what I want you to consider is that you are also holding an *invitation*. This book really invites you to enjoy a lifetime of reading.

I don't expect you to read it efficiently—cover to cover. Start by reading what looks most interesting to you. When you find something you really like, go to the library, or to a book store, and you will discover more of what you've enjoyed here. I can make that a promise because I know that these writers and poets are among the best of all time. I know, too, that the kinds of stories here—folktales, fairy tales, and fables—are so popular that they fill volumes.

And what happens when you think you have finished reading *The Children's Treasury*? Well, I don't think that will ever happen. I have read "The Village Blacksmith" by Henry Wadsworth Longfellow dozens of times, but I don't feel that I have ever "finished" reading it. I feel the same way about Robert Frost's poem "Stopping by Woods on a Snowy Evening" and . . . I know you will find your favourites, too.

So, there you have my idea of the book you are now holding—it is an invitation that you can make last forever. Have you ever had a better invitation?

Paula S. Goepfert

The Elephant's Child

This story is from a book by Rudyard Kipling called the Just So Stories. *Like the other stories in the book, it offers a wonderfully clever and funny explanation of why animals are . . . just so.*

I N THE High and Far-Off Times the Elephant, O Best Beloved, had no trunk. He had only a blackish, bulgy nose, as big as a boot, that he could wriggle about from side to side; but he couldn't pick up things with it. But there was one Elephant—a new Elephant—an Elephant's Child—who was full of 'satiable curtiosity, and that means he asked ever so many questions. *And* he lived in Africa, and he filled all Africa with his 'satiable curtiosities. He asked his tall aunt, the Ostrich, why her tail-feathers grew just so, and his tall aunt the Ostrich spanked him with her hard, hard claw. He asked his tall uncle, the Giraffe, what made his skin spotty, and his tall uncle, the Giraffe, spanked him with his hard, hard hoof. And still he was full of 'satiable curtiosity! He asked his broad aunt, the Hippopotamus, why her eyes were red, and his broad aunt, the Hippopotamus, spanked him with her broad, broad hoof; and he asked his hairy uncle, the Baboon, why melons tasted just so, and his hairy uncle, the Baboon, spanked him with his hairy, hairy paw. And *still* he was full of 'satiable curtiosity! He asked questions about everything that he saw, or heard, or felt, or smelt, or touched, and all his uncles and aunts spanked him. And still he was full of 'satiable curtiosity!

One fine morning in the middle of the Precession of the Equinoxes this 'satiable Elephant's Child asked a new fine question that he had never asked before. He asked, "What

does the Crocodile have for dinner?" Then everybody said, "Hush!" in a loud and dretful tone, and they spanked him immediately and directly, without stopping, for a long time.

By and by, when that was finished, he came upon Kolokolo Bird sitting in the middle of a wait-a-bit thorn-bush, and he said, "My father has spanked me, and my mother has spanked me; all my aunts and uncles have spanked me for my 'satiable curtiosity; and *still* I want to know what the Crocodile has for dinner!"

Then Kolokolo Bird said, with a mournful cry, "Go to the banks of the great grey-green, greasy Limpopo River, all set about with fever-trees, and find out."

That very next morning, when there was nothing left of the Equinoxes, because the Precession had preceded according to precedent, this 'satiable Elephant's Child took a hundred pounds of bananas (the little short red kind), and a hundred pounds of sugar-cane (the long purple kind), and seventeen melons (the greeny-crackly kind), and said to all his dear families, "Good-bye. I am going to the great grey-green, greasy Limpopo River, all set about with fever-trees, to find out what the Crocodile has for dinner." And they all spanked him once more for luck, though he asked them most politely to stop.

4

Then he went away, a little warm, but not at all astonished, eating melons, and throwing the rind about, because he could not pick it up.

He went from Graham's Town to Kimberley, and from Kimberley to Khama's Country, and from Khama's Country he went east by north, eating melons all the time, till at last he came to the banks of the great grey-green, greasy Limpopo River, all set about with fever-trees, precisely as Kolokolo Bird had said.

Now you must know and understand, O Best Beloved, that till that very week, and day, and hour, and minute, this 'satiable Elephant's Child had never seen a Crocodile, and did not know what one was like. It was all his 'satiable curtiosity.

The first thing that he found was a Bi-Coloured-Python-Rock-Snake curled round a rock.

"'Scuse me," said the Elephant's Child most politely, "but have you seen such a thing as a Crocodile in these promiscuous parts?"

"*Have* I seen a Crocodile?" said the Bi-Coloured-Python-Rock-Snake, in a voice of dretful scorn. "What will you ask me next?"

"'Scuse me," said the Elephant's Child, "but could you kindly tell me what he has for dinner?"

Then the Bi-Coloured-Python-Rock-Snake uncoiled himself very quickly from the rock, and spanked the Elephant's Child with his scalesome, flailsome tail.

"That is odd," said the Elephant's Child, "because my father and my mother, and my uncle and my aunt, not to mention my other aunt, the Hippopotamus, and my other uncle, the Baboon, have all spanked me for my 'satiable curtiosity—and I suppose this is the same thing."

So he said good-bye very politely to the Bi-Coloured-Python-Rock-Snake, and helped to coil him up on the rock again, and went on, a little warm, but not at all astonished, eating melons, and throwing the rind about, because he could not pick it up, till he trod on what he thought was a log of wood at the very edge of the great grey-green, greasy Limpopo River, all set about with fever-trees.

But it was really the Crocodile, O Best Beloved, and the Crocodile winked one eye—like this!

"'Scuse me," said the Elephant's Child most politely, "but do you happen to have seen a Crocodile in these promiscuous parts?"

Then the Crocodile winked the other eye, and lifted half his tail out of the mud; and the Elephant's Child stepped back most politely, because he did not wish to be spanked again.

"Come hither, Little One," said the Crocodile. "Why do you ask such things?"

"'Scuse me," said the Elephant's Child most politely, "but my father has spanked me, my mother has spanked me, not to mention my tall aunt, the Ostrich, and my tall uncle, the Giraffe, who can kick ever so hard, as well as my broad aunt, the Hippopotamus, and my hairy uncle, the Baboon, *and* including the Bi-Coloured-Python-Rock-Snake, with the scalesome, flailsome tail, just up the bank, who spanks harder than any of them; and *so*, if it's quite all the same to you, I don't want to be spanked any more."

"Come hither, Little One," said the Crocodile, "for I am the Crocodile," and he wept crocodile-tears to show it was quite true.

Then the Elephant's Child grew all breathless, and panted, and kneeled down on the bank and said, "You are the very person I have been looking for all these long days. Will you please tell me what you have for dinner?"

"Come hither, Little One," said the Crocodile, "and I'll whisper."

Then the Elephant's Child put his head down close to the Crocodile's musky, tusky mouth, and the Crocodile caught him by his little nose, which up to that very week, day, hour, and minute, had been no bigger than a boot, though much more useful.

"I think," said the Crocodile—and he said it between his teeth, like this—"I think to-day I will begin with Elephant's Child!"

At this, O Best Beloved, the Elephant's Child was much annoyed, and he said, speaking through his nose, like this, "Led go! You are hurtig be!"

Then the Bi-Coloured-Python-Rock-Snake scuffled down from the bank and said, "My young friend, if you do not now, immediately and instantly, pull as hard as ever you can, it is my opinion that your acquaintance in the large-pattern

7

leather ulster" (and by this he meant the Crocodile) "will jerk you into yonder limpid stream before you can say Jack Robinson."

This is the way Bi-Coloured-Python-Rock-Snakes always talk.

Then the Elephant's Child sat back on his little haunches, and pulled, and pulled, and pulled, and his nose began to stretch. And the Crocodile floundered into the water, making it all creamy with great sweeps of his tail, and *he* pulled, and pulled, and pulled.

And the Elephant's Child's nose kept on stretching; and the Elephant's Child spread all his little four legs and pulled, and pulled, and pulled, and his nose kept on stretching; and the Crocodile threshed his tail like an oar, and *he* pulled, and pulled, and pulled, and at each pull the Elephant's Child's nose grew longer and longer—and it hurt him hijjus!

Then the Elephant's Child felt his legs slipping, and he said through his nose, which was now nearly five feet long, "This is too butch for be!"

Then the Bi-Coloured-Python-Rock-Snake came down from the bank, and knotted himself in a double-clove-hitch round the Elephant's Child's hind-legs, and said, "Rash and inexperienced traveller, we will now seriously devote ourselves to a little high tension, because if we do not, it is my impression that yonder self-propelling man-of-war with the armour-plated upper deck" (and by this, O Best Beloved, he meant the Crocodile) "will permanently vitiate your future career."

That is the way all Bi-Coloured-Python-Rock-Snakes always talk.

So he pulled, and the Elephant's Child pulled, and the Crocodile pulled; but the Elephant's Child and the Bi-Coloured-Python-Rock-Snake pulled hardest; and at last the Crocodile let go of the Elephant's Child's nose with a plop that you could hear all up and down the Limpopo.

Then the Elephant's Child sat down most hard and sudden; but first he was careful to say "Thank you" to the Bi-Coloured-Python-Rock-Snake; and next he was kind to his

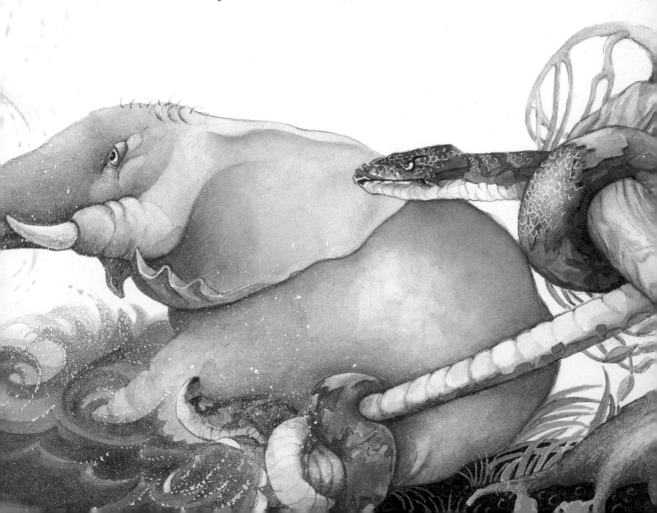

poor pulled nose, and wrapped it all up in cool banana
leaves, and hung it in the great grey-green, greasy Limpopo
to cool.

"What are you doing that for?" said the Bi-Coloured-
Python-Rock-Snake.

"'Scuse me," said the Elephant's Child, "but my nose is
badly out of shape, and I am waiting for it to shrink."

"Then you will have to wait a long time," said the
Bi-Coloured-Python-Rock-Snake. "Some people do not know
what is good for them."

The Elephant's Child sat there for three days waiting for
his nose to shrink. But it never grew any shorter, and,
besides, it made him squint. For, O Best Beloved, you will see
and understand that the Crocodile had pulled it out into a
really truly trunk same as all Elephants have to-day.

At the end of the third day a fly came and stung him on the
shoulder, and before he knew what he was doing he lifted up
his trunk and hit that fly dead with the end of it.

"'Vantage number one!" said the Bi-Coloured-Python-
Rock-Snake. "You couldn't have done that with a mere-
smear nose. Try and eat a little now."

Before he thought what he was doing the Elephant's Child

10

put out his trunk and plucked a large bundle of grass, dusted it clean against his fore-legs, and stuffed it into his own mouth.

"'Vantage number two!" said the Bi-Coloured-Python-Rock-Snake. "You couldn't have done that with a mere-smear nose. Don't you think the sun is very hot here?"

"It is," said the Elephant's Child, and before he thought what he was doing he schlooped up a schloop of mud from the banks of the great grey-green, greasy Limpopo, and slapped it on his head, where it made a cool schloopy-sloshy mud-cap all trickly behind his ears.

"'Vantage number three!" said the Bi-Coloured-Python-Rock-Snake. "You couldn't have done that with a mere-smear nose. Now how do you feel about being spanked again?"

" 'Scuse me," said the Elephant's Child, "but I should not like it at all."

"How would you like to spank somebody?" said the Bi-Coloured-Python-Rock-Snake.

"I should like it very much indeed," said the Elephant's Child.

"Well," said the Bi-Coloured-Python-Rock-Snake, "you will find that new nose of yours very useful to spank people with."

"Thank you," said the Elephant's Child, "I'll remember that; and now I think I'll go home to all my dear families and try."

So the Elephant's Child went home across Africa frisking and whisking his trunk. When he wanted fruit to eat he pulled fruit down from a tree, instead of waiting for it to fall as he used to do. When he wanted grass he plucked grass up from the ground, instead of going on his knees as he used to do. When the flies bit him he broke off the branch of a tree and used it as a fly-whisk; and he made himself a new, cool, slushy-squashy mud-cap whenever the sun was hot. When he felt lonely walking through Africa he sang to himself down his trunk, and the noise was louder than several brass bands. He went specially out of his way to find a broad Hippopotamus (she was no relation of his), and he spanked her very hard, to make sure that the Bi-Coloured-Python-Rock-Snake had spoken the truth about his new trunk. The rest of the time he picked up the melon-rinds that he had dropped on his way to the Limpopo—for he was a Tidy Pachyderm.

One dark evening he came back to all his dear families, and he coiled up his trunk and said, "How do you do?" They were very glad to see him, and immediately said, "Come here and be spanked for your 'satiable curtiosity."

"Pooh," said the Elephant's Child. "I don't think you peoples know anything about spanking; but *I* do, and I'll show you."

Then he uncurled his trunk and knocked two of his dear brothers head over heels.

"O Bananas!" said they, "where did you learn that trick, and what have you done to your nose?"

"I got a new one from the Crocodile on the banks of the great grey-green, greasy Limpopo River," said the Elephant's Child. "I asked him what he had for dinner, and he gave me this to keep."

"It looks very ugly," said his hairy uncle, the Baboon.

"It does," said the Elephant's Child. "But it's very useful," and he picked up his hairy uncle, the Baboon, by one hairy leg, and hove him into a hornets' nest.

Then that bad Elephant's Child spanked all his dear families for a long time, till they were very warm and greatly astonished. He pulled out his tall Ostrich aunt's tail-feathers; and he caught his tall uncle, the Giraffe, by the hind-leg, and dragged him through a thorn-bush; and he shouted at his broad aunt, the Hippopotamus, and blew bubbles into her ear when she was sleeping in the water after meals; but he never let any one touch Kolokolo Bird.

14

At last things grew so exciting that his dear families went off one by one in a hurry to the banks of the great grey-green, greasy Limpopo River, all set about with fever-trees, to borrow new noses from the Crocodile. When they came back nobody spanked anybody any more; and ever since that day, O Best Beloved, all the Elephants you will ever see, besides all those that you won't, have trunks precisely like the trunk of the 'satiable Elephant's Child.

A Lion and a Mouse

A MOUSE one day happened to run across the paws of a sleeping lion and wakened him. The lion, angry at being disturbed, grabbed the mouse, and was about to swallow him, when the mouse cried out, "Please, kind Sir, I didn't mean it; if you will let me go, I shall always be grateful; and, perhaps, I can help you someday." The idea that such a little thing as a mouse could help him so amused the lion that he let the mouse go. A week later the mouse heard a lion roaring loudly. He went closer to see what the trouble was and found his lion caught in a hunter's net. Remembering his promise, the mouse began to gnaw the ropes of the net and kept it up until the lion could get free. The lion then acknowledged:

Little friends might prove great friends.

A Wolf in Sheep's Clothing

A CERTAIN wolf, being very hungry, disguised himself in a sheep's skin and joined a flock of sheep. Thus, for many days he could kill and eat sheep whenever he was hungry, for even the shepherd did not find him out. One night after the shepherd had put all his sheep in the fold, he decided to kill one of his own flock for food; and without realizing what he was doing, he took out the wolf and killed him on the spot.

It really does not pay to pretend to be what you are not.

Aladdin and the Wonderful Lamp

One of the best storytellers of all time was Scheherazade. Her husband, the Sultan, customarily executed his wives the day after marriage, but Scheherazade used stories to postpone her death. Each night she told the Sultan a story—and saved the end for the next night. After a thousand and one nights, he spared her life. Together, the stories are called The Arabian Nights' Entertainments. *Here is one of Scheherazade's tales . . .*

THERE once lived a poor tailor, who had a son called Aladdin, a careless, idle boy who would do nothing but play all day long in the streets with little idle boys like himself. This so grieved the father that he died; yet, in spite of his mother's tears and prayers, Aladdin did not mend his ways. One day, when he was playing in the streets as usual, a stranger asked him his age, and if he was not the son of Mustapha the tailor. "I am, sir," replied Aladdin; "but he died a long while ago." On this the stranger, who was a famous African magician, fell on his neck and kissed him, saying, "I am your uncle, and knew you from your likeness to my brother. Go to your mother and tell her I am coming." Aladdin ran home and told his mother of his newly found uncle. "Indeed, child," she said, "your father had a brother, but I always thought he was dead." However, she prepared supper, and bade Aladdin seek his uncle, who came laden with wine and fruit. He presently fell down and kissed the place where Mustapha used to sit, bidding Aladdin's mother not to be surprised at not having seen him before, as he had been forty years out of the country. He then turned to Aladdin, and asked him his trade, at which the boy hung his

head, while his mother burst into tears. On learning that
Aladdin was idle and would learn no trade, he offered to take
a shop for him and stock it with merchandise. Next day he
bought Aladdin a fine suit of clothes and took him all over
the city, showing him the sights, and brought him home at
nightfall to his mother, who was overjoyed to see her son so
fine.

Next day the magician led Aladdin into some beautiful
gardens a long way outside the city gates. They sat down by
a fountain and the magician pulled a cake from his girdle,
which he divided between them. They then journeyed on-
wards till they almost reached the mountains. Aladdin was
so tired that he begged to go back, but the magician beguiled
him with pleasant stories, and led him on in spite of himself.
At last they came to two mountains divided by a narrow
valley. "We will go no farther," said the false uncle. "I will
show you something wonderful; only do you gather up sticks

while I kindle a fire." When it was lit the magician threw on
it a powder he had about him, at the same time saying some
magical words. The earth trembled a little and opened in
front of them, disclosing a square flat stone with a brass
ring in the middle to raise it by. Aladdin tried to run away,
but the magician caught him and gave him a blow that
knocked him down. "What have I done, uncle?" he said pite-
ously; whereupon the magician said more kindly: "Fear
nothing, but obey me. Beneath this stone lies a treasure
which is to be yours, and no one else may touch it; so you
must do exactly as I tell you." At the word treasure Aladdin
forgot his fears, and grasped the ring as he was told, saying
the names of his father and grandfather. The stone came up
quite easily, and some steps appeared. "Go down," said the
magician; "at the foot of those steps you will find an open
door leading into three large halls. Tuck up your gown and
go through them without touching anything, or you will die
instantly. These halls lead into a garden of fine fruit trees.

20

Walk on till you come to a niche in a terrace where stands a lighted lamp. Pour out the oil it contains, and bring it me." He drew a ring from his finger and gave it to Aladdin, bidding him prosper.

Aladdin found everything as the magician had said, gathered some fruit off the trees, and having got the lamp, arrived at the mouth of the cave. The magician cried out in a great hurry. "Make haste and give me the lamp." This Aladdin refused to do until he was out of the cave. The magician flew into a terrible passion, and throwing some more powder on the fire, he said something, and the stone rolled back into its place.

The magician left China forever, which plainly showed that he was no uncle of Aladdin's, but a cunning magician, who had read in his magic books of a wonderful lamp, which would make him the most powerful man in the world. Though he alone knew where to find it, he could only receive it from the hand of another. He had picked out the foolish

Aladdin for this purpose, intending to get the lamp and kill him afterwards.

For two days Aladdin remained in the dark crying and lamenting. At last he clasped his hands in prayer, and in doing so, rubbed the ring, which the magician had forgotten to take from him. Immediately an enormous and frightful genie rose out of the earth, saying: "What wouldst thou with me? I am the Slave of the Ring, and will obey thee in all things." Aladdin fearlessly replied: "Deliver me from this place!" whereupon the earth opened, and he found himself outside. As soon as his eyes could bear the light he went home, but fainted on the threshold. When he came to himself, he told his mother what had passed, and showed her the lamp and the fruits he had gathered in the garden, which were in reality precious stones. He then asked for some food. "Alas! child," she said, "I have nothing in the house, but I have spun a little cotton and will go and sell it." Aladdin bade her keep her cotton, for he would sell the lamp instead. As it was very dirty she began to rub it, that it might fetch a higher price. Instantly a hideous genie appeared and asked what she would have. She fainted away, but Aladdin, snatching the lamp, said boldly: "Fetch me something to eat!" The genie returned with a silver bowl, twelve silver plates containing rich meats, two silver cups, and two bottles of wine. Aladdin's mother, when she came to herself, said, "Whence comes this splendid feast?" "Ask not, but eat," replied Aladdin. So they sat at breakfast till it was dinner-time and Aladdin told his mother about the lamp. She begged him to sell it, and have nothing to do with devils. "No," said Aladdin, "since chance hath made us aware of its virtues, we will use it, and the ring likewise, which I shall always wear on my finger." When they had eaten all the genie had brought, Aladdin sold one of the silver plates, and so on until none were left. He then had recourse to the genie, who gave him another set of plates, and thus they lived for many years.

One day Aladdin heard an order from the Sultan proclaimed that everyone was to stay at home and close his shutters while the Princess, his daughter, went to and from the bath. Aladdin was seized by a desire to see her face, which was very difficult, as she always went veiled.

He hid himself behind the door of the bath and peeped through a chink. The Princess lifted her veil as she went in, and looked so beautiful that Aladdin fell in love with her at first sight. He went home so changed that his mother was frightened. He told her he loved the Princess so deeply that he could not live without her, and meant to ask her in marriage of her father.

His mother, on hearing this, burst out laughing; but Aladdin at last prevailed upon her to go before the Sultan and carry his request. She fetched a napkin and laid in it the magic fruits from the enchanted garden, which sparkled and shone like the most beautiful jewels. She took these with her to please the Sultan, and set out, trusting in the lamp.

The Grand Vizier and the lords of council had just gone in as she entered the hall and placed herself in front of the Sultan. He took no notice of her. She went every day for a week, and stood in the same place. When the council broke up on the sixth day the Sultan said to his Vizier: "I see a certain woman in the audience-chamber every day carrying

something in a napkin. Call her next time, that I may find out what she wants." Next day, at a sign from the Vizier, she went up to the foot of the throne and remained kneeling till the Sultan said to her: "Rise, good woman, and tell me what you want." She hesitated, so the Sultan promised to forgive her for anything she might say. She then told him of her son's violent love for the Princess. "I prayed him to forget her," she said, "but in vain; he threatened to do some desperate deed if I refused to go and ask your Majesty for the hand of the Princess. Now I pray you to forgive not me alone, but my son Aladdin." The Sultan asked her kindly what she had in the napkin, whereupon she unfolded the jewels and presented them. He was thunderstruck, and turning to the Vizier said: "What sayest thou? Ought I not to bestow the Princess on one who values her at such a price?" The Vizier, who wanted her for his own son, begged the Sultan to withhold her for three months, in the course of which he hoped his son would contrive to make him a richer

present. The Sultan granted this, and told Aladdin's mother that, though he consented to the marriage, she must not appear before him again for three months.

Aladdin waited patiently for nearly three months; but after two had elapsed, his mother, going into the city to buy oil, found everyone rejoicing, and asked what was going on. "Do you not know," was the answer, "that the son of the Grand Vizier is to marry the Sultan's daughter tonight?" Breathless, she ran and told Aladdin, who was overwhelmed at first, but presently bethought him of the lamp. He rubbed it, and the Genie appeared, saying: "What is thy will?" Aladdin replied: "The Sultan, as thou knowest, has broken his promise to me, and the Vizier's son is to have the Princess. My command is that tonight you bring hither the bride and bridegroom." "Master, I obey," said the genie. Aladdin then went to his chamber, where, sure enough, at midnight the genie transported the bed containing the Vizier's son and the Princess. "Take this new-married man," he said, "and put him outside in the cold, and return at daybreak." Whereupon the genie took the Vizier's son out of bed, leaving Aladdin with the Princess. "Fear nothing," Aladdin said to her; "you are my wife, promised to me by your unjust father, and no harm shall come to you." The Princess was too frightened to speak, and passed the most miserable night of her life, while Aladdin lay down beside her and slept soundly. At the appointed hour the genie fetched in the shivering bridegroom, laid him in his place, and transported the bed back to the palace.

Presently the Sultan came to wish his daughter good-morning. The unhappy Vizier's son jumped up and hid himself, while the Princess would not say a word, and was very sorrowful. The Sultan sent her mother to her, who said: "How comes it, child, that you will not speak to your father? What has happened?" The Princess sighed deeply, and at last told her mother how, during the night, the bed had been carried into some strange house, and what had passed there. Her mother did not believe her in the least, but bade her rise and consider it an idle dream.

The following night exactly the same thing happened, and next morning, on the Princess's refusing to speak, the Sultan threatened to cut off her head. She then confessed all, bidding him ask the Vizier's son if it were not so. The Sultan told the Vizier to ask his son, who owned the truth, adding that, dearly as he loved the Princess, he had rather die than go through another such fearful night, and wished to be separated from her. His wish was granted, and there was an end of feasting and rejoicing.

When the three months were over, Aladdin sent his mother to remind the Sultan of his promise. She stood in the same place as before, and the Sultan, who had forgotten Aladdin, at once remembered him, and sent for her. On seeing her poverty the Sultan felt less inclined than ever to keep his word, and asked his Vizier's advice, who counseled him to set so high a value on the Princess that no man living could come up to it. The Sultan then turned to Aladdin's mother, saying: "Good woman, a Sultan must remember his promises, and I will remember mine, but your son must first send me forty basins of gold brimful of jewels, carried by forty black slaves, led by as many white ones, splendidly dressed. Tell him that I await his answer!" The mother of Aladdin bowed low and went home, thinking all was lost. She gave Aladdin the message, adding: "He may wait long enough for your answer!" "Not so long, mother, as you think," her son replied. "I would do a great deal more than that for the Princess." He summoned the genie, and in a few moments the eighty slaves arrived, and filled up the small house and garden. Aladdin made them set out to the palace, two and two, followed by his mother. They were so richly dressed, with such splendid jewels in their girdles, that everyone crowded to see them and the basins of gold they carried on their heads.

They entered the palace and, after kneeling before the Sultan, stood in a half-circle round the throne with their arms crossed, while Aladdin's mother presented them to the Sultan. He hesitated no longer, but said: "Good woman, return and tell your son that I wait for him with open arms." She lost no time in telling Aladdin, bidding him make haste. But Aladdin first called the genie.

"I want a scented bath," he said, "a richly embroidered habit, a horse surpassing the Sultan's, and twenty slaves to attend me. Besides this, six slaves, beautifully dressed, to wait on my mother; and lastly, ten thousand pieces of gold in ten purses." No sooner said than done.

Aladdin mounted his horse and passed through the streets, the slaves strewing gold as they went. Those who had played with him in his childhood knew him not, he had grown so handsome. When the Sultan saw him he came down from his throne, embraced him, and led him into a hall where a feast was spread, intending to marry him to the

29

Princess that very day. But Aladdin refused, saying, "I must build a palace fit for her," and took his leave.

Once home, he said to the genie: "Build me a palace of the finest marble, set with jasper, agate, and other precious stones. In the middle you shall build me a large hall with a dome, its four walls of massy gold and silver, each side having six windows, whose lattices, all except one which is to be left unfinished, must be set with diamonds and rubies. There must be stables and horses and grooms and slaves; go and see about it!"

The palace was finished by next day, and the genie carried him there and showed him all his orders faithfully carried out, even to the laying of a velvet carpet from Aladdin's palace to the Sultan's. Aladdin's mother then dressed herself carefully, and walked to the palace with her slaves, while he followed her on horseback. The Sultan sent musicians with trumpets and cymbals to meet them, so that the air resounded with music and cheers. She was taken to the Princess, who saluted her and treated her with great honor. At night the Princess said goodbye to her father, and set out on the carpet for Aladdin's palace, with his mother at her side, and followed by the hundred slaves. She was charmed at the sight of Aladdin, who ran to receive her. "Princess," he said, "blame your beauty for my boldness if I have displeased you." She told him that, having seen him, she willingly obeyed her father in this matter. After the wedding had taken place Aladdin led her into the hall, where a feast was spread, and she supped with him, after which they danced till midnight.

Next day Aladdin invited the Sultan to see the palace. On entering the hall with the four-and-twenty windows, with their rubies, diamonds, and emeralds, he cried: "It is a world's wonder! There is only one thing that surprises me. Was it by accident that one window was left unfinished?" "No, sir, by design," returned Aladdin. "I wished your Majesty to have the glory of finishing this palace." The Sultan was pleased, and sent in the best jewelers in the city. He showed them the unfinished window, and bade them fit it up like the others. "Sir," replied their spokesman, "we cannot

find jewels enough." The Sultan had his own fetched, which
they soon used, but to no purpose, for in a month's time the
work was not half done. Aladdin, knowing that their task
was vain, bade them undo their work and carry the jewels
back, and the genie finished the window at his command.
The Sultan was surprised to receive his jewels again, and
visited Aladdin, who showed him the window finished. The
Sultan embraced him, the envious Vizier meanwhile hinting
that it was the work of enchantment.

Aladdin had won the hearts of the people by his gentle
bearing. He was made captain of the Sultan's armies, and
won several battles for him; but remained modest and
courteous as before and lived thus in peace and content for
several years.

But far away in Africa the magician remembered Aladdin
and by his magic arts discovered that Aladdin, instead of
perishing miserably in the cave, had escaped and had married a Princess with whom he was living in great honor and

31

wealth. He knew that the poor tailor's son could only have accomplished this by means of the lamp and traveled night and day till he reached the capital of China, bent on Aladdin's ruin. As he passed through the town he heard people talking everywhere about a marvelous palace.

"Forgive my ignorance," he said. "What is this palace you speak of?"

"Have you not heard of Prince Aladdin's palace," was the reply, "the greatest wonder of the world? I will direct you if you have a mind to see it."

The magician thanked him who spoke, and having seen the palace knew that it had been raised by the genie of the lamp and became half-mad with rage. He determined to get hold of the lamp and again plunge Aladdin into the deepest poverty.

Unluckily, Aladdin had gone a-hunting for eight days, which gave the magician plenty of time. He bought a dozen copper lamps, put them into a basket, and went to the palace, crying, "New lamps for old!" followed by a jeering crowd.

The Princess sitting in the hall of twenty-four windows, sent a slave to find out what the noise was about, who came back laughing, so that the Princess scolded her.

"Madam," replied the slave, "who can help laughing to see an old fool offering to exchange fine new lamps for old ones?"

Another slave, hearing this, said: "There is an old one on the cornice there which he can have." Now, this was the magic lamp, which Aladdin had left there, as he could not take it out hunting with him.

The Princess, not knowing its value, laughingly bade the slave take it and make the exchange. She went and said to the magician: "Give me a new lamp for this." He snatched it and bade the slave take her choice, amid the jeers of the crowd. Little he cared, but left off crying his lamps, and went out of the city gates to a lonely place, where he remained till nightfall, when he pulled out the lamp and rubbed it. The genie appeared and at the magician's command carried him, together with the palace and the princess in it, to a lonely place in Africa.

Next morning the Sultan looked out of the window toward Aladdin's palace and rubbed his eyes, for it was gone. He sent for the Vizier and asked what had become of the palace. The Vizier looked out too, and was lost in astonishment. He again put it down to enchantment, and this time the Sultan believed him, and sent thirty men on horseback to fetch Aladdin in chains. They met him riding home, bound him, and forced him to go with them on foot. The people, however, who loved him, followed, armed, to see that he came to no harm. He was carried before the Sultan, who ordered the executioner to cut off his head. The executioner made Aladdin kneel down, bandaged his eyes, and raised his scimitar to strike. At that instant the Vizier, who saw that the crowd had forced their way into the courtyard and were scaling the walls to rescue Aladdin, called to the executioner to stay his hand. The people, indeed, looked so threatening that the Sultan gave way and ordered Aladdin to be unbound, and pardoned him in the sight of the crowd. Aladdin now begged to know what he had done. "False wretch!" said the Sultan, "come hither," and showed him from the window the place where his palace had stood. Aladdin was so amazed that he could not say a word. "Where is my palace and my daughter?" demanded the Sultan. "For the first I am not so deeply concerned, but my daughter I must have, and you must find her or lose your head."

33

Aladdin begged for forty days in which to find her, promising if he failed, to return and suffer death at the Sultan's pleasure. His prayer was granted, and he went forth sadly from the Sultan's presence. For three days he wandered about like a madman, asking everyone what had become of his palace, but they only laughed and pitied him. He came to the banks of a river, and knelt down to say his prayers before throwing himself in. In so doing he rubbed the magic ring he still wore. The genie he had seen in the cave appeared, and asked his will. "Save my life, genie," said Aladdin, "and bring my palace back." "That is not in my power," said the genie; "I am only the Slave of the Ring; you must ask him of the lamp." "Even so," said Aladdin, "but thou canst take me to the palace, and set me down under my dear wife's window." He at once found himself in Africa, under the window of the Princess, and fell asleep out of sheer weariness.

He was awakened by the singing of the birds, and his heart was lighter. He saw plainly that all his misfortunes were owing to the loss of the lamp, and vainly wondered who had robbed him of it.

34

That morning the Princess rose earlier than she had done since she had been carried into Africa by the magician, whose company she was forced to endure once a day. She, however, treated him so harshly that he dared not live there altogether. As she was dressing, one of her women looked out and saw Aladdin.

The Princess ran and opened the window, and at the noise she made Aladdin looked up. She called to him to come to her, and great was the joy of these lovers at seeing each other again.

After he had kissed her Aladdin said: "I beg of you, Princess, in God's name, before we speak of anything else, for your own sake and mine, tell me what has become of an old lamp I left on the cornice in the hall of twenty-four windows when I went hunting."

"Alas!" she said, "I am the innocent cause of our sorrows," and told him of the exchange of the lamp.

"Now I know," cried Aladdin, "that we have to thank the African magician for this! Where is the lamp?"

"He carries it about with him," said the Princess. "I know,

for he pulled it out of his breast to show me. He wishes me to break my faith with you and marry him, saying that you were beheaded by my father's command. He is forever speaking ill of you, but I only reply to him by my tears. If I persist in doing so, I doubt not but he will use violence."

Aladdin comforted her and left her for awhile. He changed clothes with the first person he met in the town and having bought a certain powder, returned to the Princess, who let him in by a little side door. "Put on your most beautiful dress," he said to her, "and receive the magician with smiles, leading him to believe that you have forgotten me. Invite him up to sup with you and say you wish to taste the wine of his country. He will go for some and while he is gone, I will tell you what to do." She listened carefully to Aladdin and when he left her, arrayed herself gayly for the first time since she left China. She put on a girdle and headdress of diamonds, and, seeing in a glass that she was more beautiful than ever, received the magician, saying, to his great amazement: "I have made up my mind that Aladdin is dead, and that all my tears will not bring him back to me, so I am resolved to mourn no more, and have therefore invited you to sup with me; but I am tired of the wines of China, and would fain taste those of Africa." The magician flew to his cellar, and the Princess put the powder Aladdin had given her in her cup. When he returned she asked him to drink her health in the wine of Africa, handing him her cup in exchange for his, as a sign she was reconciled to him. Before drinking the magician made her a speech in praise of her beauty, but the Princess cut him short, saying: "Let us drink first, and you shall say what you will afterwards." She set her cup to her lips and kept it there, while the magician drained his to the dregs and fell back lifeless. The Princess then opened the door to Aladdin, and flung her arms round his neck; but Aladdin put her away, bidding her leave him, as he had more to do. He then went to the dead magician, took the lamp out of his vest, and bade the genie carry the palace and all in it back to China. This was done, and the Princess in her chamber only felt two little shocks, and little thought she was at home again.

36

The Sultan, who was sitting in his closet, mourning for his lost daughter, happened to look up, and rubbed his eyes, for there stood the palace as before! He hastened thither, and Aladdin received him in the hall of the four-and-twenty windows, with the Princess at his side. Aladdin told him what had happened, and showed him the dead body of the magician, that he might believe. A ten days' feast was proclaimed, and it seemed as if Aladdin might now live the rest of his life in peace; but it was not to be.

The African magician had a younger brother, who was, if possible, more wicked and more cunning than himself. He traveled to China to avenge his brother's death, and went to visit a pious woman called Fatima, thinking she might be of use to him. He entered her cell and clapped a dagger to her breast, telling her to rise and do his bidding on pain of death. He changed clothes with her, colored his face like hers, put on her veil, and murdered her, that she might tell no tales.

Then he went towards the palace of Aladdin, and all the people, thinking he was the holy woman, gathered round him, kissing his hands and begging his blessing. When he got to the palace there was such a noise going on round him that the Princess bade her slave look out of the window and ask what was the matter. The slave said it was the holy woman, curing people by her touch of their ailments, whereupon the Princess, who had long desired to see Fatima, sent for her. On coming to the Princess, the magician offered up a prayer for her health and prosperity. When he had done, the Princess made him sit by her, and begged him to stay with her always. The false Fatima, who wished for nothing better, consented, but kept his veil down for fear of discovery. The Princess showed him the hall, and asked him what he thought of it. "It is truly beautiful," said the false Fatima. "In my mind it wants but one thing." "And what is that?" said the Princess. "If only a roc's egg," replied he, "were hung up from the middle of this dome, it would be the wonder of the world."

38

After this the Princess could think of nothing but the roc's egg, and when Aladdin returned from hunting he found her in a very ill humor. He begged to know what was amiss, and she told him that all her pleasure in the hall was spoilt for the want of a roc's egg hanging from the dome. "If that is all," replied Aladdin, "you shall soon be happy." He left her and rubbed the lamp, and when the genie appeared commanded him to bring a roc's egg. The genie gave such a loud and terrible shriek that the hall shook. "Wretch!" he cried, "is it not enough that I have done everything for you, but you must command me to bring my master and hang him up in the midst of this dome? You and your wife and your palace deserve to be burnt to ashes, but that this request does not come from you, but from the brother of the African magician, whom you destroyed. He is now in your palace disguised as the holy woman—whom he murdered. He it was who put that wish into your wife's head. Take care of yourself, for he means to kill you." So saying, the genie disappeared.

Aladdin went back to the Princess, saying his head ached, and requesting that the holy Fatima should be fetched to lay her hands on it. But when the magician came near, Aladdin, seizing his dagger, pierced him to the heart. "What have you done!" cried the Princess. "You have killed the holy woman!" "Not so," replied Aladdin, "but a wicked magician," and told her of how she had been deceived.

After this Aladdin and his wife lived in peace. He succeeded the Sultan when he died, and reigned for many years, leaving behind him a long line of kings.

Lochinvar

Sir Walter Scott

O, young Lochinvar is come out of the west,
Through all the wide Border his steed was the best;
And, save his good broadsword, he weapon had none,
He rode all unarmed, and he rode all alone.
So faithful in love, and so dauntless in war,
There never was knight like the young Lochinvar.

He stayed not for brake, and he stopped not for stone,
He swam the Eske river where ford there was none;
But, ere he alighted at Netherby gate,
The bride had consented, the gallant came late;
For a laggard in love, and a dastard in war,
Was to wed the fair Ellen of brave Lochinvar.

So boldly he entered the Netherby Hall,
Among bridesmen, and kinsmen, and brothers, and all.
Then spoke the bride's father, his hand on his sword,
(For the poor craven bridegroom said never a word),
"O come ye in peace here, or come ye in war,
Or to dance at our bridal, young Lord Lochinvar?"

"I long wooed your daughter, my suit you denied;—
Love swells like the Solway, but ebbs like its tide,—
And now am I come, with this lost love of mine,
To lead but one measure, drink one cup of wine.
There are maidens in Scotland more lovely by far,
That would gladly be bride to the young Lochinvar."

The bride kissed the goblet; the knight took it up,
He quaffed off the wine, and he threw down the cup.
She looked down to blush, and she looked up to sigh,
With a smile on her lips, and a tear in her eye.
He took her soft hand, ere her mother could bar,—
"Now tread we a measure!" said young Lochinvar.

So stately his form, and so lovely her face,
That never a hall such a galliard did grace;
While her mother did fret, and her father did fume.
And the bridegroom stood dangling his bonnet and plume;
And the bride-maidens whispered, " 'Twere better by far,
To have matched our fair cousin with young Lochinvar."

One touch to her hand, and one word in her ear,
When they reached the hall-door, and the charger stood
     near
So light to the croup the fair lady he swung,
So light to the saddle before her he sprung!
"She is won! we are gone! over bank, bush, and scaur;
They'll have fleet steeds that follow," quoth young
     Lochinvar.

There was mounting 'mong Graemes of the Netherby clan;
Forsters, Fenwicks, and Musgraves, they rode and they ran;
There was racing and chasing on Cannobie Lee,
But the lost bride of Netherby ne'er did they see.
So daring in love, and so dauntless in war,
Have ye e'er heard of gallant like young Lochinvar?

The Man from Snowy River

*When you read this fast-paced Australian poem by
A.B. Paterson, you will understand why "the
bushmen love hard riding where the wild bush
horses are, / And the stock-horse snuffs the battle
with delight."*

There was movement at the station, for the word had
　　passed around
That the colt from old Regret had got away,
And had joined the wild bush horses—he was worth a
　　thousand pound,
So all the cracks had gathered to the fray.

All the tried and noted riders from the stations near and far
Had mustered at the homestead overnight,
For the bushmen love hard riding where the wild bush
　　horses are,
And the stock-horse snuffs the battle with delight.

There was Harrison, who made his pile when Pardon won
　　the cup,
The old man with his hair as white as snow;
But few could ride beside him when his blood was fairly
　　up—
He would go wherever horse and man could go.
And Clancy of the Overflow came down to lend a hand,
No better horseman ever held the reins;

For never horse could throw him while the saddle-girths
  would stand—
He learnt to ride while droving on the plains.

And one was there, a stripling on a small and weedy beast;
He was something like a racehorse undersized,
With a touch of Timor pony—three parts thoroughbred at
  least—
And such as are by mountain horsemen prized.

He was hard and tough and wiry—just the sort that won't
  say die—
There was courage in his quick impatient tread;
And he bore the badge of gameness in his bright and fiery
  eye,
And the proud and lofty carriage of his head.

But still so slight and weedy, one would doubt his power to
    stay,
And the old man said, "That horse will never do
For a long and tiring gallop—lad, you'd better stop away,
Those hills are far too rough for such as you."
So he waited, sad and wistful—only Clancy stood his
    friend—
"I think we ought to let him come," he said;
"I warrant he'll be with us when he's wanted at the end,
For both his horse and he are mountain bred.

"He hails from Snowy River, up by Kosciusko's side,
Where the hills are twice as steep and twice as rough;
Where a horse's hoofs strike firelight from the flint stones
    every stride,
The man that holds his own is good enough.
And the Snowy River riders on the mountains make their
    home,
Where the river runs those giant hills between;
I have seen full many horsemen since I first commenced to
    roam,
But nowhere yet such horsemen have I seen."

So he went;

—they found the horses by the big mimosa clump,
They raced away towards the mountain's brow,
And the old man gave his orders, "Boys, go at them from the
    jump,
No use to try for fancy riding now.
And, Clancy, you must wheel them, try and wheel them to
    the right.
Ride boldly, lad, and never fear the spills,
For never yet was rider that could keep the mob in sight,
If once they gain the shelter of those hills."

So Clancy rode to wheel them—he was racing on the wing
Where the best and boldest riders take their place,
And he raced his stock-horse past them, and he made the
    ranges ring
With the stockwhip, as he met them face to face.

Then they halted for a moment, while he swung the dreaded
    lash,
But they saw their well-loved mountain full in view,
And they charged beneath the stockwhip with a sharp and
    sudden dash,
And off into the mountain scrub they flew.

Then fast the horsemen followed, where the gorges deep
    and black
Resounded to the thunder of their tread,
And the stockwhips woke the echoes, and they fiercely
    answered back
From cliffs and crags that beetled overhead.
And upward, ever upward, the wild horses held their way,
Where mountain ash and kurrajong grew wide;
And the old man muttered fiercely, "We may bid the mob
    good day,
No man can hold them down the other side."

46

When they reached the mountain's summit, even Clancy
    took a pull—
It well might make the boldest hold their breath;
The wild hop scrub grew thickly, and the hidden ground
    was full
Of wombat holes, and any slip was death.
But the man from Snowy River let the pony have his head,
And he swung his stockwhip round and gave a cheer,
And he raced him down the mountain like a torrent down
    its bed,
While the others stood and watched in very fear.

He sent the flint-stones flying, but the pony kept his feet,
He cleared the fallen timber in his stride,
And the man from Snowy River never shifted in his seat—
It was grand to see that mountain horseman ride.
Through the stringy barks and saplings, on the rough and
    broken ground,
Down the hillside at a racing pace he went;
And he never drew the bridle till he landed safe and sound
At the bottom of that terrible descent.

He was right among the horses as they climbed the farther
    hill,
And the watchers on the mountain, standing mute,
Saw him ply the stockwhip fiercely; he was right among
    them still,
As he raced across the clearing in pursuit.
Then they lost him for a moment, where two mountain
    gullies met
In the ranges—but a final glimpse reveals
On a dim and distant hillside the wild horses racing yet,
With the man from Snowy River at their heels.

And he ran them single-handed till their sides were white
    with foam;
He followed like a bloodhound on their track,
Till they halted, cowed and beaten; then he turned their
    heads for home,
And alone and unassisted brought them back.
But his hardy mountain pony he could scarcely raise a trot,
He was blood from hip to shoulder from the spur;
But his pluck was still undaunted, and his courage fiery
    hot,
For never yet was mountain horse a cur.

And down by Kosciusko, where the pine-clad ridges raise
Their torn and rugged battlements on high,
Where the air is clear as crystal, and the white stars fairly
  blaze
At midnight in the cold and frosty sky,
And where around the Overflow the reed-beds sweep and
  sway
To the breezes, and the rolling plains are wide,
The Man from Snowy River is a household word today,
And the stockmen tell the story of his ride.

"If you talk to animals..."

Chief Dan George

If you talk to animals they will talk with you
and you will know each other.

If you do not talk to them you will not know them
and what you do not know you will fear.

What one fears one destroys.

The Train Dogs

E. Pauline Johnson

Out of the night and the north;
    Savage of breed and of bone,
Shaggy and swift comes the yelping band,
Freighters of fur from the voiceless land
    That sleeps in the Arctic zone.

Laden with skins from the north,
    Beaver and bear and raccoon,
Marten and mink from the polar belts,
Otter and ermine and sable pelts—
    The spoils of the hunter's moon.

Out of the night and the north,
    Sinewy, fearless and fleet,
Urging the pack through the pathless snow,
The Indian driver, calling low,
    Follows with moccasined feet.

Ships of the night and the north,
    Freighters on prairies and plains,
Carrying cargoes from field and flood
They scent the trail through their wild red blood,
    The wolfish blood in their veins.

The Riverbank

If you have ever felt that animals have thoughts, feelings, and jokes to share, just as people do, then you will build lasting friendships when you read The Wind in the Willows *by Kenneth Grahame. In the first chapter, which is printed here, you will meet Mole and Water Rat. When you finish reading, you will probably be curious to find out more about Ratty's companions, Badger and Toad, the other important characters in the story.*

THE MOLE had been working very hard all the morning, spring-cleaning his little home. First with brooms, then with dusters; then on ladders and steps and chairs, with a brush and a pail of whitewash; till he had dust in his throat and eyes, and splashes of whitewash all over his black fur, and an aching back and weary arms. Spring was moving in the air above and in the earth below and around him, penetrating even his dark and lowly little house with its spirit of divine discontent and longing. It was small wonder, then, that he suddenly flung down his brush on the floor, said "Bother!" and "Oh blow!" and also "Hang spring cleaning!" and bolted out of the house without even waiting to put on his coat. Something up above was calling him imperiously, and he made for the steep little tunnel which answered in his case to the graveled carriage-drive owned by animals whose residences are nearer to the sun and air. So he scraped and scratched and scrabbled and scrooged, and then he scrooged again and scrabbled and scratched and scraped, working busily with his little paws and muttering to himself, "Up we go! Up we go!" till at last, pop! his snout came out into the sunlight, and he found himself rolling in the warm grass of a great meadow.

"This is fine!" he said to himself. "This is better than whitewashing!" The sunshine struck hot on his fur, soft breezes caressed his heated brow, and after the seclusion of the cellarage he had lived in so long the carol of happy birds fell on his dulled hearing almost like a shout. Jumping off all his four legs at once, in the joy of living and the delight of spring without its cleaning, he pursued his way across the meadow till he reached the hedge on the further side.

"Hold up!" said an elderly rabbit at the gap. "Sixpence for the privilege of passing by the private road!" He was bowled over in an instant by the impatient and contemptuous Mole, who trotted along the side of the hedge chaffing the other rabbits as they peeped hurriedly from their holes to see what the row was about. "Onion-sauce! Onion-sauce!" he remarked jeeringly, and was gone before they could think of a thoroughly satisfactory reply. Then they all started grumbling at each other. "How *stupid* you are! Why didn't you tell him—" "Well, why didn't *you* say—" "You might have reminded him—" and so on, in the usual way; but, of course, it was then much too late, as is always the case.

It all seemed too good to be true. Hither and thither through the meadows he rambled busily, along the hedgerows, across the copses, finding everywhere birds building, flowers budding, leaves thrusting—everything happy, and progressive, and occupied. And instead of having an uneasy

conscience pricking him and whispering, "Whitewash!" he somehow could only feel how jolly it was to be the only idle dog among all these busy citizens. After all, the best part of a holiday is perhaps not so much to be resting yourself, as to see all the other fellows busy working.

He thought his happiness was complete when, as he meandered aimlessly along, suddenly he stood by the edge of a full-fed river. Never in his life had he seen a river before—this sleek, sinuous, full-bodied animal, chasing and chuckling, gripping things with a gurgle and leaving them with a laugh, to fling itself on fresh playmates that shook themselves free, and were caught and held again. All was a-shake and a-shiver—glints and gleams and sparkles, rustle and swirl, chatter and bubble. The Mole was be-witched, entranced, fascinated. By the side of the river he trotted as one trots, when very small, by the side of a man who holds one spellbound by exciting stories; and when

tired at last, he sat on the bank, while the river still chattered on to him, a babbling procession of the best stories in the world, sent from the heart of the earth to be told at last to the insatiable sea.

As he sat on the grass and looked across the river, a dark hole in the bank opposite, just above the water's edge, caught his eye, and dreamily he fell to considering what a nice snug dwelling-place it would make for an animal with few wants and fond of a bijou riverside residence, above flood level and remote from noise and dust. As he gazed, something bright and small seemed to twinkle down in the heart of it, vanished, then twinkled once more like a tiny star. But it could hardly be a star in such an unlikely situation; and it was too glittering and small for a glow-worm. Then, as he looked, it winked at him, and so declared itself to be an eye; and a small face began gradually to grow up round it, like a frame round a picture.

A brown little face, with whiskers.

A grave round face, with the same twinkle in its eye that had first attracted his notice.

56

Small neat ears and thick silky hair.

It was the Water Rat!

Then the two animals stood and regarded each other cautiously.

"Hullo, Mole!" said the Water Rat.

"Hullo, Rat!" said the Mole.

"Would you like to come over?" inquired the Rat presently.

"Oh, it's all very well to *talk*," said the Mole rather pettishly, he being new to a river and riverside life and its ways.

The Rat said nothing, but stooped and unfastened a rope and hauled on it; then lightly stepped into a little boat which the Mole had not observed. It was painted blue outside and white within, and was just the size for two animals; and the Mole's whole heart went out to it at once, even though he did not yet fully understand its uses.

The Rat sculled smartly across and made fast. Then he held up his forepaw as the Mole stepped gingerly down. "Lean on that!" he said. "Now then, step lively!" and the Mole to his surprise and rapture found himself actually seated in the stern of a real boat.

"This has been a wonderful day!" said he, as the Rat shoved off and took to the sculls again. "Do you know, I've never been in a boat before in all my life."

"What?" cried the Rat, openmouthed: "Never been in a— you never—well, I—what have you been doing, then?"

"Is it so nice as all that?" asked the Mole shyly, though he was quite prepared to believe it as he leaned back in his seat and surveyed the cushions, the oars, the rowlocks, and all the fascinating fittings, and felt the boat sway lightly under him.

"Nice? It's the *only* thing," said the Water Rat solemnly, as he leaned forward for his stroke. "Believe me, my young friend, there is *nothing*—absolutely nothing—half so much worth doing as simply messing about in boats. Simply messing," he went on dreamily: "messing—about—in— boats; messing—"

"Look ahead, Rat!" cried the Mole suddenly.

It was too late. The boat struck the bank full tilt. The dreamer, the joyous oarsman, lay on his back at the bottom of the boat, his heels in the air.

"—about in boats—or *with* boats," the Rat went on composedly, picking himself up with a pleasant laugh. "In or out of 'em, it doesn't matter. Nothing seems really to matter, that's the charm of it. Whether you get away, or whether you don't; whether you arrive at your destination or whether you reach somewhere else, or whether you never get anywhere at all, you're always busy, and you never do anything in particular; and when you've done it there's always something else to do, and you can do it if you like, but you'd much better not. Look here! If you've really nothing else on hand this morning, supposing we drop down the river together, and have a long day of it?"

The Mole waggled his toes from sheer happiness, spread his chest with a sigh of full contentment, and leaned back blissfully into the soft cushions. "*What* a day I'm having!" he said. "Let us start at once!"

"Hold hard a minute, then!" said the Rat. He looped the painter through a ring in his landing-stage, climbed up into his hole above, and after a short interval reappeared staggering under a fat, wicker luncheon-basket.

"Shove that under your feet," he observed to the Mole, as he passed it down into the boat. Then he untied the painter and took the sculls again.

"What's inside it?" asked the Mole, wiggling with curiosity.

"There's cold chicken inside it," replied the Rat briefly; "coldtonguecoldhamcoldbeefpickledgherkinssaladfrench rollscresssandwidgespottedmeatgingerbeerlemonadesoda-water—"

"Oh stop, stop," cried the Mole in ecstasies: "This is too much!"

"Do you really think so?" inquired the Rat seriously. "It's only what I always take on these little excursions; and the other animals are always telling me that I'm a mean beast and cut it *very* fine!"

The Mole never heard a word he was saying. Absorbed in

58

the new life he was entering upon, intoxicated with the sparkle, the ripple, the scents and the sounds and the sunlight, he trailed a paw in the water and dreamed long waking dreams. The Water Rat, like the good little fellow he was, sculled steadily on and forbore to disturb him.

"I like your clothes awfully, old chap," he remarked after some half an hour or so had passed. "I'm going to get a black velvet smoking suit myself someday, as soon as I can afford it."

"I beg your pardon," said the Mole, pulling himself together with an effort. "You must think me very rude; but all this is so new to me. So—this—is—a—River!"

"*The* River," corrected the Rat.

"And you really live by the river? What a jolly life!"

"By it and with it and on it and in it," said the Rat. "It's brother and sister to me, and aunts, and company, and food and drink, and (naturally) washing. It's my world, and I don't want any other. What it hasn't got is not worth having, and what it doesn't know is not worth knowing.

Lord! the times we've had together! Whether in winter or summer, spring or autumn, it's always got its fun and its excitements. When the floods are on in February, and my cellars and basement are brimming with drink that's no good to me, and the brown water runs by my best bedroom window; or again when it all drops away and shows patches of mud that smells like plum cake, and the rushes and weed clog the channels, and I can potter about dry-shod over most of the bed of it and find fresh food to eat, and things careless people have dropped out of boats!"

"But isn't it a bit dull at times?" the Mole ventured to ask. "Just you and the river, and no one else to pass a word with?"

"No one else to—well, I mustn't be hard on you," said the Rat with forbearance. "You're new to it, and of course you don't know. The bank is so crowded nowadays that many people are moving away altogether. Oh no, it isn't what it used to be, at all. Otters, kingfishers, dabchicks, moorhens, all of them about all day long and always wanting you to *do* something—as if a fellow had no business of his own to attend to!"

"What lies over *there*?" asked the Mole, waving a paw towards a background of woodland that darkly framed the water meadows on one side of the river.

"That? Oh that's just the Wild Wood," said the Rat shortly. "We don't go there very much, we riverbankers."

"Aren't they—aren't they very *nice* people in there?" said the Mole a trifle nervously.

"W-e-ll," replied the Rat, "let me see. The squirrels are all right. *And* the rabbits—some of 'em, but rabbits are a mixed lot. And then there's Badger, of course. He lives right in the heart of it; wouldn't live anywhere else, either, if you paid him to do it. Dear old Badger! Nobody interferes with *him*. They'd better not," he added significantly.

"Why, who *should* interfere with him?" asked the Mole.

"Well, of course—there—are others," explained the Rat in a hesitating sort of way. "Weasels—and stoats—and foxes—and so on. They're all right in a way—I'm very good friends with them—pass the time of day when we meet, and all that—but they break out sometimes, there's no denying it, and then—well, you can't really trust them, and that's the fact."

The Mole knew well that it is quite against animal etiquette to dwell on possible trouble ahead, or even to allude to it; so he dropped the subject.

"And beyond the Wild Wood again?" he asked: "Where it's all blue and dim, and one sees what may be hills or perhaps they mayn't and something like the smoke of towns, or is it only cloud-drift?"

"Beyond the Wild Wood comes the Wide World," said the Rat. "And that's something that doesn't matter, either to you or to me. I've never been there, and I'm never going, nor you either, if you've got any sense at all. Don't ever refer to it again, please. Now then! Here's our backwater at last, where we're going to lunch."

Leaving the main stream, they now passed into what seemed at first sight like a little landlocked lake. Green turf sloped down to either edge, brown snaky tree-roots gleamed below the surface of the quiet water, while ahead of them the silvery shoulder and foamy tumble of a weir, arm-in-arm with a restless dripping mill wheel, that held up in its turn a gray-gabled mill house, filled the air with a soothing murmur of sound, dull and smothery, yet with little clear voices speaking up cheerfully out of it at intervals. It was so very beautiful that the Mole could only hold up both forepaws and gasp, "Oh my! Oh my! Oh my!"

The Rat brought the boat alongside the bank, made her fast, helped the still awkward Mole safely ashore, and swung out the luncheon-basket.

The Mole begged as a favor to be allowed to unpack it all by himself; and the Rat was very pleased to indulge him, and to sprawl at full length on the grass and rest, while his excited friend shook out the tablecloth and spread it, took out all the mysterious packets one by one and arranged their contents in due order, still gasping, "Oh my! Oh my!" at each fresh revelation. When all was ready, the Rat said, "Now, pitch in, old fellow!" and the Mole was indeed very glad to obey, for he had started his spring cleaning at a very early hour that morning, as people *will* do, and had not paused for bite or sup; and he had been through a very great deal since that distant time which now seemed so many days ago.

62

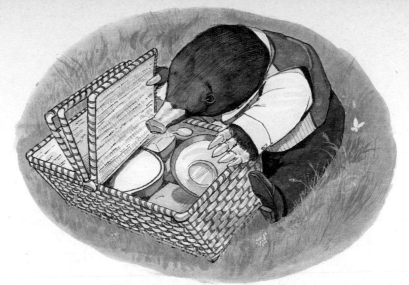

"What are you looking at?" said the Rat presently, when the edge of their hunger was somewhat dulled, and the Mole's eyes were able to wander off the tablecloth a little.

"I am looking," said the Mole, "at a streak of bubbles that I see traveling along the surface of the water. That is a thing that strikes me as funny."

"Bubbles? Oho!" said the Rat, and chirruped cheerily in an inviting sort of way.

A broad glistening muzzle showed itself above the edge of the bank, and the Otter hauled himself out and shook the water from his coat.

"Greedy beggars!" he observed, making for the provender. "Why didn't you invite me, Ratty?"

"This was an impromptu affair," explained the Rat. "By the way—my friend Mr. Mole."

"Proud, I'm sure," said the Otter, and the two animals were friends forthwith.

"Such a rumpus everywhere!" continued the Otter, "All the world seems out on the river today. I come up this backwater to try and get a moment's peace, and then stumble upon you fellows!—At least—I beg pardon—I don't exactly mean that, you know."

There was a rustle behind them, proceeding from a hedge wherein last year's leaves still clung thick, and a stripy head, with high shoulders behind it, peered forth on them.

"Come on, old Badger," shouted the Rat.

The Badger trotted forward a pace or two; then grunted, "H'm! Company," and turned his back and disappeared from view.

"That's *just* the sort of fellow he is!" observed the disappointed Rat. "Simply hates Society! Now we shan't see any more of him today. Well, tell us *who's* out on the river?"

"Toad's out, for one," replied the Otter. "In his brand-new wager-boat; new togs, new everything!"

The two animals looked at each other and laughed.

"Once, it was nothing but sailing," said the Rat. "Then he tired of that and took to punting. Nothing would please him but to punt all day and every day, and a nice mess he made of it. Last year it was houseboating, and we all had to go and stay with him in his houseboat, and pretend we liked it. He was going to spend the rest of his life in a houseboat. It's all the same whatever he takes up; he gets tired of it, and starts on something fresh."

"Such a good fellow, too," remarked the Otter reflectively: "But no stability—especially in a boat!"

From where they sat they could get a glimpse of the main stream across the island that separated them; and just then a wager-boat flashed into view, the rower—a short, stout figure—splashing badly and rolling a good deal, but working his hardest. The Rat stood up and hailed him, but Toad —for it was he—shook his head and settled sternly to his work.

"He'll be out of the boat in a minute if he rolls like that," said the Rat, sitting down again.

"Of course he will," chuckled the Otter. "Did I ever tell you that good story about Toad and the lock keeper? It happened this way. Toad . . ."

An errant mayfly swerved unsteadily athwart the current in the intoxicated fashion affected by young bloods of mayflies seeing life. A swirl of water and a "cloop!" and the mayfly was visible no more.

Neither was the Otter.

The Mole looked down. The voice was still in his ears, but the turf whereon he had sprawled was clearly vacant. Not an Otter to be seen, as far as the distant horizon.

But again there was a streak of bubbles on the surface of the river.

The Rat hummed a tune, and the Mole recollected that animal etiquette forbade any sort of comment on the sudden disappearance of one's friends at any moment, for any reason or no reason whatever.

"Well, well," said the Rat, "I suppose we ought to be moving. I wonder which of us had better pack the luncheon-basket?" He did not speak as if he was frightfully eager for the treat.

"Oh, please let me," said the Mole. So, of course, the Rat let him.

Packing the basket was not quite such pleasant work as unpacking the basket. It never is. But the Mole was bent on enjoying everything, and although just when he had got the basket packed and strapped up tightly he saw a plate staring up at him from the grass, and when the job had been done again the Rat pointed out a fork which anybody ought to have seen, and last of all, behold! the mustard pot, which he had been sitting on without knowing it—still, somehow, the thing got finished at last, without much loss of temper.

The afternoon sun was getting low as the Rat sculled gently homewards in a dreamy mood, murmuring poetry-things over to himself, and not paying much attention to Mole. But the Mole was very full of lunch, and self-satisfaction, and pride, and already quite at home in a boat (so he thought) and was getting a bit restless besides: and presently he said, "Ratty! Please, *I* want to row, now!"

The Rat shook his head with a smile. "Not yet, my young friend," he said—"wait till you've had a few lessons. It's not so easy as it looks."

The Mole was quiet for a minute or two. But he began to feel more and more jealous of Rat, sculling so strongly and so easily along, and his pride began to whisper that he could do it every bit as well. He jumped up and seized the sculls so suddenly, that the Rat, who was gazing out over the water and saying more poetry-things to himself, was taken by surprise and fell backwards off his seat with his legs in the air for the second time, while the triumphant Mole took his place and grabbed the sculls with entire confidence.

"Stop it, you *silly* ass!" cried the Rat, from the bottom of the boat. "You can't do it! You'll have us over!"

The Mole flung his sculls back with a flourish, and made a great dig at the water. He missed the surface altogether, his legs flew up above his head, and he found himself lying on the top of the prostrate Rat. Greatly alarmed, he made a grab at the side of the boat, and the next moment— sploosh!

Over went the boat, and he found himself struggling in the river.

Oh my, how cold the water was, and Oh, how *very* wet it felt. How it sang in his ears as he went down, down, down! How bright and welcome the sun looked as he rose to the surface coughing and spluttering! How black was his despair when he felt himself sinking again! Then a firm paw gripped him by the back of his neck. It was the Rat, and he was evidently laughing—the Mole could *feel* him laughing, right down his arm and through his paw, and so into his —the Mole's—neck.

The Rat got hold of a scull and shoved it under the Mole's arm; then he did the same by the other side of him and, swimming behind, propelled the helpless animal to shore, hauled him out, and set him down on the bank, a squashy, pulpy lump of misery.

When the Rat had rubbed him down a bit, and wrung some of the wet out of him, he said, "Now, then, old fellow! Trot up and down the towing-path as hard as you can, till you're warm and dry again, while I dive for the luncheon-basket."

So the dismal Mole, wet without and ashamed within, trotted about till he was fairly dry, while the Rat plunged into the water again, recovered the boat, righted her and made her fast, fetched his floating property to shore by degrees, and finally dived successfully for the luncheon-basket and struggled to land with it.

When all was ready for a start once more, the Mole, limp and dejected, took his seat in the stern of the boat; and as they set off, he said in a low voice, broken with emotion, "Ratty, my generous friend! I am very sorry indeed for my foolish and ungrateful conduct. My heart quite fails me when I think how I might have lost that beautiful luncheon-basket. Indeed, I have been a complete ass, and I know it. Will you overlook it this once and forgive me, and let things go on as before?"

"That's all right, bless you!" responded the Rat cheerily. "What's a little wet to a Water Rat? I'm more in the water than out of it most days. Don't you think any more about it; and, look here! I really think you had better come and stop with me for a little time. It's very plain and rough, you know—not like Toad's house at all—but you haven't seen that yet; still, I can make you comfortable. And I'll teach you to row, and to swim, and you'll soon be as handy on the water as any of us."

The Mole was so touched by his kind manner of speaking that he could find no voice to answer him; and he had to brush away a tear or two with the back of his paw. But the Rat kindly looked in another direction, and presently the Mole's spirits revived again, and he was even able to give some straight back-talk to a couple of moorhens who were sniggering to each other about his bedraggled appearance.

When they got home, the Rat made a bright fire in the parlor, and planted the Mole in an armchair in front of it, having fetched down a dressing gown and slippers for him, and told him river stories till suppertime. Very thrilling stories they were, too, to an earth-dwelling animal like Mole. Stories about weirs, and sudden floods, and leaping pike, and steamers that flung hard bottles—at least bottles were certainly flung, and *from* steamers, so presumably *by* them; and about herons, and how particular they were whom they spoke to; and about adventures down drains, and night fishings with Otter, or excursions far afield with Badger. Supper was a most cheerful meal; but very shortly afterwards a terribly sleepy Mole had to be escorted up-stairs by his considerate host, to the best bedroom, where he soon laid his head on his pillow in great peace and contentment, knowing that his newfound friend the River was lapping the sill of his window.

This day was only the first of many similar ones for the emancipated Mole, each of them longer and fuller of inter-est as the ripening summer moved onward. He learned to swim and to row, and entered into the joy of running water; and with his ear to the reed-stems he caught, at intervals, something of what the wind went whispering so constantly among them.

Baucis and Philemon

This ancient myth will introduce you to Jupiter, supreme god of the Romans, and to his son and messenger, Mercury. It is one of the gentlest myths you will ever read.

ON A certain hill in Phrygia stand a linden tree and an oak, enclosed by a low wall. Not far from the spot is a marsh, formerly good habitable land, but now indented with pools, the resort of fen-birds and cormorants. Once on a time, Jupiter, in human shape, visited this country, and with him his son Mercury (he of the caduceus) without his wings. They presented themselves as weary travellers, at many a door, seeking rest and shelter, but found all closed, for it was late, and the inhospitable inhabitants would not rouse themselves to open for their reception. At last a humble mansion received them, a small thatched cottage, where Baucis, a pious old dame, and her husband Philemon, united when young, had grown old together. Not ashamed of their poverty, they made it endurable by moderate desires and kind dispositions. One need not look there for master or for servant; they two were the whole household, master and servant alike.

When the two heavenly guests crossed the humble threshold, and bowed their heads to pass under the low door, the old man placed a seat, on which Baucis, bustling and attentive, spread a cloth, and begged them to sit down. Then she raked out the coals from the ashes, and kindled up a fire, fed it with leaves and dry bark, and with her scanty breath blew it into a flame. She brought out of a corner split sticks and dry branches, broke them up, and placed them under the small kettle. Her husband collected some pot-herbs in the garden, and she shred them from the stalks, and prepared them for the pot. He reached down with a forked stick a flitch of bacon hanging in the chimney, cut a small piece, and put it in the pot to boil with the herbs, setting away the rest for another time. A beechen bowl was filled with warm water, that their guests might wash. While all was doing, they beguiled the time with conversation.

On the bench designed for the guests was laid a cushion stuffed with sea weed; and a cloth, only produced on great occasions, but ancient and coarse enough, was spread over that. The old lady, with her apron on, with trembling hand set the table. One leg was shorter than the rest, but a piece of slate put under restored the level. When fixed, she rubbed the table down with some sweet-smelling herbs. Upon it she set some of chaste Minerva's olives, some cornel berries preserved in vinegar, and added radishes and cheese, with eggs lightly cooked in the ashes. All were served in earthen dishes, and an earthenware pitcher, with wooden cups, stood beside them. When all was ready, the stew, smoking hot, was set on the table. Some wine, not of the oldest, was added; and for dessert, apples and wild honey; and over and above all, friendly faces, and simple but hearty welcome.

Now while the repast proceeded, the old folks were aston-ished to see that the wine, as fast as it was poured out,

renewed itself in the pitcher, of its own accord. Struck with terror, Baucis and Philemon recognized their heavenly guests, fell on their knees, and with clasped hands implored forgiveness for their poor entertainment. There was an old goose, which they kept as the guardian of their humble cottage; and they bethought them to make this a sacrifice in honor of their guests. But the goose, too nimble, with the aid of feet and wings, for the old folks, eluded their pursuit and at last took shelter between the gods themselves. They forbade it to be slain; and spoke in these words: "We are gods. This inhospitable village shall pay the penalty of its impiety; you alone shall go free from the chastisement. Quit your house, and come with us to the top of yonder hill."

The old couple hastened to obey, and, staff in hand, labored up the steep ascent. They had reached to within an arrow's flight of the top, when turning their eyes below, they beheld all the country sunk in a lake, only their own house left standing. While they gazed with wonder at the sight, and lamented the fate of their neighbors, that old house of theirs was changed into a *temple*. Columns took the place of the corner posts, the thatch grew yellow and appeared a gilded roof, the floors became marble, the doors were enriched with carving and ornaments of gold.

Then spoke Jupiter in benignant accents: "Excellent old man, and woman worthy of such a husband, speak, tell us your wishes; what favor have you to ask of us?"

Philemon took counsel with Baucis a few moments; then declared to the gods their united wish. "We ask to be priests and guardians of this your temple; and since here we have passed our lives in love and concord, we wish that one and the same hour may take us both from life, that I may not live to see her grave, nor be laid in my own by her." Their prayer was granted. They were the keepers of the temple as long as they lived.

When grown very old, as they stood one day before the steps of the sacred edifice, and were telling the story of the place, Baucis saw Philemon begin to put forth leaves, and old Philemon saw Baucis changing in like manner. And now a leafy crown had grown over their heads, while exchanging parting words, as long as they could speak. "Farewell, dear spouse," they said together, and at the same moment the bark closed over their mouths. The Tyanean shepherd still shows the two trees, standing side by side, made out of the two good old people.

73

The Grasshopper and the Ants

O N A beautiful sunny winter day some ants had their winter store of food out to dry. A grasshopper came by and gazed hungrily at the food. As the ants paid no attention to him, he finally said, "Won't you please give me something to eat? I'm starving." "Did you not store away food last summer for use now?" asked the ants. "No," replied the grasshopper, "I was too busy enjoying myself in dancing and singing." "Well, then," said the ants, "live this winter on your dancing and singing, as we live on what we did."

No one has a right to play all the time,
or he will have to suffer for it.

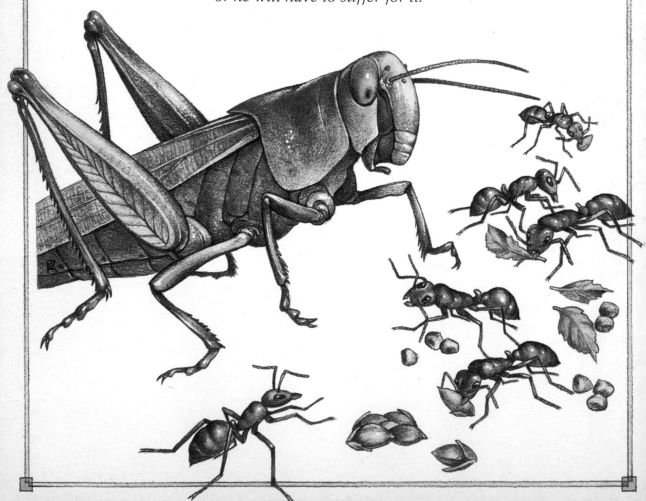

The Town Mouse and the Country Mouse

A COUNTRY mouse was very happy that his city cousin, the town mouse, had accepted his invitation to dinner. He gave his city cousin all the best food he had, such as dried beans, peas, and crusts of bread. The town mouse tried not to show how he disliked the food and picked a little here and tasted a little there to be polite. After dinner, however, he said, "How can you stand such food all the time? Still I suppose here in the country you don't know about any better. Why don't you go home with me? When you have once tasted the delicious things I eat, you will never want to come back here." The country mouse not only kindly forgave the town mouse for not liking his dinner, but even consented to go that very evening to the city with his cousin. They arrived late at night; and the city mouse, as host, took his country cousin at once to a room where there had been a big dinner. "You are tired," he said. "Rest here, and I'll bring you some real food." And he brought the country mouse such things as nuts, dates, cakes, and fruit. The country mouse thought it was all so good, he would like to stay there. But before he had a chance to say so, he heard a terrible roar, and looking up, he saw a huge creature dash into the room. Frightened half out of his wits, the country mouse ran from the table, and round and round the room, trying to find a hiding place. At last he found a place of safety. While he stood there trembling he made up his mind to go home as soon as he could get safely away; for, to himself, he said, "I'd rather have common food in safety than dates and nuts in the midst of danger."

The troubles you know are easiest to bear.

The Carefree Miller

*This French Canadian folktale is as rough
as black maple bark and full of surprises.
The tale comes from Edith Fowke's collection
Folktales of French Canada.*

ONCE there was an old man and his wife who lived happily in ease and contentment, without worry about their old age. Their only concern centred on their boy, Ti-Jean, who was intelligent but also very resourceful and hot-tempered. It was this last fault that worried them most.

One evening the father had returned from the city with a big turkey and goose. He said, "Ti-Jean, I'm giving you this goose because you've been good today. Take good care of it." Ti-Jean, who was eight or nine then, was pleased by his father's attention and resolved to take care of the goose as he'd been told.

Some time later Ti-Jean was uneasy. The goose disappeared and then returned without anyone finding where it had gone. One day when he'd gone to look for it, he suddenly heard a loud noise. Looking in the direction of the noise he saw the big turkey beating its wings, pecking at something, and crying loudly, "You'll die of it! You'll die of it!" Ti-Jean ran up and what did he see? His goose stretched out dead on a nest of eggs and the turkey attacking her, pecking her on the head and crying louder and louder, "You'll die of it! You'll die of it!"

At the sight, Ti-Jean, believing that the big turkey had killed his goose, became very angry. Seizing a heavy club he beat at the turkey, which gave its last "You'll die of it!" and sank down dead itself. That gave Ti-Jean's father and

76

mother still another reason to worry over his temper tantrums.

However, Ti-Jean was incorrigible and also, as he grew up, he became very dishonest. One of Ti-Jean's father's many occupations was that of raising and fattening pigs. He always had a large flock in a pen near a bog which was very deep. One day the father and mother went to town. The father gave Ti-Jean strict orders to take good care of the pigs, especially to be careful to keep the gate closed because of the danger that the pigs would sink in the bog nearby.

His father and mother had scarcely been gone half an hour when an animal buyer came to Ti-Jean asking if the large flock of pigs he'd seen in the pen were for sale. Ti-Jean refused at first, but the buyer persisted and offered him a good price, so he finally decided to sell but on condition that he, Ti-Jean, cut and kept the tails of the pigs. The buyer agreed. Ti-Jean cut the tail off each pig and put

the pigs in the cart of the merchant who soon disappeared with his purchase.

As soon as he'd gone Ti-Jean went to put the pigs' tails in the bog, opened the gate, and went to work. At suppertime his father came and saw the gate was open and his pigs gone. He questioned Ti-Jean but the wicked rascal said that he didn't know who had opened the gate. All he could say was that the pigs had all disappeared into the bog when he saw their tails on the surface.

Making Ti-Jean see what a disaster he'd caused, his father ordered him to pull the drowned pigs out by the tails. Perhaps by washing and bleeding them he could save a good part of the meat. With the aid of some planks Ti-Jean made a kind of floating bridge to get near the tails. Then with contortions and grimaces he pretended to try to pull the pigs out of the slough. Suddenly he seized one cut tail, pretended to fall, and upset. Then having frightened his father, Ti-Jean threw away the tails he'd caught, pretending to be in despair at not being able to succeed in his task. His father became disheartened over the loss of his pigs and scolded Ti-Jean for the rest of the night.

The next day, when his father and mother got up, Ti-Jean had disappeared. During the night he'd got up quietly, made a bundle of clothes and food, and taken to the road, determined never to return to his parents' home. His pocket well-filled with the money from the sale of the pigs, he walked for three days till he came to a flour mill where he stopped to rest. The miller, who needed a man, offered to hire him. Ti-Jean accepted immediately, for this miller had the reputation of never knowing anxiety. He was always good-humoured, without worry or trouble—they called him the carefree miller.

Three months later a surprising event happened. The king had long heard of this miller, reputed never to have known anxiety. One day the king was guided to his place and after a long conversation he said to him, "Miller, our positions in life are not equal. In spite of your poverty you have a happy life without anxiety; me, in spite of glory and grandeur, I am tired out by worries, troubles of all sorts. I

want to know if you can take part of them. Three days from now you'll have to tell me three things. Where is the centre of the earth? How much I am worth, and what I think. If you can't answer these three questions it will be the worse for you."

On these last words the king went away, leaving the miller perplexed and thinking hard. The more time passed, the more thoughtful and worried the miller became. Ti-Jean noticed the change in the miller's mood and asked the reason. When the miller told him the reason for his anxiety, Ti-Jean, who somewhat resembled the miller, offered to go to see the king in his place. The miller accepted the proposal immediately, and the next day Ti-Jean, dressed in the miller's clothes, went to the King's palace, and was brought into his presence.

"Well, miller, can you tell me where the centre of the world is?"

"Sire, my king," replied Ti-Jean, "the centre of the world is where Your Majesty puts his feet."

The king, put in good humour by this reply, smiled and said, "I'll accept that, but now tell me how much I am worth."

"Sire, my king, Your Majesty is worth twenty-nine pieces of silver."

"What!" said the king, startled. "Only twenty-nine pieces of silver? Explain that to me."

"Sire, my king, our Lord was sold for thirty pieces of silver. He was certainly worth one piece more than you."

"Bravo!" said the king, "I accept that also. Tell me now what I am thinking."

"Sire, my king, you think you're speaking to the miller, but you're speaking to Ti-Jean, his hired man."

The king, satisfied with Ti-Jean's answers, hired him to live in the castle and gave him the highest posts awarded to any servant. Later Ti-Jean went to visit his old parents, whom he found living almost in poverty. He was forgiven his past escapades and saw that they lived out their days in contentment and happiness.

The Village Blacksmith

Henry Wadsworth Longfellow

Under a spreading chestnut-tree
    The village smithy stands;
The smith, a mighty man is he,
    With large and sinewy hands;
And the muscles of his brawny arms
    Are strong as iron bands.

His hair is crisp, and black, and long,
    His face is like the tan;
His brow is wet with honest sweat,
    He earns whate'er he can,
And looks the whole world in the face,
    For he owes not any man.

Week in, week out, from morn till night,
    You can hear his bellows blow;
You can hear him swing his heavy sledge,
    With measured beat and slow,
Like a sexton ringing the village bell,
    When the evening sun is low.

And children coming home from school
    Look in at the open door;
They love to see the flaming forge,
    And hear the bellows roar,
And catch the burning sparks that fly—
    Like chaff from a threshing-floor.

He goes on Sunday to the church,
    And sits among his boys;
He hears the parson pray and preach,
    He hears his daughter's voice,
Singing in the village choir,
    And it makes his heart rejoice.

It sounds to him like her mother's voice,
    Singing in Paradise!
He needs must think of her once more,
    How in the grave she lies;
And with his hard, rough hand he wipes
    A tear out of his eyes.

Toiling,—rejoicing,—sorrowing,
    Onward through life he goes;
Each morning sees some task begin,
    Each evening sees it close;
Something attempted, something done,
    Has earned a night's repose.

Thanks, thanks to thee, my worthy friend,
    For the lesson thou hast taught!
Thus at the flaming forge of life
    Our fortunes must be wrought;
Thus on its sounding anvil shaped
    Each burning deed and thought.

Rebecca

Who slammed Doors for Fun and
Perished Miserably

Hilaire Belloc

A Trick that everyone abhors
In Little Girls is slamming Doors.
A Wealthy Banker's little Daughter
Who lived in Palace Green, Bayswater
(By name Rebecca Offendort),
Was given to this Furious Sport.
She would deliberately go
And Slam the door like Billy-Ho!
To make her Uncle Jacob start.
She was not really bad at heart,
But only rather rude and wild:
She was an aggravating child.

It happened that a Marble Bust
Of Abraham was standing just
Above the Door this little Lamb
Had carefully prepared to Slam,
And down it came! It knocked her flat!
It laid her out! She looked like that!

. . . .

Her funeral Sermon (which was long
And followed by a Sacred Song)
Mentioned her Virtues, it is true,
But dwelt upon her Vices too,
And showed the Dreadful End of One
Who goes and slams the door for Fun.

The Woman Who Flummoxed the Fairies

"Flummox" is a wonderful-sounding word that means "to confuse or embarrass." In this Scottish folktale from Sorche Nic Leodhas's book Heather and Broom, *you will see how very clever one has to be to flummox fairies.*

THERE was a woman once who was a master baker. Her bannocks were like wheaten cakes, her wheaten cakes were like the finest pastries, and her pastries werc like nothing but Heaven itself in the mouth!

Not having her match, or anything like it, in seven counties round she made a good penny by it, for there wasn't a wedding nor a christening for miles around in the countryside but she was called upon to make the cakes for it, and she got all the trade of all the gentry as well. She was fair in her prices and she was honest, too, but she was that good-hearted into the bargain. Those who could pay well she charged aplenty, but when some poor body came and begged her to make a wee bit of a cake for a celebration and timidly offered her the little money they had for it, she'd wave it away and tell them to pay her when they got the cake. Then she'd set to and bake a cake as fine and big as any she'd make for a laird, and she'd send it to them as a gift, with the best respects of her husband and herself, to the wedding pair or the parents of the baby that was to be christened, so nobody's feelings were hurt.

Not only was she a master baker, but she was the cleverest woman in the world; and it was the first that got her into trouble, but it was the second that got her out of it.

The fairies have their own good foods to eat, but they dearly love a bit of baker's cake once in a while, and will often steal a slice of one by night from a kitchen while all the folks in a house are sleeping.

In a nearby hill there was a place where the fairies lived, and of all cakes the ones the fairies liked best were the ones this master baker made. The trouble was, the taste of one was hard to come by, for her cakes were all so good that they were always eaten up at a sitting, with hardly a crumb left over for a poor fairy to find.

So then the fairies plotted together to carry the woman away and to keep her with them always just to bake cakes for them.

Their chance came not long after, for there was to be a great wedding at the castle with hundreds of guests invited, and the woman was to make the cakes. There would have to be so many of them, with so many people coming to eat them, that the woman was to spend the whole day before the wedding in the castle kitchen doing nothing but bake one cake after another!

88

The fairies learned about this from one of their number
who had been listening at the keyhole of the baker's door.
They found out, too, what road she'd be taking coming
home.

When the night came, there they were by a fairy mound
where the road went by, hiding in flower cups, and under
leaves, and in all manner of places.

When she came by they all flew out at her. "The fireflies
are gey thick the night," said she. But it was not fireflies. It
was fairies with the moonlight sparkling on their wings.

Then the fairies drifted fern seed into her eyes, and all of
a sudden she was that sleepy that she could go not one step
farther without a bit of a rest!

"Mercy me!" she said with a yawn. "It's worn myself out

89

I have this day!" And she sank down on what she took to be a grassy bank to doze just for a minute. But it wasn't a bank at all. It was the fairy mound, and once she lay upon it she was in the fairies' power.

She knew nothing about that nor anything else till she woke again, and found herself in fairyland. Being a clever woman she didn't have to be told where she was, and she guessed how she got there. But she didn't let on.

"Well now," she said happily, "and did you ever! It's all my life I've wanted to get a peep into fairyland. And here I am!"

They told her what they wanted, and she said to herself, indeed she had no notion of staying there the rest of her life! But she didn't tell the fairies that either.

"To be sure!" she said cheerfully. "Why, you poor wee things! To think of me baking cakes for everyone else, and not a one for you. So let's be at it," said she, "with no time wasted."

Then from her kittiebag that hung at her side she took a clean apron and tied it around her waist, while the fairies, happy that she was so willing, licked their lips in anticipation and rubbed their hands for joy.

"Let me see now," said she, looking around her. "Well, 'tis plain you have nothing for me to be baking a cake with. You'll just have to be going to my own kitchen to fetch back what I'll need."

Yes, the fairies could do that. So she sent some for eggs, and some for sugar, and some for flour, and some for butter, while others flew off to get a wheen of other things she told them she had to have. At last all was ready for the mixing and the woman asked for a bowl. But the biggest one they could find for her was the size of a teacup, and a wee dainty one at that.

Well then, there was nothing for it, but they must go and fetch her big yellow crockery bowl from off the shelf over the water butt. And after that it was her wooden spoons and her egg whisp and one thing and another, till the fairies were all fagged out, what with the flying back and forth, and the carrying, and only the thought of the cake to come of it kept the spirits up at all.

At last everything she wanted was at hand. The woman began to measure and mix and whip and beat. But all of a sudden she stopped.

" 'Tis no use!" she sighed. "I can't ever seem to mix a cake without my cat beside me, purring."

"Fetch the cat!" said the fairy king sharply.

So they fetched the cat. The cat lay at the woman's feet and purred, and the woman stirred away at the bowl, and for a while all was well. But not for long.

The woman let go of the spoon and sighed again. "Well now, would you think it?" said she. "I'm that used to my dog setting the time of my beating by the way he snores at every second beat that I can't seem to get the beat right without him."

"Fetch the dog!" cried the king.

So they fetched the dog and he curled up at her feet beside the cat. The dog snored, the cat purred, the woman beat the cake batter, and all was well again. Or so the fairies thought.

But no! The woman stopped again. "I'm that worrited about my babe," said she. "Away from him all night as I've been, and him with a new tooth pushing through this very week. It seems I just can't mix. . ."

"Fetch that babe!" roared the fairy king, without waiting for her to finish what she was saying. And they fetched the babe.

So the woman began to beat the batter again. But when they brought the babe, he began to scream the minute he saw her, for he was hungry, as she knew he would be, because he never would let his dadda feed him his porridge and she had not been home to do it.

"I'm sorry to trouble you," said the woman, raising her voice above the screaming of the babe, "but I can't stop beating now lest the cake go wrong. Happen my husband could get the babe quiet if . . ."

The fairies didn't wait for the king to tell them what to do. Off they flew and fetched the husband back with them. He, poor man, was all in a whirl, what with things disappearing from under his eyes right and left, and then being snatched through the air himself the way he was. But here was his wife, and he knew where she was things couldn't go far wrong. But the baby went on screaming.

So the woman beat the batter, and the baby screamed, and the cat purred, and the dog snored, and the man rubbed his eyes and watched his wife to see what she was up to. The fairies settled down, though 'twas plain to see that the babe's screaming disturbed them. Still, they looked hopeful.

Then the woman reached over and took up the egg whisp and gave the wooden spoon to the babe, who at once began to bang away with it, screaming just the same. Under cover of the screaming of the babe and the banging of the spoon and the swishing of the egg whisp the woman whispered to her husband, "Pinch the dog!"

"What?" said the man. But he did it just the same—and kept on doing it.

"Tow! Row! Row!" barked the dog, and added his voice to the babe's screams, and the banging of the wooden spoon, and the swishing of the egg whisp.

"Tread on the tail of the cat!" whispered the woman to her husband, and it's a wonder he could hear her. But he did. He had got the notion now and he entered the game for himself. He not only trod on the tail of the cat, but he kept his foot there while the cat howled like a dozen lost souls.

So the woman swished, and the baby screamed, and the wooden spoon banged, and the dog yelped, and the cat howled, and the whole of it made a terrible din. The fairies, king and all, flew round and round in distraction with their hands over their ears, for if there is one thing the fairies can't bear it's a lot of noise and there was a lot more than a

lot of noise in fairyland that day! And what's more the woman knew what they liked and what they didn't all the time!

So then the woman got up and poured the batter into two pans that stood ready. She laid by the egg whisp and took the wooden spoon away from the babe, and picking him up she popped a lump of sugar into his mouth. That surprised him so much that he stopped screaming. She nodded to her husband and he stopped pinching the dog and took his foot from the cat's tail, and in a minute's time all was quiet. The fairies stopped flying round and round and sank down exhausted.

And then the woman said, "The cake's ready for the baking. Where's the oven?"

The fairies looked at each other in dismay, and at last the fairy queen said weakly, "There isn't any oven."

"What!" exclaimed the woman. "No oven? Well then, how do you expect me to be baking the cake?"

None of the fairies could find the answer to that.

"Well then," said the woman, "you'll just have to be taking me and the cake home to bake it in my own oven, and bring me back later when the cake's all done."

The fairies looked at the babe and the wooden spoon and the egg whisp and the dog and the cat and the man. And then they all shuddered like one.

"You may all go!" said the fairy king. "But don't ask us to be taking you. We're all too tired."

"Och, you must have your cake then," said the woman, feeling sorry for them now she'd got what she wanted, which was to go back to her own home, "after all the trouble you've had for it! I'll tell you what I'll do. After it's baked, I'll be leaving it for you beside the road, behind the bank where you found me. And what's more I'll put one there for you every single week's end from now on."

The thought of having one of the woman's cakes every week revived the fairies so that they forgot they were all worn out. Or almost did.

"I'll not be outdone!" cried the fairy king. "For what you find in that same place shall be your own!"

Then the woman picked up the pans of batter, and the man tucked the bowls and spoons and things under one arm and the baby under the other. The fairy king raised an arm and the hill split open. Out they all walked, the woman with the pans of batter, the man with the bowls and the babe, and the dog and cat at their heels. Down the road they walked and back to their own house, and never looked behind them.

When they got back to their home the woman put the pans of batter into the oven, and then she dished out the porridge that stood keeping hot on the back of the fire and gave the babe his supper.

There wasn't a sound in that house except for the clock ticking and the kettle singing and the cat purring and the dog snoring. And all those were soft, quiet sounds.

"I'll tell you what," said the man at last. "It doesn't seem fair on the rest of the men that I should have the master baker and the cleverest woman in the world all in one wife."

"Trade me off then for one of the ordinary kind," said his wife, laughing at him.

"I'll not do it," said he. "I'm very well suited as I am."

So that's the way the woman flummoxed the fairies. A good thing she made out of it, too, for when the cake was baked and cooled the woman took it up and put it behind the fairy mound, as she had promised. And when she set it down she saw there a little brown bag. She took the bag up and opened it and looked within, and it was full of bright shining yellow gold pieces.

And so it went, week after week. A cake for the fairies, a bag of gold for the woman and her husband. They never saw one of the fairies again, but the bargain never was broken and they grew rich by it. So of course they lived, as why should they not, happily ever after.

Two of Everything

You must be prepared to laugh when you read this very happy Chinese folktale from Alice Ritchie's book The Treasure of Li Po.

MR. and Mrs. Hak-Tak were rather old and rather poor. They had a small house in a village among the mountains and a tiny patch of green land on the mountain side. Here they grew the vegetables which were all they had to live on, and when it was a good season and they did not need to eat up everything as soon as it was grown, Mr. Hak-Tak took what they could spare in a basket to the next village which was a little larger than theirs and sold it for as much as he could get and bought some oil for their lamp, and fresh seeds, and every now and then, but not often, a piece of cotton stuff to make new coats and trousers for himself and his wife. You can imagine they did not often get the chance to eat meat.

Now, one day it happened that when Mr. Hak-Tak was digging in his precious patch, he unearthed a big brass pot. He thought it strange that it should have been there for so long without his having come across it before, and he was disappointed to find that it was empty; still, he thought they would find some use for it, so when he was ready to go back to the house in the evening he decided to take it with him. It was very big and heavy, and in his struggles to get his arms round it and raise it to a good position for carrying, his purse, which he always took with him in his belt, fell to the ground, and, to be quite sure he had it safe, he put it inside the pot and so staggered home with his load.

As soon as he got into the house Mrs. Hak-Tak hurried from the inner room to meet him.

"My dear husband," she said, "whatever have you got there?"

"For a cooking-pot it is too big; for a bath a little too small," said Mr. Hak-Tak. "I found it buried in our vegetable patch and so far it has been useful in carrying my purse home for me."

"Alas," said Mrs. Hak-Tak, "something smaller would have done as well to hold any money we have or are likely to have," and she stooped over the pot and looked into its dark inside.

As she stooped, her hairpin—for poor Mrs. Hak-Tak had only one hairpin for all her hair and it was made of carved bone—fell into the pot. She put in her hand to get it out again, and then she gave a loud cry which brought her husband running to her side.

"What is it?" he asked. "Is there a viper in the pot?"

"Oh, my dear husband," she cried. "What can be the meaning of this? I put my hand into the pot to fetch out my hairpin and your purse, and look, I have brought out two hairpins and two purses, both exactly alike."

"Open the purse. Open both purses," said Mr. Hak-Tak. "One of them will certainly be empty."

But not a bit of it. The new purse contained exactly the same number of coins as the old one—for that matter, no one could have said which was the new and which the old—and it meant, of course, that the Hak-Taks had exactly twice as much money in the evening as they had had in the morning.

"And two hairpins instead of one!" cried Mrs. Hak-Tak, forgetting in her excitement to do up her hair which was streaming over her shoulders. "There is something quite unusual about this pot."

"Let us put in the sack of lentils and see what happens," said Mr. Hak-Tak, also becoming excited.

They heaved in the bag of lentils and when they pulled it out again—it was so big it almost filled the pot—they saw another bag of exactly the same size waiting to be pulled out in its turn. So now they had two bags of lentils instead of one.

"Put in the blanket," said Mr. Hak-Tak. "We need another blanket for the cold weather." And, sure enough, when the blanket came out, there lay another behind it.

"Put my wadded coat in," said Mr. Hak-Tak, "and then when the cold weather comes there will be one for you as well as for me. Let us put in everything we have in turn. What a pity we have no meat or tobacco, for it seems that the pot cannot make anything without a pattern."

Then Mrs. Hak-Tak, who was a woman of great intelligence, said, "My dear husband, let us put the purse in again and again and again. If we take two purses out each time we put one in, we shall have enough money by tomorrow evening to buy everything we lack."

"I am afraid we may lose it this time," said Mr. Hak-Tak, but in the end he agreed, and they dropped in the purse and pulled out two, then they added the new money to the old and dropped it in again and pulled out the larger amount twice over. After a while the floor was covered with old leather purses and they decided just to throw the money in by itself. It worked quite as well and saved trouble; every time, twice as much money came out as went in, and every time they added the new coins to the old and threw them all in together. It took them some hours to tire of this game, but at last Mrs. Hak-Tak said, "My dear husband, there is no need for us to work so hard. We shall see to it that the pot does not run away, and we can always make more money as we want it. Let us tie up what we have."

It made a huge bundle in the extra blanket and the Hak-Taks lay and looked at it for a long time before they slept, and talked of all the things they would buy and the improvements they would make in the cottage.

The next morning they rose early and Mr. Hak-Tak filled a wallet with money from the bundle and set off for the big village to buy more things in one morning than he had bought in a whole fifty years.

Mrs. Hak-Tak saw him off and then she tidied up the cottage and put the rice on to boil and had another look at the bundle of money, and made herself a whole set of new hairpins from the pot, and about twenty candles instead of the one which was all they had possessed up to now. After that she slept for a while, having been up so late the night before, but just before the time when her husband should be back, she awoke and went over to the pot. She dropped in a cabbage leaf to make sure it was still working properly, and when she took two leaves out she sat down on the floor and put her arms round it.

"I do not know how you came to us, my dear pot," she said, "but you are the best friend we ever had."

Then she knelt up to look inside it, and at that moment her husband came to the door, and, turning quickly to see all the wonderful things he had bought, she overbalanced and fell into the pot.

102

Mr. Hak-Tak put down his bundles and ran across and caught her by the ankles and pulled her out, but, oh, mercy, no sooner had he set her carefully on the floor than he saw the kicking legs of another Mrs. Hak-Tak in the pot! What was he to do? Well, he could not leave her there, so he caught her ankles and pulled, and another Mrs. Hak-Tak so exactly like the first that no one would have told one from the other, stood beside them.

"Here's an extraordinary thing," said Mr. Hak-Tak, looking helplessly from one to the other.

"I will not have a second Mrs. Hak-Tak in the house!" screamed the old Mrs. Hak-Tak.

All was confusion. The old Mrs. Hak-Tak shouted and wrung her hands and wept, Mr. Hak-Tak was scarcely calmer, and the new Mrs. Hak-Tak sat down on the floor as if she knew no more than they did what was to happen next.

"One wife is all *I* want," said Mr. Hak-Tak, "but how could I have left her in the pot?"

"Put her back in it again!" cried Mrs. Hak-Tak.

"What? And draw out two more?" said her husband. "If

two wives are too many for me, what should I do with three? No! No!" He stepped back quickly as if he was stepping away from the three wives and, missing his footing, lo and behold, he fell into the pot!

Both Mrs. Hak-Taks ran and each caught an ankle and pulled him out and set him on the floor, and there, oh, mercy, was another pair of kicking legs in the pot! Again each caught hold of an ankle and pulled, and soon another Mr. Hak-Tak, so exactly like the first that no one could have told one from the other, stood beside them.

Now the old Mr. Hak-Tak liked the idea of his double no more than Mrs. Hak-Tak had liked the idea of hers. He stormed and raged and scolded his wife for pulling him out of the pot, while the new Mr. Hak-Tak sat down on the floor beside the new Mrs. Hak-Tak and looked as if, like her, he did not know what was going to happen next.

Then the old Mrs. Hak-Tak had a very good idea. "Listen, my dear husband," she said, "now, do stop scolding and listen, for it is really a good thing that there is a new one of you as well as a new one of me. It means that you and I can go on in our usual way, and these new people, who are

ourselves and yet not ourselves, can set up house together next door to us."

And that is what they did. The old Hak-Taks built themselves a fine new house with money from the pot, and they built one just like it next door for the new couple, and they lived together in the greatest friendliness, because, as Mrs. Hak-Tak said, "The new Mrs. Hak-Tak is really more than a sister to me, and the new Mr. Hak-Tak is really more than a brother to you."

The neighbors were very much surprised, both at the sudden wealth of the Hak-Taks and at the new couple who resembled them so strongly that they must, they thought, be very close relations of whom they had never heard before. They said: "It looks as though the Hak-Taks, when they so unexpectedly became rich, decided to have two of everything, even of themselves, in order to enjoy their money more."

The Origin of Stories

The passing on of sacred stories from one generation to the next is an important part of the culture of many native Indian groups. The legend printed here, from Elizabeth Clark's Indian Legends of Canada, *tells how the tradition might have begun among the Seneca peoples.*

I N A Seneca village long ago there was a little boy whose mother and father had died when he was only a few months old. This little boy was cared for by a woman who had known his parents. She gave him the name Poyeshao, which means "Orphan Boy."

When the boy was old enough, his foster mother gave him a bow and some arrows and said, "It is time for you to learn to hunt. Tomorrow, go to the woods and kill all the birds you can find."

She took ears of dry corn, shelled off the kernels, and parched them in hot ashes from the fire. Next morning she gave the boy some of the corn for his breakfast and rolled some of it in a piece of buckskin.

"Take this with you," she said. "You'll be gone all day and you'll get hungry."

Orphan Boy started off and soon found plenty of game. At noon he sat down to rest and eat some of his corn. Then he continued hunting. When he began to head for home, he had a good string of birds.

The next morning Orphan Boy's mother said to him, "Always do your best hunting. If you become a good hunter, you'll always be well off."

Orphan Boy thought about what his mother had told him. "I'll do as she says and someday I'll be able to hunt big game." That night when he returned home, he had more

106

birds than before. His mother smiled and thanked him, saying, "Now you've begun to help me get food."

Each day Orphan Boy started off with his bow and arrows and his little bundle of corn. Each day he went farther into the woods and brought home more birds than the day before. On the ninth day he killed so many that he had to carry them home on his back. His mother tied the birds in little bundles of three and four and shared them with her neighbours.

On the tenth day the boy started off as usual and went even deeper into the woods. About noon the sinew that held the feathers to his arrow came loose. When Orphan Boy looked for a place where he could sit down and fix the arrow, he found a small clearing. Near the centre was a high, smooth, round stone with a flat top. Orphan Boy jumped up on the rock and sat down. He unwound the sinew and put it in his mouth to soften it. Then he arranged the feathers on his arrow. Just as he was about to tie them on, a voice near him asked, "Shall I tell you stories?"

107

Orphan Boy looked up, expecting to see someone. No one was there. He looked behind the stone and around it. Then he began to tie the feathers to his arrow.

"Shall I tell you stories?" asked a voice right there beside him. The boy looked in every direction but saw no one. When the voice asked again, "Shall I tell you stories?" the boy found that it came from the stone.

"What is that?" he asked. "What does it mean to tell stories?"

"It is telling what happened a long time ago. If you will give me your birds, I'll tell you stories."

"You may have the birds," Orphan Boy said.

Right away the stone began telling what happened long ago. When it finished one story, it began another. The boy sat with his head down and listened. Toward night the stone said, "We will rest now. Come again tomorrow. If anyone asks about your birds, say you've killed so many that you have to go a long way to find one."

On the way home the boy killed five or six birds. When his mother asked Orphan Boy why he had so few, he said that they were getting hard to find.

The next morning Orphan Boy started off but he forgot to hunt for birds. He was thinking of the stories the stone had told him. If a bird landed near him he shot it, but really he was heading straight to the stone.

When he got there, he put his birds on the stone and called out, "I've come back! Here are the birds. Now tell me stories."

The stone told story after story. Toward night it said, "Now we must rest until tomorrow."

On the way home the boy looked for birds, but it was late and he found only a few.

That night his mother told the neighbours, "Orphan Boy used to bring home a lot of birds, but now he brings home only four or five even after being in the woods from morning till night. Maybe he throws the birds away or gives them to some animal. Or maybe he just fools around and doesn't hunt at all."

Orphan Boy's mother hired an older boy to find out what

her foster son was doing. The next morning this boy followed Orphan Boy, keeping out of sight. Orphan Boy killed
many birds, then he suddenly took off toward the east, running as fast as he could. The older boy followed him to the
clearing in the woods. He saw Orphan Boy climb up a large
round stone and heard him talking to someone. He couldn't
see who Orphan Boy was talking to; so he went up and asked,
"What are you doing here?"

"Hearing stories," replied Orphan Boy.

"What are stories?"

"Stories tell about things that happened long ago," said
Orphan Boy. "Put your birds on this stone and say, 'I've
come to hear stories.' " The other boy did, and right away the
stone began. The boys listened until sundown. Then the
stone said, "We'll rest now. Come again tomorrow."

That night the boys returned home with only a few birds.
When Orphan Boy's mother asked the reason, the older boy
said only, "I followed him for a while. Then we hunted
together but we couldn't find any birds."

The next morning the older boy went hunting with Orphan
Boy again. By noon they each had many birds. They gave the

birds to the stone and listened to more stories. That night they tried to find birds on the way home, but it was late and they didn't find any.

Now, this went on for several days. Finally the mother hired two men to follow the two boys. The men watched the boys hunting and they followed the boys to the clearing, hiding behind trees so that they couldn't be seen. They saw the boys put their birds on the stone, then climb up and sit there with their heads down listening to a voice. Every now and then the boys said, *Mmm Hmm!* One man said to the other, "Let's go and find out who's talking to those boys."

They walked up quickly to the stone. "What are you boys doing?" they asked.

The boys were surprised, but Orphan Boy said, "You must promise not to tell anyone." When the two men had promised, Orphan Boy said, "Jump up and sit on the stone." So the men did.

Then Orphan Boy said to the stone, "Go on with the story. We are listening."

All day the four sat listening to the stone tell story after story. When it was almost night, the stone said, "Tomorrow all the people in your village must come and listen to my stories. Have each person bring something to eat. Then clear away the brush so that they can all sit on the ground near me."

That night Orphan Boy told the chief about the story-telling stone. The chief sent a runner to give the message to each family in the village.

Early next morning everyone in the village followed Orphan Boy, walking in single file through the woods. When they came to the clearing, each person put meat or bread on the stone. Then they cleared away the brush and sat down.

When all was quiet, the stone said, "Now I will tell you stories of what happened long ago. There was a world before this one. The things I am going to tell about happened in that world. Some of you will remember every word that I say, others will remember some of the words, and the rest will forget them all. From now on you must tell these stories to one another. Now listen."

110

The people bent their heads and listened to every word the stone said. Once in a while the boys said, *"Mmm Hmm!"* When the sun was almost down, the stone said, "We'll rest now. Come tomorrow and bring meat and bread."

The next day when the people returned, they found that the food they had brought the day before was gone. They put fresh food on the stone and sat down in a circle to listen.

When all was quiet, the stone began to tell stories. Late that afternoon it said, "I have finished! You must keep these stories as long as the world lasts. Tell them to your children and your grandchildren and your great-grandchildren. Some people will remember them better than others. When you go to a man or a woman to ask for one of these stories, take something to pay for it—bread or meat or whatever you have. I know all that happened in the world before this. I've told it to you. When you visit one another you must tell these things. You must remember them always. I have finished."

So it has been ever since that time. From this stone came all the knowledge that the Senecas have of the world before this one.

Proserpine

*This ancient myth will tell you how the
Greeks and the Romans explained the mystery
of the changing seasons.*

WHEN Jupiter and his brothers had defeated the Titans and banished them to Tartarus, a new enemy rose up against the gods. They were the giants Typhon, Briareus, Enceladus, and others. Some of them had a hundred arms, others breathed out fire. They were finally subdued and buried alive under Mount Ætna, where they still sometimes struggle to get loose, and shake the whole island with earthquakes. Their breath comes up through the mountain, and is what men call the eruption of the volcano.

The fall of these monsters shook the earth, so that Pluto was alarmed, and feared that his kingdom would be laid open to the light of day. Under this apprehension, he mounted his chariot, drawn by black horses, and took a circuit of inspection to satisfy himself of the extent of the damage.

While he was thus engaged, Venus, who was sitting on Mount Eryx playing with her boy Cupid, espied him, and said, "My son, take your darts with which you conquer all, even Jove himself, and send one into the breast of yonder dark monarch, who rules the realm of Tartarus. Why should he alone escape? Seize the opportunity to extend your empire and mine. Do you not see that even in heaven some despise our power? Minerva the wise, and Diana the huntress, defy us; and there is that daughter of Ceres, who threatens to follow their example. Now do you, if you have any regard for your own interest or mine, join these two in one."

112

The boy unbound his quiver, and selected his sharpest and truest arrow; then, straining the bow against his knee, he attached the string, and, having made ready, shot the arrow with its barbed point right into the heart of Pluto.

In the vale of Enna there is a lake embowered in woods, which screen it from the fervid rays of the sun, while the moist ground is covered with flowers, and Spring reigns perpetual. Here Proserpine was playing with her companions, gathering lilies and violets, and filling her basket and her apron with them, when Pluto saw her, loved her, and carried her off. She screamed for help to her mother and her companions; and when in her fright she dropped the corners of her apron and let the flowers fall, childlike she felt the loss of them as an addition to her grief. The ravisher urged on his steeds, calling them each by name, and throwing loose over their heads and necks his iron-colored reins. When he reached the River Cyane, and it opposed his passage, he struck the riverbank with his trident, and the earth opened and gave him a passage to Tartarus.

Ceres sought her daughter all the world over. Bright-haired Aurora, when she came forth in the morning, and Hesperus, when he led out the stars in the evening, found her still busy in the search. But it was all unavailing. At length weary and sad, she sat down upon a stone, and continued sitting nine days and nights, in the open air, under the sunlight and moonlight and falling showers. It was where now stands the city of Eleusis, then the home of an old man named Celeus. He was out in the field, gathering acorns and blackberries, and sticks for his fire. His little girl was driving home their two goats, and as she passed the goddess, who appeared in the guise of an old woman, she said to her, "Mother,"—and the name was sweet to the ears of Ceres, —"why do you sit here alone upon the rocks?"

The old man also stopped, though his load was heavy, and begged her to come into his cottage, such as it was. She declined, and he urged her.

114

"Go in peace," she replied, "and be happy in your daughter; I have lost mine." As she spoke, tears—or something like tears, for the gods never weep—fell down her cheeks upon her bosom.

The compassionate old man and his child wept with her. Then said he, "Come with us, and despise not our humble roof; so may your daughter be restored to you in safety."

"Lead on," said she, "I cannot resist that appeal!" So she rose from the stone and went with them.

As they walked he told her that his only son, a little boy, lay very sick, feverish and sleepless. She stooped and gathered some poppies. As they entered the cottage, they found all in great distress, for the boy seemed past hope of recovery. Metanira, his mother, received her kindly, and the goddess stooped and kissed the lips of the sick child. Instantly the paleness left his face, and healthy vigor returned to his body.

The whole family were delighted—that is, the father, mother, and little girl, for they were all; they had no servants. They spread the table, and put upon it curds and cream, apples, and honey in the comb. While they ate, Ceres mingled poppy juice in the milk of the boy. When night came and all was still, she arose, and taking the sleeping boy, moulded his limbs with her hands, and uttered over him three times a solemn charm, then went and laid him in the ashes. His mother, who had been watching what her guest was doing, sprang forward with a cry and snatched the child from the fire. Then Ceres assumed her own form, and a divine splendor shone all around.

While they were overcome with astonishment, she said, "Mother, you have been cruel in your fondness to your son. I would have made him immortal, but you have frustrated my attempt. Nevertheless, he shall be great and useful. He shall teach men the use of the plough, and the rewards which labor can win from the cultivated soil." So saying, she wrapped a cloud about her, and mounting her chariot rode away.

Ceres continued her search for her daughter, passing from land to land, and across seas and rivers, till at length she returned to Sicily, whence she at first set out, and stood by the banks of the River Cyane, where Pluto made himself a passage with his prize to his own dominions. The river nymph would have told the goddess all she had witnessed, but dared not, for fear of Pluto; so she only ventured to take up the girdle which Proserpine had dropped in her flight, and waft it to the feet of the mother. Ceres, seeing this, was no longer in doubt of her loss, but she did not yet know the cause, and laid the blame on the innocent land.

"Ungrateful soil," said she, "which I have endowed with fertility and clothed with herbage and nourishing grain, no more shall you enjoy my favors."

Then the cattle died, the plough broke in the furrow, the seed failed to come up; there was too much sun, there was too much rain; the birds stole the seeds—thistles and brambles were the only growth.

Seeing this, the fountain Arethusa interceded for the land.

"Goddess," said she, "blame not the land; it opened unwillingly to yield a passage to your daughter. I can tell you of her fate, for I have seen her. . . . While I passed through the lower parts of the earth, I saw your Proserpine. She was sad, but no longer showing alarm in her countenance. Her look was such as became a queen—the queen of Erebus; the powerful bride of the monarch of the realms of the dead."

When Ceres heard this, she stood for a while like one stupefied; then turned her chariot towards heaven, and hastened to present herself before the throne of Jove. She told the story of her bereavement, and implored Jupiter to interfere to procure the restitution of her daughter. Jupiter consented on one condition, namely, that Proserpine should not during her stay in the lower world have taken any food; otherwise, the Fates forbade her release. Accordingly, Mercury was sent, accompanied by Spring, to demand Proserpine of Pluto. The wily monarch consented; but alas! the maiden had taken a pomegranate which Pluto offered her, and had sucked the sweet pulp from a few of the seeds. This was enough to prevent her complete release; but a compromise was made, by which she was to pass half the time with her mother, and the rest with her husband Pluto.

118

Ceres allowed herself to be pacified with this arrangement, and restored the earth to her favor. Now she remembered Celeus and his family, and her promise to his infant
son Triptolemus. When the boy grew up, she taught him the
use of the plough, and how to sow the seed. She took him in
her chariot, drawn by winged dragons, through all the
countries of the earth, imparting to mankind valuable
grains, and the knowledge of agriculture. After his return,
Triptolemus built a magnificent temple to Ceres in Eleusis,
and established the worship of the goddess, under the name
of the Eleusinian mysteries, which, in the splendor and
solemnity of their observance, surpassed all other religious
celebrations among the Greeks.

The Shepherd's Boy

THERE was once a young shepherd boy who tended his sheep at the foot of a mountain near a dark forest. It was rather lonely for him all day, so he thought upon a plan by which he could get a little company and some excitement. He rushed down towards the village calling out "Wolf, wolf," and the villagers came out to meet him, and some of them stopped with him for a considerable time. This pleased the boy so much that a few days afterwards he tried the same trick, and again the villagers came to his help. But shortly after this a wolf actually did come out from the forest, and began to worry the sheep, and the boy of course cried out "Wolf, wolf," still louder than before. But this time the villagers, who had been fooled twice before, thought the boy was again deceiving them, and nobody stirred to come to his help. So the wolf made a good meal off the boy's flock, and when the boy complained, the wise man of the village said:

"A liar will not be believed, even when he speaks the truth."

Belling the Cat

L ONG ago, the mice held a general council to consider what measures they could take to outwit their common enemy, the cat. Some said this, and some said that; but at last a young mouse got up and said he had a proposal to make, which he thought would meet the case. "You will all agree," said he, "that our chief danger consists in the sly and treacherous manner in which the enemy approaches us. Now, if we could receive some signal of her approach, we could easily escape from her. I venture, therefore, to propose that a small bell be procured, and attached by a ribbon round the neck of the cat. By this means we should always know when she was about, and could easily retire while she was in the neighbourhood."

This proposal met with general applause, until an old mouse got up and said: "That is all very well, but who is to bell the cat?" The mice looked at one another and nobody spoke. Then the old mouse said:

"It is easy to propose impossible remedies."

Hansel and Grethel

The Brothers Grimm

CLOSE to a large forest there lived a woodcutter with his wife and his two children. The boy was called Hansel and the girl Grethel. They were always very poor and had very little to live on; and at one time, when there was famine in the land, the woodcutter could no longer procure their daily bread.

One night he lay in bed worrying over his troubles, and he sighed and said to his wife: "What is to become of us? How are we to feed our poor children when we have nothing for ourselves?"

"I'll tell you what, husband," answered the woman. "To-morrow morning we will take the children out quite early into the thickest part of the forest. We will light a fire and give each of them a piece of bread; then we will go to our work and leave them alone. They won't be able to find their way back, and so we shall be rid of them."

"Nay, wife," said the man. "We won't do that. I could never find it in my heart to leave my children alone in the forest; the wild animals would soon tear them to pieces."

"What a fool you are!" she said. "Then we must all four die of hunger. You may as well plane the boards for our coffins at once."

She gave him no peace until he consented. "But I grieve over the poor children all the same," said the man.

The two children could not go to sleep for hunger either, and they heard what their stepmother said to their father.

Grethel wept bitterly and said: "All is over with us now!"

"Be quiet, Grethel!" said Hansel. "Don't cry; I will find some way out of it."

When the old people had gone to sleep, he got up, put on his little coat, opened the door, and slipped out. The moon was shining brightly, and the white pebbles around the house shone like newly minted coins. Hansel stooped down and put as many into his pockets as they would hold.

Then he went back to Grethel and said: "Take comfort, little sister, and go to sleep. God won't forsake us." And then he went to bed again.

When the day broke, before the sun had risen, the woman came and said: "Get up, you lazybones; we are going into the forest to fetch wood."

Then she gave them each a piece of bread and said: "Here is something for your dinner, but mind you don't eat it before, for you'll get no more."

Grethel put the bread under her apron, for Hansel had the stones in his pockets. Then they all started for the forest.

When they had gone a little way, Hansel stopped and looked back at the cottage; he did the same thing again and again.

His father said: "Hansel, what are you stopping to look back at? Take care, and put your best foot foremost."

"Oh, Father!" said Hansel. "I am looking at my white cat. It is sitting on the roof, wanting to say good-bye to me."

"Little fool! That's no cat, it's the morning sun shining on the chimney."

But Hansel had not been looking at the cat, he had been dropping a pebble on the ground each time he stopped. When they reached the middle of the forest, their father said:

"Now children, pick up some wood, I want to make a fire to warm you."

Hansel and Grethel gathered the twigs together and soon made a huge pile. Then the pile was lighted, and when it blazed up, the woman said: "Now lie down by the fire and rest yourselves while we go and cut wood. When we have finished we will come back to fetch you."

Hansel and Grethel sat by the fire, and when dinnertime came they each ate their little bit of bread, and they thought their father was quite near because they could hear the sound of an ax. It was no ax, however, but a branch that the man had tied to a dead tree, and that blew backward and forward against it. They sat there such a long time that they got tired, their eyes began to close, and they were soon fast asleep.

When they woke up it was night. Grethel looked around her and cried: "How shall we ever get out of the wood!"

Hansel comforted her and said: "Wait a little till the moon rises, then we will soon find our way."

When the full moon rose, Hansel took his little sister's hand, and they walked on, their footsteps guided by the pebbles, which glittered like newly minted coins in the silvery light. They walked the whole night long, and at daybreak they found themselves back at their father's cottage.

126

They knocked at the door, and when the woman opened it and saw Hansel and Grethel, she said: "You bad children, why did you sleep so long in the wood? We thought you did not mean to come back anymore."

But their father was delighted, for it had gone to his heart to leave them behind alone.

Not long after they were again in great destitution, and the children heard the woman at night in bed say to their father: "We have eaten up everything again but half a loaf, and then we are at the end of everything. The children must go away. We will take them farther into the forest so that they won't be able to find their way back. There is nothing else to be done."

The man took it much to heart and said: "We had better share our last crust with the children."

But the woman would not listen to a word he said, she only scolded and reproached him. Anyone who once says "A" must also say "B," and as he had given in the first time, he had to do so the second as well. The children were again wide awake and heard what was said.

When the old people went to sleep Hansel again got up, meaning to go out and get some more pebbles, but the woman had locked the door and he couldn't get out. But he consoled his little sister and said:

"Don't cry, Grethel; go to sleep. God will help us."

In the early morning the woman made the children get up and gave them each a piece of bread, but it was smaller than the last. On the way to the forest Hansel crumbled it up in his pocket and stopped every now and then to throw a crumb onto the ground.

"Hansel, what are you stopping to look about you for?" asked his father.

"I am looking at my dove, which is sitting on the roof and wants to say good-bye to me," answered Hansel.

"Little fool!" the woman said. "That is no dove; it is the morning sun shining on the chimney."

Nevertheless, Hansel strewed the crumbs from time to time on the ground. The woman led the children far into the forest where they had never been in their lives before. Again they made a big fire, and the woman said:

"Stay where you are, children, and when you are tired you may go to sleep for a while. We are going farther on to cut wood, and in the evening when we have finished we will come back and fetch you."

At dinnertime Grethel shared what little bread she had with Hansel, for he had crumbled his up on the road. Then they went to sleep, and the evening passed, but no one came to fetch the poor children.

It was quite dark when they woke up, and Hansel cheered his little sister, saying: "Wait a bit, Grethel, till the moon rises. Then we can see the bread crumbs which I scattered to show us the way home."

When the moon rose they started, but they found no bread crumbs, for all the thousands of birds in the forest had pecked them up and eaten them.

Hansel said to Grethel: "We shall soon find the way."

But they could not find it. They walked the whole night, and all the next day from morning till night, but they could not get out of the wood.

They were very hungry, for they had nothing to eat but a few berries that they found. They were so tired that their legs would not carry them any farther, and they lay down under a tree and went to sleep.

When they woke up in the morning, it was the third day since they had left their father's cottage. They started to walk again, but they only got deeper and deeper into the wood, and if no help came they must perish.

At midday they saw a beautiful snow-white bird sitting in

a tree. It sang so beautifully that they stood still to listen to it. When it stopped, it fluttered its wings and flew around them. They followed the bird till they came to a little cottage; there, on the roof, the bird settled itself.

When they got quite near, they saw that the little house was made of bread; its roof was cake and its windows were transparent sugar.

"This will be something for us," said Hansel. "We will have a good meal. I will have a piece of the roof, Grethel, and you can have a bit of the window. It will be nice and sweet."

Hansel stretched up and broke off a piece of the roof to try what it was like. Grethel went to the window and nibbled at that. A gentle voice called out from within:

Nibbling, nibbling like a mouse,
Who's nibbling at my little house?

The children answered:

The wind, the wind doth blow
From heaven to earth below.

They went on eating without disturbing themselves. Hansel, who found the roof very good, broke off a large piece for himself; and Grethel pushed a whole round pane out of the window and sat down on the ground to enjoy it.

All at once the door opened and an old, old woman, supporting herself on a crutch, came hobbling out. Hansel and Grethel were so frightened that they dropped what they held in their hands.

But the old woman only shook her head and said: "Ah, dear children, who brought you here? Come in and stay with me; you will come to no harm."

She took them by the hand and led them into the little house. A nice dinner was set before them: pancakes and sugar, milk, apples, and nuts. After this she showed them two little white beds into which they crept and felt as if they were in Heaven.

Although the old woman appeared to be friendly, she was really a wicked old witch who was on the watch for children, and she had built the bread house on purpose to lure them to her. Whenever she could get a child into her clutches, she cooked it and ate it, and considered it a grand feast. Witches have red eyes and can't see very far, but they have keen scent like animals and can perceive the approach of human beings.

When Hansel and Grethel came near her, she laughed wickedly to herself, and said scornfully: "Now I have them, they shan't escape me."

She got up early in the morning, before the children were awake, and when she saw them sleeping, with their beautiful rosy cheeks, she murmured to herself: "They will be dainty morsels."

She seized Hansel with her bony hand and carried him off to a little stable, where she shut him up with a barred door; he might shriek as loud as he liked, she took no notice of him. Then she went to Grethel, shook her till she woke up, and cried:

"Get up, little lazybones, fetch some water and cook something nice for your brother; he is in the stable and has to be fattened. When he is nice and fat, I will eat him."

132

Grethel began to cry bitterly, but it was no use; she had to obey the witch's orders. The best food was now cooked for poor Hansel, while Grethel had only the shells of crayfish.

The old woman hobbled to the stable every morning and cried: "Hansel, put your finger out for me to feel how fat you are."

Hansel put out a knucklebone, and the old woman, whose eyes were dim, thought it was his finger and was much astonished that he did not get fat.

When four weeks had passed, and Hansel still kept thin, she became very impatient and would wait no longer for the boy to fatten.

"Now then, Grethel," she cried, "bustle along and fetch the water. Fat or thin, tomorrow I will kill Hansel and eat him."

Oh, how his poor little sister grieved! As she carried the water, the tears streamed down her cheeks.

"Dear God, help us!" she cried. "If only the wild animals in the forest had devoured us, we should, at least, have died together."

"You may spare me your lamentations; they will do you no good," said the old woman.

Early in the morning Grethel had to go out to fill the kettle with water, and then she had to kindle a fire and hang the kettle over it.

"We will bake first," said the old witch. "I have heated the oven and kneaded the dough."

She pushed poor Grethel toward the oven and said: "Creep in and see if it is properly heated, and then we will put the bread in."

She meant, when Grethel had got in, to shut the door and roast her.

But Grethel saw her intention and said: "I don't know how to get in. How am I to manage it?"

"Stupid goose!" cried the witch. "The opening is big enough; you can see that I could get into it myself."

She hobbled up and stuck her head into the oven. But Grethel gave her a push that sent the witch right in, and then she banged the door and bolted it.

"Oh! Oh!" she began to howl horribly. But Grethel ran away and left the wicked witch to perish miserably.

Grethel ran as fast as she could to the stable. She opened the door and cried: "Hansel, we are saved. The old witch is dead."

Hansel sprang out like a bird out of a cage when the door is set open. How delighted they were! They fell upon each other's necks, and kissed each other, and danced about for joy.

As they had nothing more to fear, they went into the witch's house; there they found chests in every corner full of pearls and precious stones.

"These are better than pebbles," said Hansel as he filled his pockets.

Grethel said: "I must take something home with me, too." And she filled her apron.

"But now we must go," said Hansel, "so that we may get out of this enchanted wood."

Before they had gone very far, they came to a great piece of water.

"We cannot cross," said Hansel. "I see no stepping stones and no bridge."

"And there are no boats, either," answered Grethel. "But there is a duck swimming. It may help us over if we ask it." So she cried:

> *Little duck, that cries quack, quack,*
> *Here Grethel and here Hansel stand.*
> *Quickly, take us on your back,*
> *No path nor bridge is there at hand!*

The duck came swimming toward them; Hansel got on its back and told his sister to sit on his knee.

"No," answered Grethel, "it will be too heavy for the duck; it must take us over one after the other."

The good creature did this, and when they had got safely over and walked for a while, the wood seemed to grow more and more familiar to them, and at last they saw their father's cottage in the distance. They began to run and rushed inside, where they threw their arms around their father's neck. The man had not had a single happy moment since he had deserted his children in the wood, and in the meantime his wife had died.

Grethel shook her apron and scattered the pearls and precious stones all over the floor, and Hansel added handful after handful out of his pockets.

So all their troubles came to an end, and they lived together as happily as possible.

The Brave Little Tailor

The Brothers Grimm

O NE summer morning a little tailor was sitting at his bench near the window, working cheerfully with all his might, when an old woman came down the street. She was crying, "Good jelly to sell! Good jelly to sell!"

The cry sounded pleasant in the little tailor's ear, so he put his head out the window and called out, "Here, my good woman! Come here, if you want a customer."

So the poor woman climbed the steps with her heavy basket, and was obliged to unpack and display all her pots to the tailor. He looked at every one of them and, lifting all the lids, applied his nose to each.

At last he said, "The jelly seems pretty good. You may weigh me out four half ounces, or I don't mind having a quarter of a pound."

The woman, who had expected to find a good customer, gave him what he asked for but went off angry and grumbling.

"This jelly is the very thing for me!" cried the little tailor. "It will give me strength and cunning." And he took down the bread from the cupboard, cut a big slice off the loaf and spread the jelly on it, laid it near him, and went on stitching more gallantly than ever. All the while the scent of the sweet jelly was spreading throughout the room, where there were quantities of flies. They were attracted by it and flew down to eat of it.

"Now then, who invited you here?" said the tailor, and drove the unbidden guests away. But the flies, not understanding his language, were not to be got rid of like that, and returned in larger numbers than before. Then the tailor, unable to stand it any longer, took from his chimney corner a ragged cloth.

"Now, I'll let you have it!" he said, and beat it among them unmercifully. When he ceased and counted the slain, he found seven lying dead before him.

"This is indeed somewhat," he said, wondering at his own bravery. "The whole town shall know about this."

So he hastened to cut out a belt, and he stitched it and put on it in large capitals: "Seven at one blow!"

"The town, did I say?" said the little tailor. "The whole world shall know it!" And his heart quivered with joy, like a lamb's tail.

The tailor fastened the belt round him and began to think of going out into the world, for his workshop seemed too small for his valor. So he looked about in all the house for something that would be useful to take with him, but he found nothing but an old cheese, which he put in his pocket. Outside the door he noticed that a bird had got caught in the bushes, so he took that and put it in his pocket with the cheese. Then he set out gallantly on his way, and as he was light and active he felt no fatigue.

The way led over a mountain, and when he reached the topmost peak he saw a terrible giant sitting there, and looking about him at his ease.

The tailor went bravely up to him, called out to him, and said, "Good day, comrade! There you sit looking over the wide world. I am on the way thither to seek my fortune. Have you a fancy to go with me?"

The giant looked at the tailor contemptuously and said, "You vagabond! You miserable little creature!"

"That may be," answered the little tailor, and undoing his coat he showed the giant his belt. "You can read there whether I am a man or not."

The giant read, "Seven at one blow!" And thinking it meant men that the tailor had killed, he at once felt more

respect for the little fellow. But as he wanted to test him, he took a stone and squeezed it so hard that water came out of it.

"Now you can do that," said the giant, "that is, if you have the strength for it."

"That's not much!" said the little tailor. "I call that play." And he put his hand in his pocket and took out the cheese and squeezed it till the whey ran out of it.

"Well," said he, "what do you think of that?"

The giant did not know what to say to it, for he could not have believed it of the little man. Then the giant took up a stone and threw it so high that it was nearly out of sight.

"Now, little fellow, suppose you do that!"

"Well thrown!" said the tailor. "But the stone fell back to earth again. I will throw you one that will never come back." So he felt in his pocket, took out the bird, and threw it into the air. And the bird, when it found itself at liberty, took wing, flew off, and returned no more.

"What do you think of that, comrade?" asked the tailor.

"There is no doubt that you can throw," said the giant. "Now we will see if you can carry."

He led the little tailor to a mighty oak tree which had been felled and was lying on the ground, and said, "Now, if you are strong enough, help me to carry this tree out of the wood."

"Willingly," answered the little man. "You take the trunk on your shoulders and I will take the branches with all their foliage. That is by far the biggest end."

So the giant took the trunk on his shoulders, and the tailor seated himself on a branch. And the giant, who could not see what he was doing, had the whole tree to carry, and the little man on it as well. And the little man was very cheerful and merry and whistled the tune, *"There were three tailors riding by,"* as if carrying the tree was mere child's play.

The giant, when he had struggled on under his heavy load a part of the way, was tired out and cried, "Look here, I must let go the tree!"

The tailor jumped off quickly. Then, taking hold of the tree with both arms as if he were carrying it, he said to the giant, "You see you can't carry the tree, though you are such a big fellow!"

They went on together a little farther and presently they came to a cherry tree. And the giant took hold of the topmost branches, where the ripest fruit hung, and pulling them downward gave them to the tailor to hold, bidding him eat. But the little tailor was much too weak to hold the tree, and as the giant let go, the tree sprang back and the tailor was thrown up into the air.

And when he dropped down again without any damage, the giant said to him, "How is this? Haven't you strength enough to hold such a weak sprig as that?"

"It is not strength that is lacking," answered the little tailor. "How should it to one who has slain seven at one blow? I just jumped over the tree because the hunters are shooting down there in the bushes. Why don't you jump it too?"

The giant made the attempt and, not being able to vault the tree, he remained hanging in the branches, so that once more the little tailor got the better of him.

Then said the giant, "As you are such a gallant fellow, suppose you come with me to our den and stay the night."

The tailor was quite willing and followed him. When they reached the den, there sat some other giants by the fire and all gladly welcomed him.

The little tailor looked round and thought, "There is more elbow room here than in my workshop."

The giant showed him a bed and told him he had better lie down on it and go to sleep. The bed, however, was too big for the tailor, so he did not stay in it but crept into a corner to sleep. As soon as it was midnight the giant got up, took a great staff of iron and beat the bed through with one stroke, and supposed he had made an end of that grasshopper of a tailor. Very early in the morning the giants went into the wood and forgot all about the little tailor, and when they saw him coming after them alive and merry, they were terribly frightened. And thinking he was going to kill them, they ran away in all haste.

So the little tailor marched on, always following his nose. And after he had gone a great way he entered the courtyard belonging to a king's palace, and there he felt so overpowered with fatigue that he lay down and fell asleep. In the meanwhile came various people, who looked at him very curiously and read on his belt, "Seven at one blow!"

"Oh," said they, "why should this great lord come here in time of peace? What a mighty champion he must be!"

Then they went and told the King about him. They thought that if war should break out what a worthy and useful man he would be, and he ought not to be allowed to depart at any price. The King then summoned his council and sent one of his courtiers to the little tailor to beg him, as soon as he should wake up, to consent to serve in the King's army. So the messenger stood and waited at the sleeper's side until he began to stretch his limbs and to open his eyes, and then he carried his answer back. "That was the reason for which I came," the little tailor had said. "I am ready to enter the King's service."

So he was received into it very honourably, and a separate dwelling was set apart for him.

But the rest of the soldiers were very much set against the little tailor, and they wished him a thousand miles away.

"What shall be done about it?" they said among themselves. "If we pick a quarrel and fight with him, then seven of us will fall at each blow. That will be of no good to us."

So they came to a resolution, and went all together to the King to ask for their discharge.

"We never intended," said they, "to serve with a man who kills seven at a blow."

The King felt sorry to lose all his faithful servants because of one man. He wished that he had never seen him, and would willingly get rid of him if he might. But he did not dare to dismiss the little tailor for fear he should kill all the King's people and place himself upon the throne. He thought a long while about it, and at last made up his mind what to do.

He sent for the little tailor and told him that as he was so great a warrior he had a proposal to make to him. He told him that in a wood in his dominions dwelt two giants who did great damage by robbery, murder, and fire, and that no man dared go near them for fear of his life. But that if the tailor should overcome and slay both these giants the King would give him his only daughter in marriage and half his kingdom as dowry, and that a hundred horsemen should go with him to give him assistance.

"That would be a fine thing for a man like me," thought the little tailor. "A beautiful princess and half a kingdom are not to be had every day."

So he said to the King, "Oh yes, I can soon overcome the giants, and yet I have no need of the hundred horsemen. He who can kill seven at one blow has no need to be afraid of two."

So the little tailor set out and the hundred horsemen followed him.

When he came to the border of the wood he said to his escort, "Stay here while I go to attack the giants."

Then he sprang into the wood and looked about him right and left. After a while he caught sight of the two giants. They were lying down under a tree asleep, and snoring so that all the branches shook. The little tailor, all alert, filled both his pockets with stones and climbed up into the tree, and made his way to an overhanging bough so that he could seat himself just above the sleepers. And from there he let one stone after another fall on the chest of one of the giants.

For a long time the giant was quite unaware of this, but at last he woke up and pushed his comrade and said, "What are you hitting me for?"

"Are you dreaming?" said the other. "I am not touching you." And they composed themselves again to sleep, and the tailor let fall a stone on the other giant.

"What can that be?" cried he. "What are you casting at me?"

"I am casting nothing at you," answered the first, grumbling.

They disputed about it for a while, but as they were tired they gave it up at last, and their eyes closed once more. Then the little tailor began his game anew. He picked out a heavier stone and threw it down with force upon the first giant's chest.

"This is too much!" cried he, and sprang up like a madman and struck his companion such a blow that the tree shook above them. The other paid him back with ready coin, and they fought with such fury that they tore up trees by their roots to use for weapons against each other, so that at last both of them lay dead upon the ground. And now the little tailor got down. "What a lucky thing," he said, "that the tree I was sitting in did not get torn up, too! Or else I should have had to jump from one tree to another."

Then he drew his sword and gave each of the giants a few hacks in the breast, and went back to the horsemen and said, "The deed is done. I have made an end of both of them, though it went hard with me. In the struggle they rooted up trees to defend themselves, but it was of no use. They had to do with a man who can kill seven at one blow."

"Then are you not wounded?" asked the horsemen.

"Nothing of the sort!" answered the tailor. "They have not injured a hair."

The horsemen still would not believe it and rode into the wood to see, and there they found the giants wallowing in their blood, and all about them lying the uprooted trees. The little tailor then claimed the promised boon, but the King repented of his offer and again sought how to rid himself of the hero.

"Before you can possess my daughter and the half of my kingdom," said he to the tailor, "you must perform another heroic act. In the wood lives a unicorn who does great damage. You must capture him."

"A unicorn does not strike more terror into me than two giants. Seven at one blow! That is my way," was the tailor's answer.

So taking a rope and an ax with him, he went out into the wood and told those who were ordered to attend him to wait outside. He had not far to seek. The unicorn soon came out and sprang at him, as if he would make an end of him without delay.

"Softly, softly!" said the tailor. "Most haste, worst speed." And he remained standing until the animal came quite near; then he slipped quickly behind a tree. The unicorn ran with all his might against the tree and stuck his horn so deep into the trunk that he could not get it out again, and so was captured.

"Now I have you," said the tailor, coming out from behind the tree. And putting the rope around the unicorn's neck, he took the ax and cut free the horn, and when all his party was assembled he brought the animal to the King.

The King did not yet wish to give him the promised reward and set him a third task to do. Before the wedding could take place the tailor was to secure a wild boar which had done a great deal of damage in the wood.

The huntsmen were to accompany him and help him.

"All right," said the tailor. "This is child's play."

But he did not take the huntsmen into the wood, and they were all the better pleased, for the wild boar had many a time before received them in such a way that they had no fancy to disturb him.

When the boar caught sight of the tailor he ran at him with
foaming mouth and gleaming tusks to bear him to the
ground, but the nimble hero rushed into a chapel which
chanced to be near and jumped quickly out a window on the
other side. The boar ran after him, and when he got inside
the tailor shut the door after him, and there he was im-
prisoned, for the creature was too big and unwieldy to jump
out the window too.

Then the tailor called the huntsmen that they might see
the prisoner with their own eyes. And then he betook himself
to the King, who now, whether he liked it or not, was obliged
to fulfill his promise and give him his daughter and the half
of his kingdom. But if he had known that the great warrior
was only a little tailor he would have taken it still more to
heart.

152

So the wedding was celebrated with great splendor and little joy, and the tailor was made into a king. One night the young Queen heard her husband talking in his sleep and saying, "Boy, make me that waistcoat and patch me those breeches, or I will wrap my yardstick about your shoulders!"

And as she perceived of what low birth her husband was, she went to her father the next morning and told him all, and begged him to set her free from a man who was nothing better than a tailor.

The King bade her be comforted, saying, "Tonight leave your bedroom door open. My guards shall stand outside, and when he is asleep they shall come in and bind him and carry him off to a ship that will take him to the other side of the world."

So the wife felt consoled, but the King's water bearer, who had been listening all the while, went to the little tailor and disclosed to him the whole plan.

"I shall put a stop to all this," said he.

At night he lay down as usual in bed, and when his wife thought that he was asleep she got up, opened the door, and lay down again. The little tailor, who only made believe to be asleep, began to murmur plainly.

"Boy, make me that waistcoat and patch me those breeches, or I will wrap my yardstick about your shoulders! I have slain seven at one blow, killed two giants, caught a unicorn, and taken a wild boar. And shall I be afraid of those who are standing outside of my room door?"

And when they heard the tailor say this, a great fear seized the guards. They fled away as if they had been wild hares and none of them would venture to attack him.

And so the little tailor all his lifetime remained a king.

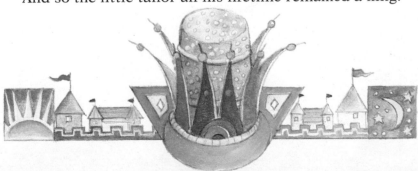

The Highwayman

Alfred Noyes

The wind was a torrent of darkness among the gusty trees.
The moon was a ghostly galleon tossed upon cloudy seas.
The road was a ribbon of moonlight over the purple moor,
And the highwayman came riding—
      Riding—riding—
The highwayman came riding, up to the old inn-door.

He'd a French cocked-hat on his forehead, a bunch of lace at
  his chin,
A coat of the claret velvet, and breeches of brown doe-skin.
They fitted with never a wrinkle. His boots were up to the
  thigh.
And he rode with a jewelled twinkle,
      His pistol butts a-twinkle,
His rapier hilt a-twinkle, under the jewelled sky.

Over the cobbles he clattered and clashed in the dark
  inn-yard,
And he tapped with his whip on the shutters, but all was
  locked and barred.
He whistled a tune to the window, and who should be
  waiting there
But the landlord's black-eyed daughter,
      Bess, the landlord's daughter,
Plaiting a dark red love-knot into her long black hair.

And dark in the dark old inn-yard a stable-wicket creaked
Where Tim the ostler listened. His face was white and
 peaked.
His eyes were hollows of madness, his hair like mouldy hay,
But he loved the landlord's daughter,
  The landlord's red-lipped daughter.
Dumb as a dog he listened, and he heard the robber say—

"One kiss, my bonny sweetheart, I'm after a prize to-night,
But I shall be back with the yellow gold before the morning
 light;
Yet, if they press me sharply, and harry me through the day,
Then look for me by moonlight,
  Watch for me by moonlight,
I'll come to thee by moonlight, though hell should bar the
 way."

He rose upright in the stirrups. He scarce could reach her
 hand,
But she loosened her hair in the casement. His face burnt
 like a brand
As the black cascade of perfume came tumbling over his
 breast;
And he kissed its waves in the moonlight,
  (Oh, sweet, black waves in the moonlight!)
Then he tugged at his rein in the moonlight, and galloped
 away to the west.

He did not come in the dawning. He did not come at noon;
And out of the tawny sunset, before the rise of the moon,
When the road was a gypsy's ribbon, looping the purple
 moor,
A red-coat troop came marching—
  Marching—marching—
King George's men came marching, up to the old inn-door.

They said no word to the landlord. They drank his ale
  instead.
But they gagged his daughter, and bound her, to the foot of
  her narrow bed.
Two of them knelt at her casement, with muskets at their
  side!
There was death at every window;
        And hell at one dark window;
For Bess could see, through her casement, the road that *he*
  would ride.

They had tied her up to attention, with many a sniggering
  jest.
They had bound a musket beside her, with the muzzle
  beneath her breast!
"Now, keep good watch!" and they kissed her. She heard
  the doomed man say—
Look for me by moonlight;
        Watch for me by moonlight;
I'll come to thee by moonlight, though hell should bar the
  way!

She twisted her hands behind her; but all the knots held
  good!
She writhed her hands till her fingers were wet with sweat
  or blood!
They stretched and strained in the darkness, and the hours
  crawled by like years,
Till, now, on the stroke of midnight,
      Cold, on the stroke of midnight,
The tip of one finger touched it! The trigger at least was
  hers!

The tip of one finger touched it. She strove no more for the
  rest.
Up, she stood up to attention, with the muzzle beneath her
  breast,
She would not risk their hearing; she would not strive
  again;
For the road lay bare in the moonlight;
      Blank and bare in the moonlight;
And the blood of her veins, in the moonlight, throbbed to
  her love's refrain.

158

Tlot-tlot; tlot-tlot! Had they heard it? The horse-hoofs
   ringing clear;
Tlot-tlot; tlot-tlot, in the distance? Were they deaf that they
   did not hear?
Down the ribbon of moonlight, over the brow of the hill,
The highwayman came riding—
         Riding—riding—
The red-coats looked to their priming! She stood up,
   straight and still.

Tlot-tlot, in the frosty silence! *Tlot-tlot*, in the echoing
   night!
Nearer he came and nearer. Her face was like a light.
Her eyes grew wide for a moment; she drew one last deep
   breath,
Then her finger moved in the moonlight,
         Her musket shattered the moonlight,
Shattered her breast in the moonlight and warned
   him—with her death.

He turned. He spurred to the west; he did not know who
    stood
Bowed, with her head o'er the musket, drenched with her
    own blood!
Not till the dawn he heard it, and his face grew grey to hear
How Bess, the landlord's daughter,
        The landlord's black-eyed daughter,
Had watched for her love in the moonlight, and died in the
    darkness there.

Back, he spurred like a madman, shouting a curse to the
    sky,
With the white road smoking behind him and his rapier
    brandished high.
Blood-red were his spurs in the golden noon; wine-red was
    his velvet coat;
When they shot him down on the highway,
        Down like a dog on the highway,
And he lay in his blood on the highway, with the bunch of
    lace at his throat.

160

And still of a winter's night, they say, when the wind is in
    the trees,
When the moon is a ghostly galleon tossed upon cloudy
    seas,
When the road is a ribbon of moonlight over the purple
    moor,
A highwayman comes riding—
        Riding—riding—
A highwayman comes riding, up to the old inn-door.

Over the cobbles he clatters and clangs in the dark
    inn-yard.
And he taps with his whip on the shutters, but all is locked
    and barred.
He whistles a tune to the window, and who should be
    waiting there
But the landlord's black-eyed daughter,
        Bess, the landlord's daughter,
Plaiting a dark red love-knot into her long black hair.

The Wizard

Jack Prelutsky

The wizard, watchful, waits alone
within his tower of cold gray stone
and ponders in his wicked way
what evil deeds he'll do this day.
He's tall and thin, with wrinkled skin,
a tangled beard hangs from his chin,
his cheeks are gaunt, his eyes set deep,
he scarcely eats, he needs no sleep.

His fingers wave arcane commands,
ten bony sticks on withered hands,
his flowing cloak is smirched with grime,
he's worn it since the dawn of time.
Upon his hat, in silver lines
are pictured necromantic signs,
symbols of the awesome power
of the wizard, alone in his cold stone tower.

He scans his mystic stock in trade—
charms to fetch a demon's aid,
seething stews of purplish potions,
throbbing thaumaturgic lotions,
supernatural tracts and tomes
replete with lore of elves and gnomes,
talismans, amulets, willowy wand
to summon spirits from beyond.

162

He spies a bullfrog by the door
and stooping, scoops it off the floor.
He flicks his wand, the frog's a flea
through elemental sorcery,
the flea hops once, the flea hops twice,
the flea becomes a pair of mice
that dive into a bubbling brew,
emerging as one cockatoo.

The wizard laughs a hollow laugh,
the soaking bird's reduced by half,
and when, perplexed, it starts to squawk,
the wizard turns it into chalk
with which he deftly writes a spell
that makes the chalk a silver bell
which tinkles in the ashen air
till flash . . . a fire burns brightly there.

He gestures with an ancient knack
to try to bring the bullfrog back.
Another flash! . . . no flame now burns
as once again the frog returns,
but when it bounds about in fear,
the wizard shouts, "Begone from here,"
and midway through a frightened croak
it vanishes in clouds of smoke.

The wizard smirks a fiendish smirk
reflecting on the woes he'll work
as he consults a dusty text
and checks which hex he'll conjure next.
He may pluck someone off the spot
and turn him into . . . who knows what?
Should you encounter a toad or lizard,
look closely . . . it may be the work of the wizard.

The Miraculous Hind

*For perhaps a thousand years, Hungarians have
been telling their children the wonderful legend of
"The Miraculous Hind," a tale which many
scholars believe describes the early history
of the Hungarians. Here is the legend, retold by
Elizabeth Cleaver. . . .*

L ET me tell you a tale of an adventurous hunt for a
Miraculous Hind by my people, the Hungarians.

Long, long ago, near the Ural Mountains there
lived a king named Menrót and his wife Enéh. Enéh and
Menrót had many children. Two of their sons, Hunor and
Magyar, grew up to be fine and mighty hunters. One day,
Hunor and Magyar decided to hold a great hunt, and began
their elaborate preparations. Both brothers chose fifty of
their finest men to accompany them. The hundred men
spent many hours sharpening arrowheads and spear tips
and sabre blades. Even the hunting hounds felt the excitement and grew restless as they waited for the hunt to begin. Hunor and Magyar chose their finest clothes to wear.
They wore fitted jackets, called *dolmány*, adorned with
braiding and beautifully worked jewelled buttons. Over the
dolmany they wore sleeved mantles called *mente*. From
their belts and sword chains hung sabres studded with
precious stones. On their caps they wore an *aigrette*. The
men wore wide white gathered pantaloons called *gatya*.
And some had ornate *szür* mantles.

At dawn, with trumpets sounding and sabres flashing, a
procession of one hundred horsemen set out, and at its head
were Hunor and Magyar. Suddenly a stag and a hind
appeared. Magyar's arrow flashed into the air and pierced
the stag's heart. The stag fell to the ground, and a bluebird
fluttered high into the sky as it died. But the beautiful wild

hind escaped into the forest. They followed the hind for the rest of the day, and all the next. They crossed a desert and approached a sea, but the hind remained beyond the reach of their arrows. At sundown they reached the shores of the Kur River, and the hind disappeared. Hunor said, "We shall camp here." Magyar answered, "At daybreak we shall continue the chase." Planning to find their direction the next day, all the horsemen dismounted and prepared to camp for the night. In the windy, cool dawn one of the horsemen spotted the hind on the other bank of the river. Hunor and Magyar and all their hundred horsemen quickly saddled their horses and swam the Kur River to follow the hind. They crossed desert plains, where there was no grass and not a drop of water to drink. Then they came to a land where great pools of oil burned and cast a fiery glow in the night sky.

Every evening when the weary horsemen made their camp, they were disappointed and tired of their hunt.

But each morning the excitement caught them again with the sense of great adventure. By now they were very far from home, for they had reached the Sea of Azov. The mysterious hind was often in view, but once, when the hunters approached it, a thick mist descended, hiding everything from sight. When the sun burst through the mist, the hunters could see once more, but the hind had disappeared. The horsemen looked everywhere for her tracks in the forest . . . among bushes . . . in groves of willow trees . . . and poplars. Then they realized that they were lost. They had travelled too far. Magyar asked, "Who knows the way home in this endless world?" Hunor thought and answered, "Let us settle here in this land to which the miraculous hind has led us. The grass is like silk. The water is sweet and sweet sap drips like syrup from the trees. The blue rivers have shining fish and wild game is plentiful." So Hunor and Magyar and their hundred horsemen settled and made camp. Once rested, they longed for a new adventure and so descended on the plains where the horses were able to gallop freely . . . and the air smelled sweet with hay, and the scented wind brushed their faces.

At twilight, the magic time between day and night, a strange thing happened. As if in a dream—the men began to hear music like rippling waves drifting through the woods, stirring dewdrops on the blades of grass. Quickly the men finished their supper around their campfires . . . and rode off to find where the music came from. They came upon a tent woven from the strands of the mist. All around it fairy maidens danced and sang. Many fairy maidens lived in these woods, and every evening they all danced in the mist. The daughters of kings Dúl and Belár also danced here. The two fairest and prettiest of all were the daughters of King Dúl. Hunor and Magyar decided they should all choose maidens for themselves. Hunor chose one of King Dúl's fair daughters to be his wife . . . and Magyar chose the other. Then each of the hundred horsemen chose a wife. Together they all rode off into the starry night . . . to the land where the grass is like silk, the water is sweet, and sweet sap drips like syrup from the trees —where the blue river has shining fish, and wild game is plentiful. Here is where Hunor and Magyar and their one hundred horsemen and their wives made their home. Their children and their children's children formed the Hungarians.

The Ugly Duckling

Hans Christian Andersen

I T WAS glorious out in the country. It was summer, and the cornfields were yellow, and the oats were green; the hay had been put up in stacks in the green meadows, and the stork went about on his long red legs, and chattered Egyptian, for this was the language he had learned from his good mother. All around the fields · and meadows were great forests, and in the midst of these forests lay deep lakes. Yes, it was really glorious out in the country. In the midst of the sunshine there lay an old farm, surrounded by deep canals, and from the wall down to the water grew great burdocks, so high that little children could stand upright under the loftiest of them. It was just as wild there as in the deepest wood. Here sat a Duck upon her nest, for she had to hatch her young ones; but she was almost tired out before the little ones came; and then she so seldom had visitors. The other ducks liked better to swim about in the canals than to run up to sit down under a burdock, and cackle with her.

At last one egg shell after another burst open. "Piep! piep!" it cried, and in all the eggs there were little creatures that stuck out their heads.

"Rap! rap!" they said; and they all came rapping out as fast as they could, looking all round them under the green leaves; and the mother let them look as much as they chose, for green is good for the eyes.

"How wide the world is!" said the young ones, for they

168

certainly had much more room now than when they were in the eggs.

"Do you think this is all the world?" asked the mother. "That extends far across the other side of the garden, quite into the parson's field, but I have never been there yet. I hope you are all together," she continued, and stood up. "No, I have not all. The largest egg still lies there. How long is that to last? I am really tired of it." And she sat down again.

"Well, how goes it?" asked an old Duck who had come to pay her a visit.

"It lasts a long time with that one egg," said the Duck who sat there. "It will not burst. Now, only look at the others; are they not the prettiest ducks one could possibly see? They are all like their father: the bad fellow never comes to see me."

"Let me see the egg which will not burst," said the old

visitor. "Believe me, it is a turkey's egg. I was once cheated in that way, and had much anxiety and trouble with the young ones, for they are afraid of the water. I could not get them to venture in. I quacked and clucked, but it was no use. Let me see the egg. Yes, that's a turkey's egg! Let it lie there, and teach the other children to swim."

"I think I will sit on it a little longer," said the Duck. "I've sat so long now that I can sit a few days more."

"Just as you please," said the old Duck; and she went away.

At last the great egg burst. "Piep! piep!" said the little one, and crept forth. It was very large and very ugly. The Duck looked at it.

"It's a very large duckling," said she; "none of the others look like that: can it really be a turkey chick? Now we shall soon find it out. It must go into the water, even if I have to thrust it in myself."

The next day the weather was splendidly bright, and the sun shone on all the green trees. The Mother Duck went down to the water with all her little ones. Splash she jumped into the water. "Quack! quack!" she said, and one duckling after another plunged in. The water closed over their heads, but they came up in an instant, and swam capitally; their legs went of themselves, and there they were all in the water. The ugly gray Duckling swam with them.

"No, it's not a turkey," said she; "look how well it can use its legs, and how upright it holds itself. It is my own child! On the whole it's quite pretty, if one looks at it rightly. Quack! quack! come with me, and I'll lead you out into the great world, and present you in the poultry yard; but keep close to me, so that no one may tread on you, and take care of the cats!"

And so they came into the poultry yard. There was a terrible riot going on in there, for two families were quarrelling about an eel's head, and the cat got it after all.

"See, that's how it goes in the world!" said the Mother Duck; and she whetted her beak, for she, too, wanted the eel's head. "Only use your legs," she said. "See that you can

170

bustle about, and bow your heads before the old Duck
yonder. She's the grandest of all here; she's of Spanish
blood—that's why she's so fat; and do you see, she has a red
rag around her leg; that's something particularly fine, and
the greatest distinction a duck can enjoy: it signifies that
one does not want to lose her, and that she's to be recognized by man and beast. Shake yourselves—don't turn in
your toes; a well brought up duck turns its toes quite out,
just like father and mother, so! Now bend your necks and
say 'Rap!' ''

And they did so; but the other ducks round about looked
at them, and said quite boldly:

"Look there! Now we're to have these hanging on as if
there were not enough of us already! And—fie!—how that
Duckling yonder looks; we won't stand that!'' And one duck
flew up immediately, and bit it in the neck.

"Let it alone,'' said the mother; "it does no harm to any
one.''

"Yes, but it's too large and peculiar,'' said the Duck who
had bitten it; "and therefore it must be buffeted.''

"Those are pretty children that the mother has there,''

171

said the old Duck with the rag round her leg. "They're all pretty but that one; that was a failure. I wish she could alter it."

"That cannot be done, my lady," replied the Mother Duck. "It is not pretty, but it has a really good disposition, and swims as well as any other; I may even say it swims better. I think it will grow up pretty, and become smaller in time; it has lain too long in the egg, and therefore is not properly shaped." And then she pinched it in the neck, and smoothed its feathers. "Moreover, it is a drake," she said, "and therefore it is not of so much consequence. I think he will be very strong: he makes his way already."

"The other ducklings are graceful enough," said the old Duck. "Make yourself at home; and if you find an eel's head, you may bring it to me."

And now they were at home. But the poor Duckling which had crept last out of the egg, and looked so ugly, was bitten and pushed and jeered at, as much by the ducks as by the chickens.

"It is too big!" they all said. And the turkey cock, who had been born with spurs, and therefore thought himself an emperor, blew himself up like a ship in full sail, and bore straight down upon it; then he gobbled, and grew quite red in the face. The poor Duckling did not know where it should stand or walk; it was quite melancholy because it looked ugly, and was scoffed at by the whole yard.

So it went on the first day; and afterward it became worse and worse. The poor Duckling was hunted about by every one; even its brothers and sisters were quite angry with it, and said, "If the cat would only catch you, you ugly creature!" And the mother said, "If you were only far away!" And the ducks bit it, and the chickens beat it, and the girl who had to feed the poultry kicked at it with her foot.

Then it ran and flew over the fence, and the little birds in the bushes flew up in fear.

"That is because I am so ugly!" thought the Duckling; and it shut its eyes, but flew on farther; thus it came out

into the great moor, where the wild ducks lived. Here it lay the whole night long; and it was weary and downcast.

Toward morning the wild ducks flew up, and looked at their new companion.

"What sort of a one are you?" they asked; and the Duckling turned in every direction, and bowed as well as it could. "You are remarkably ugly!" said the Wild Ducks. "But that is very indifferent to us, so long as you do not marry into our family."

Poor thing! It certainly did not think of marrying, and only hoped to obtain leave to lie among the reeds and drink some of the swamp water.

Thus it lay two whole days; then came thither two wild geese, or, properly speaking, two wild ganders. It was not long since each had crept out of an egg, and that's why they were so saucy.

"Listen, comrade," said one of them. "You're so ugly that I like you. Will you go with us, and become a bird of passage? Near here, in another moor, there are a few sweet lovely wild geese, all unmarried, and all able to say 'Rap!' You've a chance of making your fortune, ugly as you are!"

"Piff! paff!" resounded through the air; and the two ganders fell down dead in the swamp, and the water became blood-red. "Piff! paff!" it sounded again, and whole flocks of wild geese rose up from the reeds. And then there was another report. A great hunt was going on. The hunters were lying in wait all round the moor, and some were even sitting up in the branches of the trees, which spread far over the reeds. The blue smoke rose up like clouds among the dark trees, and was wafted far away across the water; and the hunting dogs came—splash, splash!—into the swamp, and the rushes and the reeds bent down on every side. That was a fright for the poor Duckling! It turned its head, and put it under its wing; but at that moment a frightful great dog stood close by the Duckling. His tongue hung far out of his mouth and his eyes gleamed horrible and ugly; he thrust out his nose close against the Duckling, showed his sharp teeth, and—splash, splash!—on he went, without seizing it.

"Oh, Heaven be thanked!" sighed the Duckling. "I am so ugly that even the dog does not like to bite me!"

And so it lay quiet, while the shots rattled through the reeds and gun after gun was fired. At last, late in the day, silence was restored; but the poor Duckling did not dare to rise up; it waited several hours before it looked round, and then hastened away out of the moor as fast as it could. It ran on over field and meadow; there was such a storm raging that it was difficult to get from one place to another.

Toward evening the Duckling came to a little miserable peasant's hut. This hut was so dilapidated that it did not know on which side it should fall; and that's why it remained standing. The storm whistled round the Duckling in such a way that the poor creature was obliged to sit down, to stand against it; and the tempest grew worse and worse. Then the Duckling noticed that one of the hinges of the door had given way, and the door hung so slanting that the Duckling could slip through the crack into the room.

Here lived a woman, with her Tom Cat and her Hen. And the Tom Cat, whom she called Sonnie, could arch his back and purr, he could even give out sparks; but for that one had to stroke his fur the wrong way. The Hen had quite little short legs, and therefore she was called Chickabiddy-shortshanks; she laid good eggs, and the woman loved her as her own child.

In the morning the strange Duckling was at once noticed, and the Tom Cat began to purr, and the Hen to cluck.

"What's this?" said the woman, and looked all round; but she could not see well, and therefore she thought the Duckling was a fat duck that had strayed. "This is a rare prize!" she said. "Now I shall have duck's eggs. I hope it is not a drake. We must try that."

And so the Duckling was admitted on trial for three weeks; but no eggs came. And the Tom Cat was master of the house, and the Hen was the lady, and always said, "We and the world!" for she thought they were half the world, and by far the better half. The Duckling thought one might have a different opinion, but the Hen would not allow it.

"Can you lay eggs?" she asked.

"No."

"Then you'll have the goodness to hold your tongue."

And the Tom Cat said, "Can you curve your back, and purr, and give out sparks?"

"No."

"Then you cannot have any opinion of your own when sensible people are speaking."

And the Duckling sat in a corner and was melancholy; then the fresh air and the sunshine streamed in; and it was seized with such a strange longing to swim on the water, that it could not help telling the Hen of it.

"What are you thinking of?" cried the Hen. "You have nothing to do, that's why you have these fancies. Purr or lay eggs, and they will pass over."

"But it is so charming to swim on the water!" said the Duckling, "so refreshing to let it close above one's head, and to dive down to the bottom."

"Yes, that must be a mighty pleasure truly," quoth the Hen. "I fancy you must have gone crazy. Ask the Cat about it—he's the cleverest animal I know—ask him if he likes to swim on the water, or to dive down: I won't speak about myself. Ask our mistress, the old woman; no one in the world is cleverer than she. Do you think she has any desire to swim, and to let the water close above her head?"

"You don't understand me," said the Duckling.

"We don't understand you? Then pray who is to understand you? You surely don't pretend to be cleverer than the Tom Cat and the woman—I won't say anything of myself. Don't be conceited, child, and be grateful for all the kindness you have received. Did you not get into a warm room, and have you not fallen into company from which you may learn something? But you are a chatterer, and it is not pleasant to associate with you. You may believe me, I speak for your good. I tell you disagreeable things, and by that one may always know one's true friends! Only take care that you learn to lay eggs, or to purr and give out sparks!"

"I think I will go out into the wide world," said the Duckling.

"Yes, do go," replied the Hen.

And the Duckling went away. It swam on the water, and

dived, but it was slighted by every creature because of its ugliness.

Now came the autumn. The leaves in the forest turned yellow and brown; the wind caught them so that they danced about, and up in the air it was very cold. The clouds hung low, heavy with hail and snowflakes, and on the fence stood the raven, crying, "Croak! croak!" for mere cold; yes, it was enough to make one feel cold to think of this. The poor little Duckling certainly had not a good time. One evening—the sun was just setting in his beauty—there came a whole flock of great handsome birds out of the bushes; they were dazzlingly white, with long flexible necks; they were swans. They uttered a very peculiar cry, spread forth their glorious great wings, and flew away from that cold region to warmer lands, to fair, open lakes. They mounted so high, so high! and the ugly little Duckling felt quite strangely as it watched them. It turned round and

round in the water like a wheel, stretched out its neck
toward them, and uttered such a strange loud cry as frightened itself. Oh! it could not forget those beautiful, happy
birds; and so soon as it could see them no longer, it dived
down to the very bottom, and when it came up again, it was
quite beside itself. It knew not the name of those birds, and
knew not whither they were flying; but it loved them more
than it had ever loved any one. It was not at all envious of
them. How could it think of wishing to possess such loveli-
ness as they had? It would have been glad if only the ducks
would have endured its company—the poor, ugly creature!

And the winter grew cold, very cold! The Duckling was
forced to swim about in the water, to prevent the surface
from freezing entirely; but every night the hole in which it
swam about became smaller and smaller. It froze so hard
that the icy covering crackled again; and the Duckling was
obliged to use its legs continually to prevent the hole from
freezing up. At last it became exhausted, and lay quite still,
and thus froze fast into the ice.

Early in the morning a peasant came by, and when he
saw what had happened, he took his wooden shoe, broke
the ice crust to pieces, and carried the Duckling home to
his wife. Then it came to itself again. The children wanted
to play with it; but the Duckling thought they would do it
an injury, and in its terror fluttered up into the milk pan, so
that the milk spurted down into the room. The woman

clapped her hands, at which the Duckling flew down into the butter tub, and then into the meal barrel and out again. How it looked then! The woman screamed, and struck at it with the fire tongs; the children tumbled over one another in their efforts to catch the Duckling; and they laughed and screamed finely! Happily the door stood open, and the poor creature was able to slip out between the shrubs into the newly fallen snow; and there it lay quite exhausted.

But it would be too melancholy if I were to tell all the misery and care which the Duckling had to endure in the hard winter. It lay out on the moor among the reeds when the sun began to shine again and the larks to sing: it was a beautiful spring.

Then all at once the Duckling could flap its wings: they beat the air more strongly than before, and bore it strongly away; and before it well knew how all this happened, it found itself in a great garden, where the elder-trees smelt sweet, and bent their long green branches down to the canal that wound through the region. Oh, here it was so beautiful, such a gladness of spring! and from the thicket came three glorious white swans; they rustled their wings, and swam lightly on the water. The Duckling knew the splendid creatures, and felt oppressed by a peculiar sadness.

"I will fly away to them, to the royal birds! and they will kill me, because I, that am so ugly, dare to approach them. But it is of no consequence! Better to be killed by them than to be pursued by ducks, and beaten by fowls, and pushed about by the girl who takes care of the poultry yard, and to suffer hunger in winter!" And it flew out into the water, and swam toward the beautiful swans: these looked at it, and came sailing down upon it with outspread wings. "Kill me!" said the poor creature, and bent its head down upon the water, expecting nothing but death. But what was this that it saw in the clear water? It beheld its own image; and, lo! it was no longer a clumsy dark gray bird, ugly and hateful to look at, but—a swan!

It matters nothing if one is born in a duck-yard, if one has only lain in a swan's egg.

It felt quite glad at all the need and misfortune it had suffered; now it realized its happiness in all the splendor that surrounded it. And the great swans swam round it, and stroked it with their beaks.

Into the garden came little children, who threw bread and corn into the water; and the youngest cried, "There is a new one!" and the other children shouted joyously, "Yes, a new one has arrived!" And they clapped their hands and danced about, and ran to their father and mother; and bread and cake were thrown into the water; and they all said, "The new one is the most beautiful of all! so young and handsome!" and the old swans bowed their heads before him.

Then he felt quite ashamed, and hid his head under his wing, for he did not know what to do; he was so happy, and yet not at all proud. He thought how he had been persecuted and despised; and now he heard them saying that he was the most beautiful of all birds. Even the elder-tree bent its branches straight down into the water before him, and the sun shone warm and mild. Then his wings rustled, he lifted his slender neck, and cried rejoicingly from the depths of his heart:

"I never dreamed of so much happiness when I was still the ugly Duckling!"

The Owl and the Pussy-Cat

Edward Lear

The Owl and the Pussy-cat went to sea
   In a beautiful pea-green boat:
They took some honey, and plenty of money
   Wrapped up in a five-pound note.
The Owl looked up to the stars above,
   And sang to a small guitar,
"O lovely Pussy, O Pussy, my love,
   What a beautiful Pussy you are,
       You are,
       You are!
   What a beautiful Pussy you are!"

Pussy said to the Owl, "You elegant fowl,
   How charmingly sweet you sing!
Oh! let us be married; too long we have tarried:
   But what shall we do for a ring?"
They sailed away, for a year and a day,
   To the land where the bong-tree grows;
And there in a wood a Piggy-wig stood,
   With a ring at the end of his nose,
       His nose,
       His nose,
   With a ring at the end of his nose.

182

"Dear Pig, are you willing to sell for one shilling
   Your ring?" Said the Piggy, "I will."
So they took it away, and were married next day
   By the turkey who lives on the hill.
They dined on mince and slices of quince,
   Which they ate with a runcible spoon;
And hand in hand, on the edge of the sand,
   They danced by the light of the moon,
       The moon,
       The moon,
   They danced by the light of the moon.

How Glooskap Found the Summer

All the Eastern Woodlands Indians of Canáda and the United States knew Glooskap—a hero who was both kind and powerful, both teacher and protector. The Glooskap legend printed here is from Godfrey Leland's book The Algonquin Legends of New England.

IN THE long-ago time before the first white men came to live in the New World, and when people lived always in the early red morning before sunrise, a mighty race of Indians lived in the northeastern part of the New World. Nearest the sunrise were they, and they called themselves Wawaniki—Children of Light. Glooskap was their lord and master. He was ever kind to his people, and did many great works for them.

Once, in Glooskap's day, it grew very cold; snow and ice were everywhere, fires would not give enough warmth; the corn would not grow, and his people were perishing with cold and famine. Then Glooskap went very far north where all was ice. He came to a wigwam in which he found a giant, a great giant —for he was Winter. It was his icy breath that had frozen all the land. Glooskap entered the wigwam and sat down. Then Winter gave him a pipe, and as he smoked, the giant told tales of the olden times when he, Winter, reigned everywhere; when all the land was silent, white, and beautiful. The charm fell upon Glooskap; it was the frost charm. As the giant talked on and on, Glooskap fell asleep; and for six months he slept like a bear; then the charm fled, as he was too strong for it, and he awoke.

Soon after he awoke, his talebearer, Tatler the Loon, a wild bird who lived on the shores of the lakes, brought him strange news. He told of a country far off to the south where it was always warm: there lived a queen, who could easily overcome the giant, Winter. So Glooskap, to save his people from cold and famine and death, decided to go and find the queen.

Far off to the seashore he went, and sang the magic song which the whales obey. Up came his old friend, Blob the Whale. She was Glooskap's carrier and bore him on her back when he wished to go far out to sea. Now the whale always had a strange law for travelers. She said to Glooskap, "You must shut your eyes tight while I carry you; to open them is dangerous; if you do that, I am sure to go aground on a reef or sand-bar, and cannot get off, and you may be drowned."

Glooskap got on her back, and for many days the whale swam, and each day the water grew warmer and the air more balmy and sweet, for it came from spicy shores. The odors were no longer those of salt, but of fruits and flowers.

Soon they found themselves in shallow waters. Down in the sand the clams were singing a song of warning. "O big Whale," they sang, "keep out to sea, for the water here is shallow."

The whale said to Glooskap, who understood the language of all creatures, "What do they say?"

But Glooskap, wishing to land at once, said, "They tell you to hurry, for a storm is coming."

Then the whale hurried until she was close to the land, and Glooskap opened his left eye and peeped. At once the whale stuck hard and fast on the beach, so that Glooskap, leaping from her head, walked ashore on dry land.

The whale, thinking she could never get off, was very angry. But Glooskap put one end of his strong bow against the whale's jaw, and taking the other end in his hands, he placed his feet against the high bank, and with a mighty push, he sent her out into the deep water. Then, to keep peace with the whale, he threw her a pipe and a bag of Indian tobacco, and the whale, pleased with the gift, lighted the pipe and sailed far out to sea.

Far inland strode Glooskap and at every step it grew warmer, and the flowers began to come up and talk with him. He came to where there were many fairies dancing in the forest. In the center of the group was one fairer than all the others; her long brown hair was crowned with flowers and her arms filled with blossoms. She was the queen Summer.

Glooskap knew that here at last was the queen who by her charm could melt old Winter's heart, and force him to leave. He caught her up, and kept her by a crafty trick. The Master cut a moose-hide into a long cord; as he ran away with Summer, he let the end trail behind him. The Fairies of Light pulled at the cord, but as Glooskap ran, the cord ran out, and though they pulled, he left them far behind.

So at last he came to the lodge of old Winter, but now he had Summer in his bosom; and Winter welcomed him, for he hoped to freeze Glooskap to sleep again.

But this time the Master did the talking. This time his charm was the stronger, and ere long the sweat ran down Winter's face; he knew that his power was gone; and the charm of Frost was broken. His icy tent melted. Then Summer used her strange power and everything awoke. The grass grew, the fairies came out, and the snow ran down the rivers, carrying away the dead leaves. Old Winter wept, seeing his power gone.

But Summer, the queen, said, "I have proved that I am more powerful than you. I give you now all the country to the far North for your own, and there I shall never disturb you. Six months of every year you may come back to Glooskap's country and reign as of old, but you will be less severe. During the other six months, I myself will come from the South and rule the land."

Old Winter could do nothing but accept her offer. In the late autumn he comes back to Glooskap's country and reigns six months; but his rule is softer than in olden times. And when he comes, Summer runs home to the warm Southland. But at the end of six months, she always comes back to drive old Winter away to his own land, to awaken the northern land, and to give it the joys that only she, the queen, can give. And so, in Glooskap's old country, Winter and Summer, the hoary old giant and the beautiful fairy queen, divide the rule of the land between them.

Mutt Makes His Mark

Mutt is the sort of dog who forces people to rethink their opinions about animals. "Is Mutt really a dog?" you will ask, when you read about him. The answer is yes. Mutt was, in fact, a real dog who lived in Saskatoon, Canada, with a boy named Farley Mowat. As an adult, Mowat wrote books about his prairie boyhood and Mutt. The story printed here is from The Dog Who Wouldn't Be.

IT ALL began on one of those blistering July days when the prairie pants like a dying coyote, the dust lies heavy, and the air burns the flesh it touches. On such days those with good sense retire to the cellar caverns that are euphemistically known in Canada as beer parlors. These are all much the same across the country—ill-lit and crowded dens, redolent with the stench of sweat, spilled beer, and smoke—but they are, for the most part, moderately cool. And the insipid stuff that passes for beer is usually ice cold.

On this particular day five residents of the city, dog fanciers all, had forgathered in a beer parlor. They had just returned from witnessing some hunting-dog trials held in Manitoba, and they had brought a guest with them. He was a rather portly gentleman from the state of New York, and he had both wealth and ambition. He used his wealth lavishly to further his ambition, which was to raise and own the finest retrievers on the continent, if not in the world. Having watched his own dogs win the Manitoba trials, this man had come on to Saskatoon at the earnest invitation of the local men, in order to see what kind of dogs they bred, and to buy some if he fancied them.

He had not fancied them. Perhaps rightfully annoyed at having made the trip in the broiling summer weather to no good purpose, he had become a little overbearing in his manner. His comments when he viewed the local kennel dogs had been acidulous, and scornful. He had ruffled the local breeders' feelings, and as a result they were in a mood to do and say foolish things.

The visitor's train was due to leave at 4 P.M., and from 12:30 until 3 the six men sat cooling themselves internally, and talking dogs. The talk was as heated as the weather. Inevitably Mutt's name was mentioned, and he was referred to as an outstanding example of that rare breed, the Prince Albert retriever.

The stranger hooted. "Rare breed!" he cried. "I'll say it must be rare! I've never even heard of it."

The local men were incensed by this big-city skepticism. They immediately began telling tales of Mutt, and if they laid it on a little, who can blame them? But the more stories they told, the louder grew the visitor's mirth and the more pointed his disbelief. Finally someone was goaded a little too far.

"I'll bet you," Mutt's admirer said truculently, "I'll bet you a hundred dollars this dog can outretrieve any damn dog in the whole United States."

Perhaps he felt that he was safe, since the hunting season was not yet open. Perhaps he was too angry to think.

The stranger accepted the challenge, but it did not seem as if there was much chance of settling the bet. Someone said as much, and the visitor crowed.

"You've made your brag," he said. "Now show me."

There was nothing for it then but to seek out Mutt and hope for inspiration. The six men left the dark room and braved the blasting light of the summer afternoon as they made their way to the public library.

The library stood, four-square and ugly, just off the main thoroughfare of the city. The inevitable alley behind it was shared by two Chinese restaurants and by sundry other merchants. My father had his office in the rear of the library building overlooking the alley. A screened door gave access to whatever air was to be found trapped and roasted in the narrow space behind the building. It was through this rear door that the delegation came.

From his place under the desk Mutt barely raised his head to peer at the newcomers, then sank back into a comatose state of near oblivion engendered by the heat. He probably heard the mutter of talk, the introductions, and the slightly strident tone of voice of the stranger, but he paid no heed.

Father, however, listened intently. And he could hardly control his resentment when the stranger stooped, peered beneath the desk, and was heard to say, *"Now* I recognize the breed—Prince Albert rat hound did you say it was?"

My father got stiffly to his feet. "You gentlemen wish a demonstration of Mutt's retrieving skill—is that it?" he asked.

A murmur of agreement from the local men was punctuated by a derisive comment from the visitor. "Test him," he said offensively. "How about that alley there—it must be full of rats."

Father said nothing. Instead he pushed back his chair and, going to the large cupboard where he kept some of his shooting things so that they would be available for after-work excursions, he swung wide the door and got out his gun case. He drew out the barrels, fore and end, and stock and assembled the gun. He closed the breech and tried the triggers, and at that familiar sound Mutt was galvanized into life and came scuffling out from under the desk to stand with twitching nose and a perplexed air about him.

He had obviously been missing something. This wasn't the hunting season. But—the gun was out.

He whined interrogatively and my father patted his head. "Good boy," he said, and then walked to the screen door with Mutt crowding against his heels.

By this time the group of human watchers was as perplexed as Mutt. The six men stood in the office doorway and watched curiously as my father stepped out on the porch, raised the unloaded gun, leveled it down the alley toward the main street, pressed the triggers, and said in a quiet voice, "Bang—bang— go get 'em boy!"

To this day Father maintains a steadfast silence as to what his intentions really were. He will not say that he expected the result that followed, and he will not say that he did not expect it.

Mutt leaped from the stoop and fled down that alleyway at his best speed. They saw him turn the corner into the main street, almost causing two elderly women to collide with one another. The watchers saw the people on the far side of the street stop, turn to stare, and then stand as if petrified. But Mutt himself they could no longer see.

He was gone only about two minutes, but to the group upon the library steps it must have seemed much longer. The man from New York had just cleared his throat preparatory to a new and even more amusing sally, when he saw something that made the words catch in his gullet.

They all saw it—and they did not believe.

Mutt was coming back up the alley. He was trotting. His head and tail were high—and in his mouth was a magnificent ruffed grouse. He came up the porch stairs nonchalantly, laid the bird down at my father's feet, and with a satisfied sigh crawled back under the desk.

194

There was silence except for Mutt's panting. Then one of the local men stepped forward as if in a dream, and picked up the bird.

"Already stuffed, by God!" he said, and his voice was hardly more than a whisper.

It was then that the clerk from Ashbridge's Hardware arrived. The clerk was disheveled and mad. He came bounding up the library steps, accosted Father angrily, and cried:

"That damn dog of yours—you ought to keep him locked up. Come bustin' into the shop a moment ago and snatched the stuffed grouse right out of the window. Mr Ashbridge's fit to be tied. Was the best bird in his whole collection. . . ."

I do not know if the man from New York ever paid his debt. I do know that the story of that day's happening passed into the nation's history, for the Canadian press picked it up from the *Star-Phoenix*, and Mutt's fame was carried from coast to coast across the land.

That surely was no more than his due.

The Dog and His Shadow

A DOG, carrying a piece of meat in his mouth, was crossing a stream on a narrow footbridge. He happened to look into the water and there he saw his shadow, but he thought it another dog with a piece of meat larger than his. He made a grab for the other dog's meat; but in doing so, of course, he dropped his own, and therefore was without any.

Greediness may cause one to lose everything.

The Goose with the Golden Eggs

O NCE upon a time a man had a goose that laid a golden egg every day. Although he was gradually becoming rich, he grew impatient. He wanted to get all his treasure at once; therefore he killed the Goose. Cutting her open, he found her—just like any other goose. He learned to his sorrow:

It takes time to win success.

The Elephant
and His Son

Storytellers have been creating fables for
thousands of years—and they are still popular.
Here is a modern fable from Arnold Lobel's very
wise book called, simply, Fables.

T HE ELEPHANT and his son were spending an
evening at home. Elephant Son was singing a song.
"You must be silent," said Father Elephant.
"Your papa is trying to read his newspaper. Papa cannot
listen to a song while he is reading his newspaper."

"Why not?" asked Elephant Son.

"Because Papa can think about only one thing at a time,
that is why," said Father Elephant.

Elephant Son stopped singing. He sat quietly. Father
Elephant lit a cigar and went on reading.

After a while, Elephant Son asked, "Papa, can you still
think about only one thing at a time?"

"Yes, my boy," said Father Elephant, "that is correct."

"Well then," said Elephant Son, "you might stop thinking
about your newspaper and begin to think about the slipper
that is on your left foot."

"But my boy," said Father Elephant, "Papa's newspaper
is far more important and interesting and informative than
the slipper that is on his left foot."

"That may be true," said Elephant Son, "but while your
newspaper is not on fire from the ashes of your cigar, the
slipper that is on your left foot certainly is!"

Father Elephant ran to put his foot in a bucket of water.
Softly, Elephant Son began to sing again.

Knowledge will not always take the place
of simple observation.

Snow-White and the Seven Dwarfs

The Brothers Grimm

IT WAS in the middle of winter, when the broad flakes of snow were falling around, that a certain queen sat working at a window, the frame of which was made of fine black ebony; and as she was looking out upon the snow, she pricked her finger, and three drops of blood fell upon it. Then she gazed thoughtfully upon the red drops which sprinkled the white snow, and said, "Would that my little daughter may be as white as that snow, as red as the blood, and as black as the ebony window-frame!"

And so the little girl grew up. Her skin was as white as snow, her cheeks as rosy as blood, and her hair as black as ebony; and she was called Snow-White.

But this queen died; and the king soon married another wife, who was very beautiful, but so proud that she could not bear to think that any one could surpass her. She had a magical mirror, to which she used to go and gaze upon herself in it, and say,

> *"Mirror, Mirror on the wall*
> *Who is fairest of us all?"*

And the glass answered,

> *"Thou, queen, art fairest of them all."*

But Snow-White grew more and more beautiful; and when she was seven years old, she was as bright as the day,

and fairer than the queen herself. Then the glass one day answered the queen, when she went to consult it as usual,

"Queen, you are full fair, 'tis true,
But Snow-White fairer is than you."

When the queen heard this she turned pale with rage and envy; and called to one of her servants and said, "Take Snow-White away into the wide wood, that I may never see her more." Then the servant led Snow-White away; but his heart melted when she begged him to spare her life, and he said, "I will not hurt thee, thou pretty child." So he left her by herself, and though he thought it most likely that the wild beasts would tear her in pieces, he felt as if a great weight were taken off his heart when he had made up his mind not to kill her, but leave her to her fate.

Then poor Snow-White wandered along through the wood in great fear; and the wild beasts roared about her, but none did her any harm. In the evening she came to a little cottage, and went in there to rest herself, for her little feet would carry her no further. Everything was spruce and neat in the cottage. On the table was spread a white cloth, and there were seven little plates with seven little loaves, and seven little glasses, and knives and forks laid in order; and by the wall stood seven little beds. Then, as she was very hungry, she picked a little piece off each loaf, and drank a very little from each glass; and after that she thought she would lie down and rest. So she tried all the little beds; and one was too long, and another was too short, till at last the seventh suited her; and there she laid herself down, and went to sleep.

Presently in came the masters of the cottage, who were seven little dwarfs that lived among the mountains, and dug and searched about for gold. They lighted up their seven lamps, and saw directly that all was not right. The first said, "Who has been sitting on my stool?" The second,

"Who has been eating off my plate?" The third, "Who has been picking my bread?" The fourth, "Who has been meddling with my spoon?" The fifth, "Who has been handling my fork?" The sixth, "Who has been cutting with my knife?" The seventh, "Who has been drinking from my glass?" Then the first looked round and said, "Who has been lying on my bed?" And the rest came running to him, and every one cried out that somebody had been upon his bed. But the seventh saw Snow-White, and called all his brethren to come and see her; and they cried out with wonder and astonishment, and brought their lamps to look at her, and said, "Oh, what a lovely child she is!" And they were delighted to see her, and took care not to wake her;

and the seventh dwarf slept an hour with each of the other dwarfs in turn, till the night was gone.

In the morning Snow-White told them all her story; and they pitied her, and said if she would keep all things in order, and cook and wash, and knit and spin for them, she might stay where she was, and they would take good care of her. Then they went out all day long to their work, seeking for gold and silver in the mountains; and Snow-White remained at home; and they warned her, and said, "The queen will soon find out where you are, so take care and let no one in."

But the queen, now that she thought Snow-White was dead, believed that she was certainly the handsomest lady in the land; and she went to her mirror and said,

"Mirror, Mirror on the wall
  Who is fairest of us all?"

And the mirror answered,

"Queen, thou art of beauty rare,
  But Snow-White living in the glen
  With the seven little men
  Is a thousand times more fair."

Then the queen was very much alarmed; for she knew that the glass always spoke the truth, and was sure that the servant had betrayed her. And she could not bear to think that any one lived who was more beautiful than she was; so she disguised herself as an old pedlar and went her way over the hills to the place where the dwarfs dwelt. Then she knocked at the door, and cried, "Fine wares to sell!" Snow-White looked out at the window, and said, "Good-day, good-woman; what have you to sell?" "Good wares, fine wares," said she; "laces and bobbins of all colors." "I will let the old lady in; she seems to be a very good sort of body," thought Snow-White; so she ran down, and unbolted the door. "Bless me!" said the old woman, "how badly your stays are laced! Let me lace them up with one of my nice new laces." Snow-White did not dream of any mischief; so she stood up before the old woman, who set to work so nimbly, and pulled the lace so tight, that Snow-White lost her breath, and fell down as if she were dead. "There's an end of all thy beauty," said the spiteful queen, and went away home.

In the evening the seven dwarfs returned; and I need not say how grieved they were to see their faithful Snow-White

stretched upon the ground motionless, as if she were quite dead. However, they lifted her up, and when they found what was the matter, they cut the lace; and in a little time she began to breathe, and soon came to life again. Then they said, "The old woman was the queen herself; take care another time, and let no one in when we are away."

When the queen got home, she went straight to her glass, and spoke to it as usual; but to her great surprise it still said,

"Queen, thou art of beauty rare,
But Snow-White living in the glen
With the seven little men,
Is a thousand times more fair."

Then the blood ran cold in her heart with spite and malice to see that Snow-White still lived; and she dressed herself up again in a disguise, but very different from the one she wore before, and took with her a poisoned comb. When she reached the dwarfs' cottage, she knocked at the door, and cried, "Fine wares to sell!" But Snow-White said, "I dare not let any one in." Then the queen said, "Only look at my beautiful combs"; and gave her the poisoned one. And it looked so pretty that Snow-White took it up and put it into her hair to try it. But the moment it touched her head the poison was so powerful that she fell down senseless. "There you may lie," said the queen, and went her way. But by good luck the dwarfs returned very early that evening, and when they saw Snow-White lying on the ground, they guessed what had happened, and soon found the poisoned comb. When they took it away, she recovered, and told them all that had passed; and they warned her once more not to open the door to any one.

Meantime the queen went home to her glass, and trembled with rage when she received exactly the same answer as before; and she said, "Snow-White shall die, if it costs me my life." So she went secretly into a chamber, and prepared a poisoned apple. The outside looked very rosy and tempting, but whoever tasted it was sure to die. Then she dressed herself up as a peasant's wife, and travelled over the hills to the dwarfs' cottage, and knocked at the door; but Snow-White put her head out of the window and said, "I dare not let any one in, for the dwarfs have told me not." "Do as you please," said the old woman, "but at any rate take this pretty apple; I will make you a present of it." "No," said Snow-White, "I dare not take it." "You silly girl!" answered the other, "what are you afraid of? Do you think it is poisoned? Come! Do you eat one part, and I will eat the other." Now the apple was so prepared that one side

207

was good, though the other side was poisoned. Then Snow-White was very much tempted to taste, for the apple looked exceedingly nice; and when she saw the old woman eat, she could refrain no longer. But she had scarcely put the piece into her mouth, when she fell down dead upon the ground. "This time nothing will save you," said the queen; and she went home to her glass and at last it said,

"Thou, queen, art the fairest of them all."

And then her envious heart was glad, and as happy as such a heart could be.

When evening came, and the dwarfs returned home, they found Snow-White lying on the ground. No breath passed her lips, and they were afraid that she was quite dead. They lifted her up, and combed her hair, and washed her face with water; but all was in vain, for the little girl seemed quite dead. So they laid her down upon a bier, and all seven watched and bewailed her three whole days; and then they proposed to bury her; but her cheeks were still rosy, and her face looked just as it did while she was alive; so they said, "We will never bury her in the cold ground." And they made a coffin of glass, so that they might still look at her, and wrote her name upon it, in golden letters, and that she was a king's daughter. And the coffin was placed upon the hill, and one of the dwarfs always sat by it and watched. And the birds of the air came too, and bemoaned Snow-White; first of all came an owl, and then a raven, but at last came a dove.

And thus Snow-White lay for a long, long time, and still looked as though she were only asleep; for she was even now as white as snow, and as red as blood, and as black as ebony. At last a prince came and called at the dwarfs' house; and he saw Snow-White, and read what was written in golden letters. Then he offered the dwarfs money, and earnestly prayed them to let him take her away; but they said, "We will not part with her for all the gold in the world." At last, however, they had pity on him, and gave him the coffin; but the moment he lifted it up to carry it home with him, the piece of apple fell from between her lips, and Snow-White awoke, and said, "Where am I?" And the prince answered, "Thou art safe with me." Then he told her all that had happened, and said, "I love you better than all the world. Come with me to my father's palace, and you shall be my wife." And Snow-White consented, and went home with the prince; and everything was prepared with great pomp and splendour for their wedding.

To the feast was invited, among the rest, Snow-White's old enemy, the queen; and as she was dressing herself in fine rich clothes, she looked in the glass, and said,

"Mirror, Mirror on the wall,
Who is fairest of us all?"

And the glass answered,

"O Queen, although you are of beauty rare
The young queen is a thousand times more fair."

When she heard this, she started with rage; but her envy and curiosity were so great, that she could not help setting out to see the bride. And when she arrived, and saw that it was no other than Snow-White, who, as she thought, had been dead a long while, she choked with passion, and fell ill and died. But Snow-White and the prince lived and reigned happily over that land many, many years.

Rapunzel

The Brothers Grimm

ONCE upon a time there lived a man and his wife, who had long wished for a child, but all in vain. And, it so happened that at the back of their house was a little window which overlooked a beautiful garden full of the finest vegetables and flowers. But there was a high wall round it, and no one ventured there, for it belonged to a witch of great power of whom all the world was afraid.

One day when the wife was standing at the window, and looking into the garden, she saw a bed filled with the finest rampion; and it looked so fresh and green that she began to wish for some; and at length she longed for it greatly. This went on for days, and as she knew she could not get the rampion, she pined away, and grew pale and miserable. The man was uneasy, and he asked, "What is the matter, dear wife?"

"Oh," answered she, "I shall die unless I can have some of that rampion to eat that grows in the garden at the back of our house."

The man, who loved her very much, thought to himself, "Rather than lose my wife I will get the rampion, cost what it will."

So in the twilight he climbed over the wall into the witch's garden, plucked hastily a handful of rampion, and brought it to his wife. She made a salad of it at once; and ate to her heart's content. She liked it so much, and it tasted so good, that the next day she longed for it thrice as much as she had before; if she was to have any rest the man must climb over the wall once more. So he went in the twilight again; and as he was climbing back, he saw the witch standing before him, and was terribly frightened, as she cried, with angry eyes, "How dare you climb over into my garden like a thief, and steal my rampion! It shall be the worse for you!"

"Oh," answered he, "be merciful rather than just; I have only done it through necessity. My wife saw your rampion from our window, and became possessed with so great a longing for it that she would have died if she could not have some to eat."

Then the witch said, "If it is all as you say you may have as much rampion as you like, on one condition—the child that will come into the world must be given to me. It shall go well with the child, and I will care for it like a mother."

In his distress the man promised everything, and when the time came and the child was born the witch appeared, and gave the child the name of Rapunzel (which is the same as rampion). Then she took it away with her.

Rapunzel grew to be the most beautiful child in the world. When she was twelve years old the witch shut her up in a tower in the midst of a wood. It had neither steps nor door, only one small window above.

When the witch wished to be let in, she would stand below and cry, "Rapunzel, Rapunzel! Let down thy hair!"

Rapunzel had beautiful long hair that shone like gold. When she heard the voice of the witch she would undo the fastening of the upper window, unbind the plaits of her hair, and let it fall down twenty ells below, and the witch would climb up by it.

They had lived thus a few years when it happened that the King's son came riding through the wood. He came to the tower; and as he drew near he heard a voice singing so sweetly that he stood still and listened. It was Rapunzel. In her loneliness she tried to pass away the time with sweet songs. The King's son wished to go in to her, and sought to find a door in the tower, but there was none. So he rode home, but the song had entered his heart, and every day he went into the wood and listened to it.

Once, as he was standing there under a tree, he saw the witch come up, and he listened while she called out, "O Rapunzel, Rapunzel! Let down thy hair."

Then he saw how Rapunzel let down her long tresses, and how the witch climbed up by them and went in to her, and he said to himself, "Since that is the ladder I will climb it, and seek my fortune." And the next day, as soon as it began to grow dusk, he went to the tower and cried, "O Rapunzel, Rapunzel! Let down thy hair."

And she let down her hair, and the King's son climbed up by it.

Rapunzel was greatly terrified when she saw that a man had come in to her, for she had never seen one before. But the King's son began speaking so kindly to her, telling her how her singing had entered into his heart, so that he could have no peace until he had seen her himself, that Rapunzel forgot her terror. When he asked her to take him for her husband, she saw that he was young and beautiful, and she thought to herself, "I certainly like him much better than old mother Gothel."

She put her hand into his hand, and said, "I would willingly go with thee, but I do not know how I shall get out. Each time thou comest, bring a silken rope, and I will make a ladder. When it is quite ready I will use it to get down out of the tower, and thou shalt take me away on thy horse." They agreed that he should come to her every evening, as the old woman only came in the daytime.

Now the witch knew nothing of all this until one day when Rapunzel said to her unwittingly, "Mother Gothel, how is it that you climb up here so slowly, and the King's son is with me in a moment?"

"O wicked child," cried the witch, "what is this I hear! I thought I had hidden thee from all the world, and now thou hast betrayed me!"

In her anger she seized Rapunzel by her beautiful hair, struck her several times with her left hand, and then grasping a pair of shears in her right—snip, snap—she cut, and the beautiful locks lay on the ground. The witch was so hardhearted that she took Rapunzel and put her in a waste and desert place, where the young girl lived in great woe and misery.

216

On the evening of the same day on which she took Rapunzel away she went back to the tower and made fast the severed lock of hair to the window hasp.

The King's son came and cried, "Rapunzel, Rapunzel! Let down thy hair."

The witch let down the hair, and the King's son climbed up. But instead of his dearest Rapunzel he found the witch looking at him with her wicked glittering eyes.

"Aha!" cried she, mocking him, "you came for your darling, but the sweet bird sits no longer in the nest. She sings no more. The cat has got her, and will scratch out your eyes as well! Rapunzel is lost to you; you will see her no more."

The King's son was beside himself with grief, and in his agony he sprang from the tower. He escaped with his life, but the thorns on which he fell put out his eyes. He wandered blindly through the wood, eating nothing but roots and berries, and doing nothing but lamenting and weeping for the loss of his dearest wife.

He wandered for several years in this misery until one day he came to the desert place where Rapunzel lived with her twin children. She had borne him a boy and a girl. At first he heard a voice that he thought he knew, and when he reached the place from which it seemed to come Rapunzel recognized him, and fell on his neck and wept. When her tears touched his eyes they became clear again, and he could see as well as ever.

He took her and the children to his kingdom, where he was received with great joy, and there they lived long and happily.

A Mad Tea-Party

One hot afternoon, a girl named Alice followed a smartly dressed white rabbit down a rabbit hole and found Wonderland. You will learn all of what happened to her there if you read Alice's Adventures in Wonderland *by Lewis Carroll. "A Mad Tea-Party" (which Alice finds by following directions from a Cheshire Cat) will give you a good introduction to Wonderland, a place of the impossible.*

THERE was a table set out under a tree in front of the house, and the March Hare and the Hatter were having tea at it: a Dormouse was sitting between them, fast asleep, and the other two were using it as a cushion, resting their elbows on it, and talking over its head. "Very uncomfortable for the Dormouse," thought Alice; "only as it's asleep, I suppose it doesn't mind."

The table was a large one, but the three were all crowded together at one corner of it. "No room! No room!" they cried out when they saw Alice coming. "There's *plenty* of room!" said Alice indignantly, and she sat down in a large armchair at one end of the table.

"Have some wine," the March Hare said in an encouraging tone.

Alice looked all round the table, but there was nothing on it but tea. "I don't see any wine," she remarked.

"There isn't any," said the March Hare.

"Then it wasn't very civil of you to offer it," said Alice angrily.

"It wasn't very civil of you to sit down without being invited," said the March Hare.

"I didn't know it was *your* table," said Alice: "it's laid for a great many more than three."

"Your hair wants cutting," said the Hatter. He had been looking at Alice for some time with great curiosity, and this was his first speech.

"You should learn not to make personal remarks," Alice said with some severity: "It's very rude."

The Hatter opened his eyes very wide on hearing this; but all he *said* was, "Why is a raven like a writing desk?"

"Come, we shall have some fun now!" thought Alice. "I'm glad they've begun asking riddles—I believe I can guess that," she added aloud.

"Do you mean that you think you can find out the answer to it?" said the March Hare.

"Exactly so," said Alice.

"Then you should say what you mean," the March Hare went on.

"I do," Alice hastily replied; "at least—I mean what I say —that's the same thing, you know."

"Not the same thing a bit!" said the Hatter. "Why, you might just as well say that 'I see what I eat' is the same thing as 'I eat what I see'!"

"You might just as well say," added the March Hare, "that 'I like what I get' is the same thing as 'I get what I like'!"

"You might just as well say," added the Dormouse, which seemed to be talking in its sleep, "that 'I breathe when I sleep' is the same thing as 'I sleep when I breathe'!"

"It *is* the same thing with you," said the Hatter, and here the conversation dropped, and the party sat silent for a minute, while Alice thought over all she could remember about ravens and writing desks, which wasn't much.

The Hatter was the first to break the silence. "What day of the month is it?" he said, turning to Alice: he had taken his watch out of his pocket, and was looking at it uneasily, shaking it every now and then, and holding it to his ear.

Alice considered a little, and then said, "The fourth."

"Two days wrong!" sighed the Hatter. "I told you butter wouldn't suit the works!" he added, looking angrily at the March Hare.

"It was the *best* butter," the March Hare meekly replied.

"Yes, but some crumbs must have got in as well," the Hatter grumbled: "you shouldn't have put it in with the bread knife."

The March Hare took the watch and looked at it gloomily: then he dipped it into his cup of tea, and looked at it again: but he could think of nothing better to say than his first remark, "It was the *best* butter, you know."

Alice had been looking over his shoulder with some curiosity. "What a funny watch!" she remarked. "It tells the day of the month, and doesn't tell what o'clock it is!"

"Why should it?" muttered the Hatter. "Does *your* watch tell you what year it is?"

"Of course not," Alice replied very readily: "but that's because it stays the same year for such a long time together."

"Which is just the case with *mine*," said the Hatter.

Alice felt dreadfully puzzled. The Hatter's remark seemed to her to have no sort of meaning in it, and yet it was certainly English. "I don't quite understand you," she said, as politely as she could.

"The Dormouse is asleep again," said the Hatter, and he poured a little hot tea upon its nose.

221

The Dormouse shook its head impatiently, and said, without opening its eyes, "Of course, of course: just what I was going to remark myself."

"Have you guessed the riddle yet?" the Hatter said, turning to Alice again.

"No, I give it up," Alice replied. "What's the answer?"

"I haven't the slightest idea," said the Hatter.

"Nor I," said the March Hare.

Alice sighed wearily. "I think you might do something better with the time," she said, "than wasting it in asking riddles that have no answers."

"If you knew Time as well as I do," said the Hatter, "you wouldn't talk about wasting *it*. It's *him*."

"I don't know what you mean," said Alice.

"Of course you don't!" the Hatter said, tossing his head contemptuously. "I daresay you never even spoke to Time!"

"Perhaps not," Alice cautiously replied; "but I know I have to beat time when I learn music."

"Ah! That accounts for it," said the Hatter. "He won't stand beating. Now, if you only kept on good terms with him,

he'd do almost anything you liked with the clock. For instance, suppose it were nine o'clock in the morning, just time to begin lessons: you'd only have to whisper a hint to Time, and round goes the clock in a twinkling! Half-past one, time for dinner!"

("I only wish it was," the March Hare said to itself in a whisper.)

"That would be grand, certainly," said Alice thoughtfully; "but then—I shouldn't be hungry for it, you know."

"Not at first, perhaps," said the Hatter: "but you could keep it to half-past one as long as you liked."

"Is that the way *you* manage?" Alice asked.

The Hatter shook his head mournfully. "Not I!" he replied. "We quarreled last March—just before *he* went mad, you know—" (pointing with his teaspoon at the March Hare)

"—it was at the great concert given by the Queen of Hearts, and I had to sing

> 'Twinkle, twinkle, little bat!
> How I wonder what you're at!'

You know the song, perhaps?"

"I've heard something like it," said Alice.

"It goes on, you know," the Hatter continued, "in this way:

> 'Up above the world you fly,
> Like a tea-tray in the sky.
> Twinkle, twinkle—' "

Here the Dormouse shook itself, and began singing in its sleep, *"Twinkle, twinkle, twinkle, twinkle—"* and went on so long that they had to pinch it to make it stop.

"Well, I'd hardly finished the first verse," said the Hatter, "when the Queen bawled out, 'He's murdering the time! Off with his head!' "

"How dreadfully savage!" exclaimed Alice.

"And ever since that," the Hatter went on in a mournful tone, "he won't do a thing I ask! It's always six o'clock now."

A bright idea came into Alice's head. "Is that the reason so many tea things are put out here?" she asked.

"Yes, that's it," said the Hatter with a sigh: "it's always teatime, and we've no time to wash the things between whiles."

"Then you keep moving round, I suppose?" said Alice.

"Exactly so," said the Hatter: "as the things get used up."

"But what happens when you come to the beginning again?" Alice ventured to ask.

"Suppose we change the subject," the March Hare interrupted, yawning. "I'm getting tired of this. I vote the young lady tells us a story."

"I'm afraid I don't know one," said Alice, rather alarmed at the proposal.

"Then the Dormouse shall!" they both cried. "Wake up, Dormouse!" And they pinched it on both sides at once.

The Dormouse slowly opened its eyes. "I wasn't asleep," it said in a hoarse, feeble voice, "I heard every word you fellows were saying."

224

"Tell us a story!" said the March Hare.

"Yes, please do!" pleaded Alice.

"And be quick about it," added the Hatter, "or you'll be asleep again before it's done."

"Once upon a time there were three little sisters," the Dormouse began in a great hurry; "and their names were Elsie, Lacie, and Tillie; and they lived at the bottom of a well—"

"What did they live on?" said Alice, who always took a great interest in questions of eating and drinking.

"They lived on treacle," said the Dormouse, after thinking a minute or two.

"They couldn't have done that, you know," Alice gently remarked. "They'd have been ill."

"So they were," said the Dormouse; "*very* ill."

Alice tried a little to fancy to herself what such an extraordinary way of living would be like, but it puzzled her too much: so she went on: "But why did they live at the bottom of a well?"

"Take some more tea," the March Hare said to Alice, very earnestly.

"I've had nothing yet," Alice replied in an offended tone: "so I can't take more."

"You mean you can't take *less*," said the Hatter: "It's very easy to take *more* than nothing."

225

"Nobody asked *your* opinion," said Alice.

"Who's making personal remarks now?" the Hatter asked triumphantly.

Alice did not quite know what to say to this: so she helped herself to some tea and bread-and-butter, and then turned to the Dormouse, and repeated her question. "Why did they live at the bottom of a well?"

The Dormouse again took a minute or two to think about it, and then said, "It was a treacle well."

"There's no such thing!" Alice was beginning very angrily, but the Hatter and the March Hare went "Sh! Sh!" and the Dormouse sulkily remarked, "If you can't be civil, you'd better finish the story for yourself."

"No, please go on!" Alice said very humbly. "I won't interrupt you again. I daresay there may be *one*."

"One, indeed!" said the Dormouse indignantly. However, he consented to go on. "And so these three little sisters —they were learning to draw, you know—"

"What did they draw?" said Alice, quite forgetting her promise.

"Treacle," said the Dormouse, without considering at all, this time.

"I want a clean cup," interrupted the Hatter: "let's all move one place on."

He moved on as he spoke, and the Dormouse followed him: the March Hare moved into the Dormouse's place, and Alice rather unwillingly took the place of the March Hare. The Hatter was the only one who got any advantage from the change; and Alice was a good deal worse off than before, as the March Hare had just upsct the milk jug into his plate.

Alice did not wish to offend the Dormouse again, so she began very cautiously: "But I don't understand. Where did they draw the treacle from?"

"You can draw water out of a water well," said the Hatter; "so I should think you could draw treacle out of a treacle well—eh, stupid?"

"But they were *in* the well," Alice said to the Dormouse, not choosing to notice this last remark.

"Of course they were," said the Dormouse: "well in."

This answer so confused poor Alice that she let the Dormouse go on for some time without interrupting it.

"They were learning to draw," the Dormouse went on, yawning and rubbing its eyes, for it was getting very sleepy;

227

"and they drew all manner of things—everything that begins with an M—"

"Why with an M?" said Alice.

"Why not?" said the March Hare.

Alice was silent.

The Dormouse had closed its eyes by this time, and was going off into a doze; but, on being pinched by the Hatter, it woke up again with a little shriek, and went on: "—that begins with an M, such as mousetraps, and the moon, and memory, and muchness—you know you say things are 'much of a muchness'—did you ever see such a thing as a drawing of a muchness!"

"Really, now you ask me," said Alice, very much confused, "I don't think—"

"Then you shouldn't talk," said the Hatter.

This piece of rudeness was more than Alice could bear: she got up in great disgust, and walked off: the Dormouse fell asleep instantly, and neither of the others took the least notice of her going, though she looked back once or twice, half hoping that they would call after her: the last time she saw them, they were trying to put the Dormouse into the teapot.

"At any rate I'll never go *there* again!" said Alice, as she picked her way through the wood. "It's the stupidest tea party I ever was at in all my life!"

Stopping by Woods on a Snowy Evening

Robert Frost

Whose woods these are I think I know.
His house is in the village though;
He will not see me stopping here
To watch his woods fill up with snow.

My little horse must think it queer
To stop without a farmhouse near
Between the woods and frozen lake
The darkest evening of the year.

He gives his harness bells a shake
To ask if there is some mistake.
The only other sound's the sweep
Of easy wind and downy flake.

The woods are lovely, dark and deep,
But I have promises to keep,
And miles to go before I sleep.
And miles to go before I sleep.

The Miller, His Son, and the Ass

A MILLER with his son were one time driving an ass to market to sell it. Some young people passing by made fun of them for walking when the ass might be carrying one of them. Upon hearing them, the father had the boy get on the ass and was walking along happily until an old man met them. "You lazy rascal," he called to the boy, "to ride and let your poor old father walk!" The son, red with shame, quickly climbed off the ass and insisted that his father ride. Not long after, they met another who cried out, "How selfish that father is—to ride and let his young son walk!"

At that the miller took his son up on the ass with himself, thinking he had at last done the right thing. But alas, he hadn't, for the next person they met was more critical than the others. "You should be ashamed of yourself," he said, "to be both riding that poor little beast; you are much better able to carry *it*."

Discouraged but willing to do right, the miller and his son got off the ass, bound its legs together on a long pole, and thus carried it on to the market. When they entered town, however, they made such a funny sight that crowds gathered about them laughing and shouting. This noise frightened the ass so much that he kicked himself free and, tumbling into the river, was drowned. The miller, now disgusted, called to his son to come along, and they rushed back home. "Well," said the father, "we have lost the ass, but we have learned one thing—that when one tries to please everybody, he pleases none, not even himself."

The Hare and the Tortoise

A HARE was once boasting about how fast he could run when a tortoise, overhearing him, said, "I'll run you a race." "Done," said the hare and laughed to himself; "but let's get the fox for a judge." The fox consented and the two started. The hare quickly outran the tortoise, and knowing he was far ahead, lay down to take a nap. "I can soon pass the tortoise whenever I awaken." But unfortunately, the hare overslept himself; therefore when he awoke, though he ran his best, he found the tortoise was already at the goal.

Slow and steady wins the race.

The Cat and the Pain-killer

Many an adult would return to childhood for the privilege of spending even one day with Tom Sawyer. The reading public first met Tom with the publication of Mark Twain's The Adventures of Tom Sawyer *in 1876. The book brims with antics, good fun, and truly hair-raising adventure. The section below will introduce you to Tom, who lives with his Aunt Polly and his snivelling cousin Sid and dreams of having Becky Thatcher be his sweetheart.*

ONE of the reasons why Tom's mind had drifted away from its secret troubles was that it had found a new and weighty matter to interest itself about. Becky Thatcher had stopped coming to school. Tom had struggled with his pride a few days, and tried to "whistle her down the wind," but failed. He began to find himself hanging around her father's house, nights, and feeling very miserable. She was ill. What if she should die! There was distraction in the thought. He no longer took an interest in war, nor even in piracy. The charm of life was gone; there was nothing but dreariness left. He put his hoop away, and his bat; there was no joy in them any more. His aunt was concerned. She began to try all manner of remedies on him. She was one of those people who are infatuated with patent medicines and all new-fangled methods of producing health or mending it. She was an inveterate experimenter in these things. When something fresh in this line came out she was in a fever, right away, to try it; not on herself, for she was never ailing, but on anybody else that came handy. She was a subscriber for all the "Health" periodicals and phrenological frauds; and the solemn ignorance they were inflated with was breath to her nostrils. All the "rot" they contained about ventilation, and how to go to bed, and how to get up, and what to eat, and what to drink, and how much exercise to take, and what frame of mind to keep oneself in, and what sort of clothing to wear, was all gospel to her, and she never observed that her health-journals of the current month customarily upset everything they had recommended the month before. She was as simple-hearted and honest as the day was long, and so she was an easy victim. She gathered together her quack periodicals and quack medicines, and thus armed with death, went about on her pale horse, metaphorically speaking, with "hell following after." But she never suspected that she was not an angel of healing and the balm of Gilead in disguise, to the suffering neighbors.

The water treatment was new, now, and Tom's low condition was a windfall to her. She had him out at daylight every morning, stood him up in the woodshed and drowned him with a deluge of cold water; then she scrubbed him down with a towel like a file, and so brought him to; then she rolled him up in a wet sheet and put him away under blankets till she sweated his soul clean and "the yellowish stains of it came through his pores"—as Tom said.

Yet notwithstanding all this, the boy grew more and more melancholy and pale and dejected. She added hot baths, sitz baths, shower baths, and plunges. The boy remained as dismal as a hearse. She began to assist the water with a slim oatmeal diet and blister-plasters. She calculated his capacity as she would a jug's, and filled him up every day with quack cure-alls. Tom had become indifferent to persecution by this time. This phase filled the old lady's heart with consternation. This indifference must be broken up at any cost. Now she heard of Pain-killer for the first time. She ordered a lot at once. She tasted it and was filled with gratitude. It was simply fire in a liquid form. She dropped the water treatment and everything else, and pinned her faith to Pain-killer. She gave Tom a teaspoonful and watched with the deepest anxiety for the result. Her troubles were instantly at rest, her soul at peace again; for the "indifference" was broken up. The boy could not have shown a wilder heartier interest if she had built a fire under him.

234

Tom felt that it was time to wake up; this sort of life might
be romantic enough, in his blighted condition, but it was
getting to have too little sentiment and too much distracting
variety about it. So he thought over various plans for relief,
and finally hit upon that of professing to be fond of Pain-
killer. He asked for it so often that he became a nuisance,
and his aunt ended by telling him to help himself and quit
bothering her. If it had been Sid, she would have had no
misgivings to alloy her delight; but since it was Tom, she

235

watched the bottle clandestinely. She found that the medicine did really diminish, but it did not occur to her that the boy was mending the health of a crack in the sitting-room floor with it.

One day Tom was in the act of dosing the crack when his aunt's yellow cat came along, purring, eyeing the teaspoon avariciously, and begging for a taste. Tom said: "Don't ask for it unless you want it, Peter." But Peter signified that he did want it.

"You better make sure."

Peter was sure.

"Now you've asked for it, and I'll give it to you because there ain't anything mean about *me*; but if you find you don't like it, you musn't blame anybody but your own self."

236

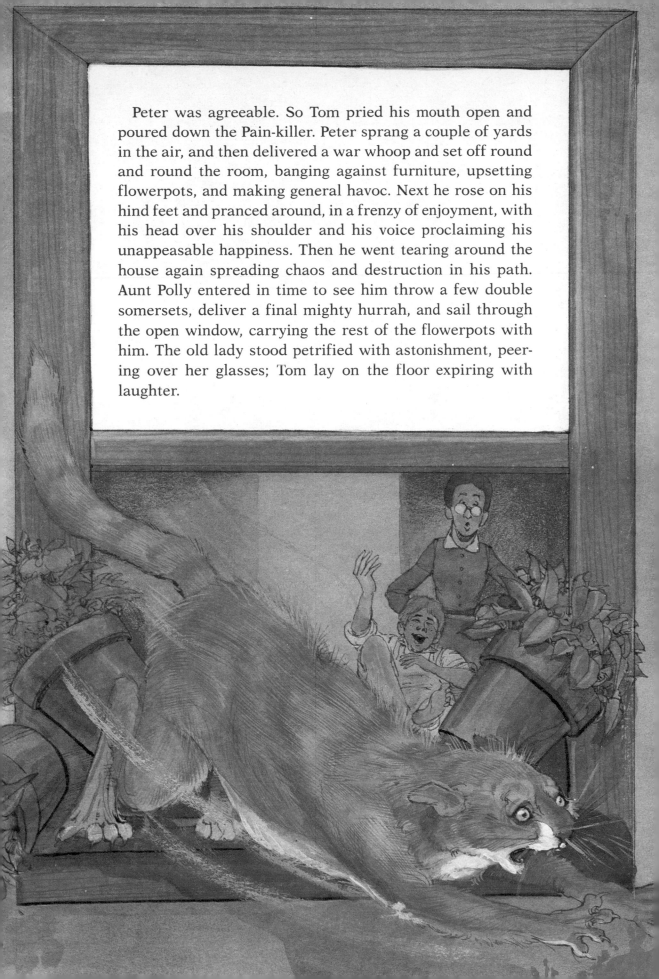

Peter was agreeable. So Tom pried his mouth open and poured down the Pain-killer. Peter sprang a couple of yards in the air, and then delivered a war whoop and set off round and round the room, banging against furniture, upsetting flowerpots, and making general havoc. Next he rose on his hind feet and pranced around, in a frenzy of enjoyment, with his head over his shoulder and his voice proclaiming his unappeasable happiness. Then he went tearing around the house again spreading chaos and destruction in his path. Aunt Polly entered in time to see him throw a few double somersets, deliver a final mighty hurrah, and sail through the open window, carrying the rest of the flowerpots with him. The old lady stood petrified with astonishment, peering over her glasses; Tom lay on the floor expiring with laughter.

"Tom, what on earth ails that cat?"

"I don't know, aunt," gasped the boy.

"Why, I never see anything like it. What *did* make him act so?"

" 'Deed I don't know, Aunt Polly; cats always act so when they're having a good time."

"They do, do they?" There was something in the tone that made Tom apprehensive.

"Yes'm. That is, I believe they do."

"You do?"

"Yes'm."

The old lady was bending down, Tom watching, with interest emphasized by anxiety. Too late he divined her

238

"drift." The handle of the telltale teaspoon was visible under the bed-valance. Aunt Polly took it, held it up. Tom winced, and dropped his eyes. Aunt Polly raised him by the usual handle —his ear—and cracked his head soundly with her thimble.

"Now, sir, what did you want to treat that poor dumb beast so for?"

"I done it out of pity for him—because he hadn't any aunt."

"Hadn't any aunt!—you numskull. What has that got to do with it?"

"Heaps. Because if he'd 'a' had one she'd 'a' burnt him out herself! She'd 'a' roasted his bowels out of him 'thout any more feeling than if he was a human!"

Aunt Polly felt a sudden pang of remorse. This was putting the thing in a new light; what was cruelty to a cat *might* be cruelty to a boy, too. She began to soften; she felt sorry. Her eyes watered a little, and she put her hand on Tom's head and said gently:

"I was meaning for the best, Tom. And, Tom, it *did* do you good."

Tom looked up in her face with just a perceptible twinkle peeping through his gravity:

"I know you was meaning for the best, auntie, and so was I with Peter. It done *him* good, too. I never see him get around so since—"

"Oh, go 'long with you, Tom, before you aggravate me again. And you try and see if you can't be a good boy, for once, and you needn't take any more medicine."

Introduction
to Songs of Innocence

William Blake

Piping down the valleys wild,
Piping songs of pleasant glee,
On a cloud I saw a child,
And he laughing said to me:

"Pipe a song about a Lamb!"
So I piped with merry cheer.
"Piper, pipe that song again";
So I piped: he wept to hear.

"Drop thy pipe, thy happy pipe;
Sing thy songs of happy cheer";
So I sang the same again,
While he wept with joy to hear.

"Piper, sit thee down and write
In a book, that all may read."
So he vanished from my sight,
And I plucked a hollow reed,

And I made a rural pen,
And I stained the water clear,
And I wrote my happy songs
Every child may joy to hear.

Eeyore Loses a Tail and Pooh Finds One

Winnie-the-Pooh seems to have gotten a reputation for being a cute little bear for very small children to love. Now, this is not fair to Pooh. When you read the story below from A.A. Milne's book Winnie-the-Pooh, *see if you don't agree that Pooh is also a kind and imaginative bear you can love reading about all your life.*

THE OLD Grey Donkey, Eeyore, stood by himself in a thistly corner of the forest, his front feet well apart, his head on one side, and thought about things. Sometimes he thought sadly to himself, "Why?" and sometimes he thought, "Wherefore?" and sometimes he thought, "Inasmuch as which?"—and sometimes he didn't quite know what he *was* thinking about. So when Winnie-the-Pooh came stumping along, Eeyore was very glad to be able to stop thinking for a little, in order to say "How do you do?" in a gloomy manner to him.

"And how are you?" said Winnie-the-Pooh.

Eeyore shook his head from side to side.

"Not very how," he said. "I don't seem to have felt at all how for a long time."

"Dear, dear," said Pooh, "I'm sorry about that. Let's have a look at you."

So Eeyore stood there, gazing sadly at the ground, and Winnie-the-Pooh walked all round him once.

"Why, what's happened to your tail?" he said in surprise.

"What *has* happened to it?" said Eeyore.

"It isn't there!"

"Are you sure?"

"Well, either a tail *is* there or it isn't there. You can't make a mistake about it. And yours *isn't* there!"

"Then what is?"

"Nothing."

"Let's have a look," said Eeyore, and he turned slowly round to the place where his tail had been a little while ago, and then, finding that he couldn't catch it up, he turned round the other way, until he came back to where he was at first, and then he put his head down and looked between his front legs, and at last he said, with a long, sad sigh, "I believe you're right."

"Of course I'm right," said Pooh.

"That Accounts for a Good Deal," said Eeyore gloomily. "It Explains Everything. No Wonder."

"You must have left it somewhere," said Winnie-the-Pooh.

"Somebody must have taken it," said Eeyore. "How Like Them," he added, after a long silence.

Pooh felt that he ought to say something helpful about it, but didn't quite know what. So he decided to do something helpful instead.

"Eeyore," he said solemnly, "I, Winnie-the-Pooh, will find your tail for you."

"Thank you, Pooh," answered Eeyore. "You're a real friend," said he. "Not like Some," he said.

So Winnie-the-Pooh went off to find Eeyore's tail.

It was a fine spring morning in the forest as he started out. Little soft clouds played happily in a blue sky, skipping from time to time in front of the sun as if they had come to put it out, and then sliding away suddenly so that the next might have his turn. Through them and between them the sun shone bravely; and a copse which had worn its firs all the year round seemed old and dowdy now beside the new green lace which the beeches had put on so prettily. Through copse and spinney marched Bear; down open slopes of gorse and heather, over rocky beds of streams, up steep banks of sandstone into the heather again; and so at last, tired and hungry, to the Hundred Acre Wood. For it was in the Hundred Acre Wood that Owl lived.

"And if anyone knows anything about anything," said Bear to himself, "it's Owl who knows something about something," he said, "or my name's not Winnie-the-Pooh," he said. "Which it is," he added. "So there you are."

Owl lived at The Chestnuts, an old-world residence of great charm, which was grander than anybody else's, or seemed so to Bear, because it had both a knocker *and* a bell-pull. Underneath the knocker there was a notice which said:

PLES RING IF AN RNSER IS REQIRD.

Underneath the bell-pull there was a notice which said:

PLEZ CNOKE IF AN RNSR IS NOT REQID.

These notices had been written by Christopher Robin, who was the only one in the forest who could spell; for Owl, wise though he was in many ways, able to read and write and spell his own name WOL, yet somehow went all to pieces over delicate words like MEASLES and BUTTERED TOAST.

Winnie-the-Pooh read the two notices very carefully, first from left to right, and afterwards, in case he had missed some of it, from right to left. Then, to make quite sure, he knocked and pulled the knocker, and he pulled and knocked the bell-rope, and he called out in a very loud voice, "Owl! I

require an answer! It's Bear speaking." And the door opened, and Owl looked out.

"Hallo, Pooh," he said. "How's things?"

"Terrible and Sad," said Pooh, "because Eeyore, who is a
friend of mine, has lost his tail. And he's Moping about it.
So could you very kindly tell me how to find it for him?"

"Well," said Owl, "the customary procedure in such
cases is as follows."

"What does Crustimoney Proseedcake mean?" said Pooh.
"For I am a Bear of Very Little Brain, and long words
Bother me."

"It means the Thing to Do."

"As long as it means that, I don't mind," said Pooh
humbly.

244

"The thing to do is as follows. First, Issue a Reward. Then——"

"Just a moment," said Pooh, holding up his paw. "*What* do we do to this—what you were saying? You sneezed just as you were going to tell me."

"I *didn't* sneeze."

"Yes, you did, Owl."

"Excuse me, Pooh, I didn't. You can't sneeze without knowing it."

"Well, you can't know it without something having been sneezed."

"What I *said* was, 'First *Issue* a Reward.' "

"You're doing it again," said Pooh sadly.

"A Reward!" said Owl very loudly. "We write a notice to say that we will give a large something to anybody who finds Eeyore's tail."

"I see, I see," said Pooh, nodding his head. "Talking about large somethings," he went on dreamily, "I generally have a small something about now—about this time in the morning," and he looked wistfully at the cupboard in the corner of Owl's parlour; "just a mouthful of condensed milk or what not, with perhaps a lick of honey——"

"Well, then," said Owl, "we write out this notice, and we put it up all over the forest."

"A lick of honey," murmured Bear to himself, "or—or not, as the case may be." And he gave a deep sigh, and tried very hard to listen to what Owl was saying.

But Owl went on and on, using longer and longer words, until at last he came back to where he started, and he explained that the person to write out this notice was Christopher Robin.

"It was he who wrote the ones on my front door for me. Did you see them, Pooh?"

For some time now Pooh had been saying "Yes" and "No" in turn, with his eyes shut, to all that Owl was saying, and having said, "Yes, yes," last time, he said "No, not at all," now, without really knowing what Owl was talking about.

"Didn't you see them?" said Owl, a little surprised. "Come and look at them now."

So they went outside. And Pooh looked at the knocker and the notice below it, and he looked at the bell-rope and the notice below it, and the more he looked at the bell-rope, the more he felt that he had seen something like it, somewhere else, sometime before.

"Handsome bell-rope, isn't it?" said Owl.

Pooh nodded.

"It reminds me of something," he said, "but I can't think what. Where did you get it?"

"I just came across it in the Forest. It was hanging over a bush, and I thought at first somebody lived there, so I rang it, and nothing happened, and then I rang it again very loudly, and it came off in my hand, and as nobody seemed to want it, I took it home, and——"

"Owl," said Pooh solemnly, "you made a mistake. Somebody did want it."

"Who?"

"Eeyore. My dear friend Eeyore. He was—he was fond of it."

"Fond of it?"

"Attached to it," said Winnie-the-Pooh sadly.

So with these words he unhooked it, and carried it back to Eeyore; and when Christopher Robin had nailed it on in its right place again, Eeyore frisked about the forest,

waving his tail so happily that Winnie-the-Pooh came over all funny, and had to hurry home for a little snack of something to sustain him. And, wiping his mouth half an hour afterwards, he sang to himself proudly:

> *Who found the Tail?*
>   "I," said Pooh,
> "At a quarter to two
>   (Only it was quarter to eleven really),
> *I* found the Tail!"

Mother to Son

Langston Hughes

Well, son, I'll tell you:
Life for me ain't been no crystal stair.
It's had tacks in it,
And splinters,
And boards torn up,
And places with no carpet on the floor—
Bare.
But all the time
I'se been a-climbin' on,
And reachin' landin's,
And turnin' corners,
And sometimes goin' in the dark
Where there ain't been no light.
So boy, don't you turn back.
Don't you set down on the steps
'Cause you finds it's kinder hard.
Don't you fall now—
For I'se still goin', honey,
I'se still climbin',
And life for me ain't been no crystal stair.

Dreams

Langston Hughes

Hold fast to dreams
For if dreams die
Life is a broken-winged bird
That cannot fly.

Hold fast to dreams
For when dreams go
Life is a barren field
Frozen with snow.

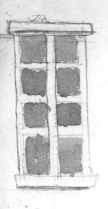

The General's Horse

This Spanish folktale from Robert Davis's book
Padre Porko, the Gentlemanly Pig *will introduce*
you to one of the most unlikely and likeable
characters in folklore—Señor Don Padre Porko,
special friend and protector of orphans and
animals.

I
T WAS a misty-moisty evening. The drops of rain
fell from the tips of the leaves, with a "plop," into
the puddles underneath. The wind blew the branches of the umbrella pine against the windows of the Padre's
house. It was the sort of weather when no person or animal
was willingly out-of-doors. The honest creatures of the air,
the forest and the earth had long been asleep.

The Widow Hedge-Hog had washed the supper dishes,
swept the hearth with her tail, warmed the Padre's flannel
pajamas, and gone home to her family under the apple tree.

Before his fire the Padre dozed. He had eaten three plates
of heavenly stewed carrots for his supper, and every now
and then he rubbed his stomach gently, to help them digest.
The tapping of the branches on the window and the falling
of the rain made a soothing music. Upon the shelf above the
chimney stood a polished red apple. The Padre was trying
to decide whether he should eat the apple or smoke his pipe
before crawling into bed for a good night's sleep.

"Rat-a-tat-tat-tat," suddenly sounded the knocker on his
door.

"My Goodness Gracious," he exclaimed, pushing his feet
into his red slippers. "Who can be out on a night like this?
It must be someone in real trouble."

251

"Who is there?" he called, putting his sensitive nose to the keyhole. He could learn more through his nose than many people can learn through their ears and eyes.

"It is Antonio, the stable-boy from the General's."

"Come in, come in," invited the Padre, seating himself again, and taking out his pipe.

The door opened and a dripping figure stepped inside. Very politely he waited on the door-mat, his cap in his hand.

"Your Honor will please to excuse me for coming so late," he said. "But it was only tonight that the General said he would send me away in disgrace. My Grandmother told me that Your Honor is the Godfather of all Spanish boys who do not have real fathers, so you will please to excuse my coming."

The Padre was reaching up for the red apple. "She told you the truth, Antonio. You sit here and eat this apple, while I put tobacco in my pipe." With a skillful movement of his left hind foot the Padre kicked dry branches upon the fire.

252

"And don't be in any hurry, Antonio. Take all the time you need. Tell me the very worst. Whatever the trouble, we can put it right."

"It is about the white horse," Antonio began, "the fat, white one, that the General rides in parades, at the head of his soldiers. He can't walk. It is his left front hoof." The boy gulped it out in a single breath.

"They say that it is my fault, that I made him fall when I rode him for exercise. But it's not true. I always go slowly, and turn corners at a walk."

"Let's go and see," said the Padre, going to the closet for his rubber coat. "And here's a cape for you to put around your shoulders."

Once at the General's, the Padre and Antonio hung their wet things in the harness-room and unhooked the door of the box stall where the white horse lived. He was a superb animal, but he stood with one front foot off the floor.

"Excuse me, Your Excellency, but can you tell me the cause of Your Excellency's lameness?"

253

The great beast pricked up his ears. "The cause of it!" he snorted. "Why a three-day-old colt would know that much, and yet these stupid doctors and professors have been pestering me for two weeks. A wire nail has gone into the tender center of my foot. It has no head. You cannot see it. The idiots, and they pretend to know so much."

"I thought as much," murmured the Padre, sympathetically. "And will Your Excellency co-operate with us, if we try to get the nail out?"

"Won't I, though!" The horse snorted again. "Why, I haven't been able to touch this foot to the ground for sixteen days."

"This is a case for the Rat Family, and for no one else," said the Padre to himself. He trotted over to a hole in the stable floor. His voice, as he leaned over the opening, was a soft whine through his nose. "Is the lady of the house at home?"

A gray muzzle appeared. "I am only a poor widow, Don Porko; my husband was caught in a trap last harvest time. But if my children and a poor soul like me can be of any help to you, you are more than welcome to our best."

"Indeed you can, Mrs. Furrynose," said the Padre with enthusiasm. "We animals are going to do what none of the veterinary professors knew how to do. Listen carefully. Of all the rats in this town which one has the strongest teeth?" Other heads had joined Mother Furrynose at the opening, and now they all answered in a single unanimous squeak, "Uncle Israel, down at the flour-mill."

"Good," said the Padre. "And now, Mrs. Furrynose, I want you to listen once more. Will you send your oldest boy for Uncle Israel right away? Tell him that Padre Porko needs all the husky boy and girl rats in this town at the General's stable in half-an-hour."

Before the Padre had finished his request, a sleek rat was out of the hole and running toward the door. "You can count on us, Chief," he called.

255

Hardly ten minutes had passed when a peculiar noise was heard outside the stable. It was like the wind blowing the dry leaves in October. It was a rustling, a bustling, a scratching, a scraping, a marching of countless feet. Uncle Israel entered at the head of his tribe. He was an old-fashioned Quaker rat, gray and gaunt, and the size of a half-grown kitten. When he smiled he showed his remarkable teeth, sharp as razors and the color of ivory. He motioned to his brown-coated army and they lined up in rows around the wall, watching him and the Padre with shoe-button eyes.

"I'm not so strong as I used to be," apologized Uncle Israel, "except for my teeth. I don't want to boast, but none of these young rats can hold on to things as hard as I can. As soon as I got your message I brought my relatives. We will do anything you say, Padre." The rows of heads nodded in agreement.

"Thank you for coming, Uncle Israel," said the Padre. "In a minute I'll explain what our work is going to be. First we must tell the General's horse our plan."

He stood by the shoulder of the white horse and spoke in his most persuasive way. "Your Excellency, we are ready for the operation that will cure your foot. But we must be sure of your co-operation. It may hurt, I'm afraid, especially at first."

"It can't hurt more than my hoof aches right now. Go ahead," said the horse.

"We must uncover the end of the nail so that Uncle Israel can grip it in his beautiful teeth. Please bend back your foot."

The General's horse rested his foot on the straw, with the under side showing, and Uncle Israel, placing one paw on either edge of the tender V, began to gnaw, his teeth cutting in like a machine. Presently he sat up, squeaking excitedly. "I have it. It's right there. It's like a piece of wire. But I can get a good hold on it. What next, Padre?"

"Antonio," ordered the Padre, "bring the halters that hang in the harness room, and tie the ropes one to the other. And you, Uncle Israel, slip your head through this

loop in the leather. We will run the long rope out across the
stable floor so that everyone can find a hold. Take your
time, Uncle Israel, everything depends upon your teeth.
When you are ready for us to pull, wiggle your tail.''

Things worked like clock-work. Uncle Israel held on.
Three hundred young rats strained and pulled on the rope.
The General's horse winced with the pain. The Padre walked up and down like a captain in a battle. But the nail in the
foot of the white horse did not budge.

Padre Porko had an idea. ''Widow Furrynose, what would
give you the most pleasure in the world?''

The lady replied quickly. ''To bury that deceitful black
cat up at the miller's.'' Everybody sat up and clapped his
paws.

''Well, young people,'' said the Padre, ''think that you are
pulling the hearse to the graveyard, and that the miller's
black cat is in it. Wouldn't you manage to get that hearse to
the graveyard? Pull like that.''

The floor of the barn seemed alive. It was a rippling,
gray-brown carpet of straining small bodies. The teeth of

Uncle Israel were locked in a death grip. Padre Porko walked back and forth, singing, "Horrible cat, get her buried, haul the hearse."

And, inch by inch, a long, thin, villainous nail came out of the horse's foot.

Then what a racket! Everyone was squirming, and squeaking, and jumping and rolling over, and tickling and nipping tails, and telling how strong he was. The white horse and Antonio admired Uncle Israel's teeth. And all of his nephews and nieces and grandchildren were so proud of him that they kissed him on both whiskers. Padre Porko kept repeating, "I'm proud of you. Great work! I always say that we animals can do anything, if we will work together."

But it was the General's horse who brought the evening to its perfect close. He whinnied into the Padre's ear, "Please translate to Antonio that if he will unlock the oat box I'm sure our friends would enjoy a light lunch. The General himself would be the first to propose it. He will be very thankful when he visits the stable tomorrow and finds me trotting on four legs."

Mrs. Furrynose and Uncle Israel had the young people sit in circles of ten, while Antonio passed the refreshments, pouring a little pile of oats in the center of each circle. Over three hundred guests were served but their table manners were excellent. No one snatched or grabbed, or gobbled his food. Everyone said, "If you please," and "Thank you," and "Excuse me for talking when my mouth is full."

When the crunching was at its height, Uncle Israel made a speech. "Padre Porko, Your Excellency, and friends, relatives and neighbors, this is a proud and happy night for me. In all my life my teeth never did such good work before. They helped this noble white horse, and they enabled us rats to aid the Padre in one of his kind acts. But, also, tonight, my teeth brought me to the attention of a lovely lady, Madame Furrynose, and I am delighted to say that she will not be a widow much longer. One and all, you are invited to the wedding, which will be held next Sunday afternoon in the flour-mill, while the miller is at church. And the Padre Porko has promised to send word to all dogs

260

and cats of the town that none of our guests are to be caught while going, coming or at the party." A hurricane of cheers and clapping followed the speech.

The pink nose of the white horse pushed through the window of this stall, and the merrymakers looked up. "May I, too, offer a wedding present to these worthy friends? Every night I will leave a handful of grain in the corner of my manger. They will find it there for their midnight lunch. A wedding pair with such polite manners can be trusted not to disturb the repose of a hard-working old horse."

The morning sun crept along the stable wall until it shone directly upon the sleeping Antonio. He sat up and rubbed his eyes. How did it happen that he was not in his bed, but in the box stall of the General's horse? And the horse was stamping with the foot that had been lame. Queerer still, the grain box was open and half the oats were gone. And what was the meaning of the four halter ropes tied together?

These are questions which Antonio never could answer. But when he told his story to his children, he was no longer a stable boy. He was the head trainer of all the General's racing horses.

The Charge of the Light Brigade

Alfred, Lord Tennyson

[BALACLAVA, OCTOBER 25, 1852]

Half a league, half a league,
  Half a league onward,
All in the valley of Death
  Rode the six hundred.
"Forward, the Light Brigade!
Charge for the guns!" he said:
Into the valley of Death
  Rode the six hundred.

"Forward, the Light Brigade!"
Was there a man dismayed?
Not though the soldier knew
  Some one had blundered:
Theirs not to make reply,
Theirs not to reason why,
Theirs but to do and die:
Into the valley of Death
  Rode the six hundred.

Cannon to right of them,
Cannon to left of them,
Cannon in front of them
 Volleyed and thundered;
Stormed at with shot and shell,
Boldly they rode and well,
Into the jaws of Death,
Into the mouth of Hell
 Rode the six hundred.

Flashed all their sabres bare,
Flashed as they turned in air
Sabring the gunners there,
Charging an army, while
   All the world wondered:
Plunged in the battery-smoke
Right through the line they broke;
Cossack and Russian
Reeled from the sabre-stroke,
   Shattered and sundered.
Then they rode back, but not,
   Not the six hundred.

Cannon to right of them,
Cannon to left of them,
Cannon behind them
   Volleyed and thundered;
Stormed at with shot and shell,
While horse and hero fell,
They that had fought so well
Back from the mouth of Hell,
All that was left of them,
   Left of six hundred.

When can their glory fade?
O the wild charge they made!
   All the world wondered.
Honor the charge they made!
Honor the Light Brigade,
   Noble six hundred!

Song of the Witches

William Shakespeare

Double, double toil and trouble;
Fire burn and caldron bubble.
Fillet of a fenny snake,
In the caldron boil and bake;
Eye of newt and toe of frog,
Wool of bat and tongue of dog,
Adder's fork and blind-worm's sting,
Lizard's leg and howlet's wing,
For a charm of powerful trouble,
Like a hell-broth boil and bubble.

Double, double toil and trouble;
Fire burn and caldron bubble.
Cool it with a baboon's blood,
Then the charm is firm and good.

Alligator Pie

Dennis Lee

Alligator pie, alligator pie,
If I don't get some I think I'm gonna die.
Give away the green grass, give away the sky,
But don't give away my alligator pie.

Alligator stew, alligator stew,
If I don't get some I don't know what I'll do.
Give away my furry hat, give away my shoe,
But don't give away my alligator stew.

Alligator soup, alligator soup,
If I don't get some I think I'm gonna droop.
Give away my hockey-stick, give away my hoop,
But don't give away my alligator soup.

Young Black Beauty

When Black Beauty *was first published, over a hundred years ago, it carried a subtitle—*The Autobiography of a Horse. *The book was written by Anna Sewell as a protest against what she saw as Victorian England's cruelty to horses, but* Black Beauty *is really a moving and timeless story. In the first three chapters, which are printed below, Black Beauty introduces himself.*

My Early Home

THE FIRST place that I can well remember was a large pleasant meadow with a pond of clear water in it. Some shady trees leaned over it, and rushes and water lilies grew at the deep end. Over the hedge on one side we looked into a plowed field, and on the other we looked over a gate at our master's house, which stood by the roadside. At the top of the meadow was a plantation of fir trees, and at the bottom there was a swiftly running brook overhung by a steep bank.

While I was young I lived upon my mother's milk, as I could not eat grass. In the daytime I ran by her side, and at night I lay down close by her. When it was hot, we used to stand by the pond in the shade of the trees, and when it was cold, we had a nice warm shed near the plantation.

As soon as I was old enough to eat grass, my mother went out to work in the daytime and came back in the evening.

There were six young colts in the meadow besides me. They were older than I was; some were nearly as large as grown-up horses. I ran with them and had great fun. We used to gallop all together round and round the field, as hard as we could go. Sometimes we had rather rough play, for the older colts would frequently bite and kick as well as gallop.

One day when there was a good deal of kicking, my mother whinnied to me to come to her, and then she said, "I wish you to pay attention to what I am going to say to you. The colts who live here are very good colts, but they are cart-horse colts, and, of course, they have not learned manners. You have been well bred and well born. Your father has a great name in these parts, and your grandfather won the cup two years at the Newmarket races; your grandmother had the sweetest temper of any horse I ever knew, and I think you have never seen me kick or bite. I hope you will grow up gentle and good, and never learn bad ways. Do your work with a will, lift your feet up well when you trot, and never bite or kick even in play."

I have never forgotten my mother's advice. I knew she was a wise old horse, and our master thought a great deal of her. Her name was Duchess, but many is the time he called her Pet.

Our master was a good, kind man. He gave us good food, good lodging, and kind words. He spoke as kindly to us as he did to his little children. We were all fond of him, and my mother loved him very much. When she saw him at the gate, she would neigh with joy and trot up to him. He would pat and stroke her and say, "Well, old Pet, and how is your little Darkie?" I was a dull black, so he called me Darkie. Then he would give me a piece of bread, which was very good, and sometimes he brought a carrot for my mother. All the horses would come to him, but I think we were his favorites. My mother always took him to town on a market day in a light gig.

There was a plowboy, Dick, who sometimes came into our field to pluck blackberries from the hedge. When he had eaten all he wanted, he would have what he called fun with the colts, throwing stones and sticks at them to make them gallop. We did not much mind him, for we could gallop off. But sometimes a stone would hit and hurt us.

270

One day he was at this game and did not know that the master was in the next field. But he was there, watching what was going on. Over the hedge he jumped in a snap, and, catching Dick by the arm, he gave him such a box on the ears as made him roar with pain and surprise. As soon as we saw the master, we trotted up nearer so that we could see what went on.

"Bad boy!" he said. "Bad boy to chase the colts. This is not the first time nor the second, but it shall be the last! There! Take your money and go home. I shall not want you on my farm again."

So we never saw Dick anymore. Old Daniel, the man who looked after the horses, was just as gentle as our master, so we were well off.

The Hunt

I WAS two years old when a circumstance happened which I have not forgotten. It was early in the spring. There had been a little frost in the night, and a light mist still hung over the plantations and meadows. The other colts and I were feeding at the lower part of the field when we heard, in the distance, what sounded like the cry of dogs. The oldest of the colts raised his head, pricked his ears, and said, "There are the hounds!" He immediately cantered off, followed by the rest of us, to the upper part of the field where we could look over the hedge and see several fields beyond. My mother and an old riding horse of our master's were also standing near and seemed to know all about it.

"They have found a hare," said my mother. "If they come this way, we shall see the hunt."

And soon the dogs were all tearing down the field of young wheat next to ours. I never heard such a noise as they made. They did not bark, nor howl, nor whine, but kept up a "Yo! Yo-o-o! Yo! Yo-o-o!" at the top of their voices. After them came a number of men on horseback, some of them in green coats, all galloping as fast as they could. The old horse snorted and looked eagerly after them, and we young colts wanted to be galloping after them, but they were soon away into the fields lower down. Here it seemed as if they had come to a stand. The dogs left off barking, and ran about every way with their noses to the ground.

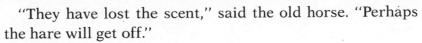

"They have lost the scent," said the old horse. "Perhaps the hare will get off."

"What hare?" I said.

"Oh! I don't know *what* hare. Likely enough it may be one of our own hares out of the plantation. Any hare they can find will do for the dogs and men to run after."

Before long the dogs began their "Yo! Yo-o-o!" again. And back they came all together at full speed, making straight for our meadow at the part where the high bank and hedge overhang the brook.

"Now we shall see the hare," said my mother. And just then a hare, wild with fright, rushed by.

On came the dogs! They burst over the bank, leaped the stream, and came dashing across the field, followed by the huntsmen. Six or eight men leaped their horses over, close upon the dogs. The hare tried to get through the fence. It was too thick, and she turned sharp round to make for the road. But it was too late. The dogs were upon her with their wild cries. We heard one shriek, and that was the end of the hare.

One of the huntsmen rode up and whipped off the dogs, who would soon have torn her to pieces. He held her up by the leg, torn and bleeding, and all the gentlemen seemed well pleased.

As for me, I was so astonished that I did not at first see what was going on by the brook. But when I did look, there was a sad sight. Two fine horses were down; one was struggling in the stream, and the other was groaning on the grass. One of the riders was getting out of the water covered with mud. The other lay quite still.

"His neck is broken," said my mother.

"And serves him right, too," said one of the colts.

I thought the same, but my mother did not join with us.

"Well, no," she said. "You must not say that. But though I am an old horse, and have seen and heard a great deal, I never yet could make out why men are so fond of this sport. They often hurt themselves, often spoil good horses and tear up the fields, and all for a hare or a fox or a stag that they could get more easily some other way. But we are only horses and don't know."

While my mother was saying this, we stood and looked on. Many of the riders had gone to the young man. But my master, who had been watching what was going on, was the first to raise him. His head fell back and his arms hung down, and everyone looked very serious. There was no noise now. Even the dogs were quiet and seemed to know that something was wrong. They carried him to our master's house. I heard afterward that it was young George Gordon, the squire's only son, a fine, tall young man, and the pride of his family.

There was now riding off in all directions to the doctor's, to the farrier's, and no doubt to Squire Gordon's, to let him know about his son. When Mr. Bond, the farrier, came to look at the black horse that lay groaning on the grass, he felt him all over and shook his head; one of his legs was broken. Then someone ran to our master's house and came back with a gun. Presently there was a loud bang and a dreadful shriek, and then all was still. The black horse moved no more.

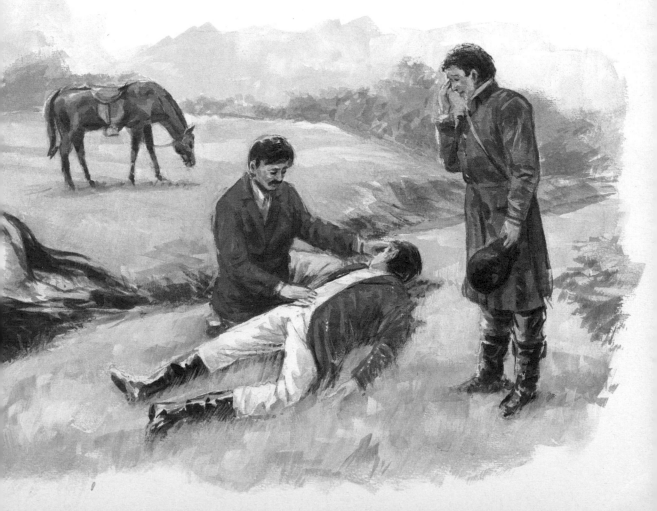

My mother seemed much troubled. She said she had known that horse for years, and that his name was Rob Roy. He was a good, bold horse, and there was no vice in him. She never would go to that part of the field afterward.

Not many days after, we heard the church bell tolling for a long time. Looking over the gate, we saw a long, strange black coach that was covered with black cloth and was drawn by black horses. After that came another and another and another, and all were black, while the bell kept tolling, tolling. They were carrying young Gordon to the churchyard to bury him. He would never ride again.

What they did with Rob Roy I never knew. But 'twas all for one little hare.

My Breaking In

I WAS now beginning to grow handsome; my coat had grown fine and soft, and was bright black. I had one white foot and a pretty white star on my forehead. I was thought very handsome.

My master would not sell me till I was four years old. He said lads ought not to work like men, and colts ought not to work like horses till they were quite grown up.

When I was four years old, Squire Gordon came to look at me. He examined my eyes, my mouth, and my legs. He felt them all down, and then I had to walk and trot and gallop before him. He seemed to like me and said, "When he has been well broken in, he will do very well." My master said he would break me in himself, as he should not like me to be frightened or hurt.

He lost no time about it, for the next day he began.

Everyone may not know what breaking in is; therefore I will describe it. It means to teach a horse to wear a saddle and bridle and to carry on his back a man, woman, or child;

277

to go just the way his rider wishes, and to go quietly. Besides this, he has to learn to wear a collar, a crupper, and a breeching, and to stand still while they are put on; then to have a cart or a chaise fixed behind him, so that he cannot walk or trot without dragging it after him. And he must go fast or slow, as his driver wishes. He must never start at what he sees, nor speak to other horses, nor bite, nor kick, nor have any will of his own; but always do his master's will, even though he may be very tired or hungry. But the worst of all is, when his harness is once on, he may neither jump for joy nor lie down for weariness. So you see this breaking in is a great thing.

I had, of course, long been used to a halter and a headstall, and to being led about in the field and lanes quietly. But now I was to have a bit and a bridle. My master gave me some oats as usual, and after a good deal of coaxing he got the bit into my mouth and the bridle fixed.

But it was a nasty thing! Those who have never had a bit in their mouths cannot think how bad it feels. A great piece of cold hard steel as thick as a man's finger is pushed into one's mouth, between one's teeth, and over one's tongue! Its ends come out at the corner of your mouth and are held fast there by straps over your head, under your throat, round your nose, and under your chin, so that in no way in the world can you get rid of the nasty hard thing. It is very bad! Yes, very bad!

At least I thought so; but I knew my mother always wore one when she went out, and all horses did when they were grown up. So, what with the nice oats, and what with my master's pats, kind words, and gentle ways, I learned to wear my bit and bridle.

Next came the saddle, but that was not half so bad. My master put it on my back very gently, while old Daniel held my head. He then made the girths fast under my body, patting and talking to me all the time. Then I had a few oats, then a little leading about. This he did every day, till I began to look for the oats and the saddle.

At length, one morning my master got on my back and rode me round the meadow on the soft grass. It certainly did

278

feel queer. But I must say I felt rather proud to carry my master, and as he continued to ride me a little every day, I soon became accustomed to it.

The next unpleasant business was putting on the iron shoes; that, too, was very hard at first. My master went with me to the smith's forge, to see that I was not hurt or got any fright. The blacksmith took my feet in his hand, one after the other, and cut away some of the hoof. It did not pain me, so I stood still on three legs till he had done them all. Then he took a piece of iron the shape of my foot, and clapped it on, and drove some nails through the shoe quite into my hoof, so that the shoe was firmly on. My feet felt very stiff and heavy, but in time I got used to it.

And now, having got so far, my master went on to break me to harness; there were more new things to wear. First, a stiff, heavy collar just on my neck, and a bridle with great side-pieces against my eyes, called blinkers. And blinkers they were, for I could not see on either side, but only straight in front of me. Next there was a small saddle with a nasty stiff

strap that went right under my tail. That was the crupper. I hated the crupper—to have my long tail doubled up and poked through a strap was almost as bad as the bit. I never felt more like kicking, but of course I could not kick such a good master.

So in time I got used to everything and could do my work as well as my mother.

I must not forget to mention one part of my training, which I have always considered a very great advantage. My master sent me for a fortnight to a neighbouring farmer's, who had a meadow which was skirted on one side by the railway. Here were some sheep and cows, and I was turned in among them.

I shall never forget the first train that ran by. I was feeding quietly near the pales which separated the meadow from the railway, when I heard a strange sound at a distance. Before I knew whence it came—with a rush and a clatter and a puffing out of smoke—a long black train of something flew up and was gone, almost before I could draw my breath. I turned and galloped to the farther side of the meadow as fast as I could go, and there I stood snorting with astonishment

and fear. In the course of the day many other trains went by, some more slowly. These drew up at the station close by and sometimes made an awful shriek and groan before they stopped. I thought it very dreadful, but the cows went on eating very quietly and hardly raised their heads as the black frightful thing came puffing and grinding past.

For the first few days I could not feed in peace; but as I found that this terrible creature never came into the field or did me any harm, I began to disregard it. Very soon I cared as little about a train passing as the cows and sheep did.

Since then I have seen many horses much alarmed and restive at the sight or sound of a steam engine. But thanks to my good master's care, I am as fearless at railway stations as in my own stable.

Now, if anyone wants to break in a young horse well, that is the way.

My master often drove me in double harness with my mother, because she was steady and could teach me how to go better than a strange horse. She told me the better I behaved, the better I should be treated, and that it was wisest to do my best to please my master.

"But," said she, "there are a great many kinds of men. There are good, thoughtful men like our master, that any horse may be proud to serve; but there are bad, cruel men, who never ought to have a horse or dog to call their own. Besides, there are a great many foolish men, vain, ignorant, and careless, who never trouble themselves to think. These spoil more horses than all, just for want of sense. They don't mean it, but they do it for all that. I hope you will fall into good hands; but a horse never knows who may buy him or who may drive him. It is all chance for us.

"But still I say, do your best wherever it is and keep up your good name."

The Bremen Town Musicians

The Brothers Grimm

A CERTAIN man had an ass which for many years carried sacks to the mill without tiring. At last, however, its strength was worn out and it was no longer of any use for work. Accordingly, its master began to ponder as to how best to cut down its keep. But the ass, seeing there was mischief in the air, ran away and started on the road to Bremen. There he thought he could become a town musician.

When he had been traveling a short time, he fell in with a hound, who was lying panting on the road as though he had run himself off his legs.

"Well, what are you panting so for, Growler?" said the ass.

"Ah," said the hound, "just because I am old, and every day I get weaker. And also, because I can no longer keep up with the pack, my master wanted to kill me, so I took my departure. But now how am I to earn my bread?"

"Do you know what?" said the ass. "I am going to Bremen and shall there become a town musician. Come with me and take your part in the music. I shall play the lute, and you shall beat the kettledrum."

The hound agreed and they went on.

A short time afterwards they came upon a cat sitting in the road, with a face as long as a wet week.

"Well, why are you so cross, Whiskers?" asked the ass.

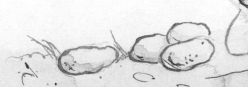

"Who can be cheerful when he is out at elbows?" said the cat. "I am getting on in years and my teeth are blunted, and I prefer to sit by the stove and purr instead of hunting round after mice. Just because of this my mistress wanted to drown me. I made myself scarce, but now I don't know where to turn."

"Come with us to Bremen," said the ass. "You are a great hand at serenading, so you can become a town musician."

The cat consented and joined them.

Next the fugitives passed by a yard where a barnyard fowl was sitting on the door, crowing with all its might.

"You crow so loud you pierce one through and through," said the ass. "What is the matter?"

"Why? Because Sunday visitors are coming tomorrow, the mistress has no pity, and she has ordered the cook to make me into soup. So I shall have my neck wrung tonight. Now I am crowing with all my might while I can."

"Come along, Red-comb," said the ass. "You had much better come with us. We are going to Bremen and you will find a much better fate there. You have a good voice, and when we make music together there will be quality in it."

The cock allowed himself to be persuaded and they all four went off together. They could not, however, reach the town in one day, and by evening they arrived at a wood, where they determined to spend the night. The ass and the hound lay down under a big tree. The cat and the cock settled themselves in the branches, the cock flying right up to the top, which was the safest place for him. Before going to sleep he looked round once more in every direction. Suddenly it seemed that he saw a light burning in the distance. He called out to his comrades that there must be a house not far off, for he saw a light.

"Very well," said the ass. "Let us set out and make our way to it, for the entertainment here is very bad."

The hound thought some bones or meat would suit him too, so they set out in the direction of the light. They soon saw it shining more clearly and getting bigger and bigger, till they reached a brightly lighted robbers' den. The ass, being the tallest, approached the window and looked in.

"What do you see, old Jackass?" asked the cock.

"What do I see?" answered the ass. "Why, a table spread with delicious food and drink, and robbers seated at it enjoying themselves."

"That would just suit us," said the cock.

"Yes, if we were only there," answered the ass.

Then the animals took counsel as to how to set about driving the robbers out. At last they hit upon a plan.

The ass was to take up his position with his forefeet on the window sill, the hound was to jump on his back, the cat to climb up onto the hound, and last of all the cock was to up and perch on the cat's head. When they were thus arranged, at a given signal they all began to perform their music. The ass brayed, the hound barked, the cat mewed, and the cock crowed. Then they dashed through the window, shivering the panes. The robbers jumped up at the terrible noise. They thought nothing less than that the devil

was coming in upon them and fled into the wood in the greatest alarm. Then the four animals sat down to table and helped themselves according to taste, and they ate as though they had been starving for weeks. When they had finished, they extinguished the light and looked for sleeping places, each one to suit his taste.

The ass lay down on a pile of straw, the hound behind the door, the cat on the hearth near the warm ashes, and the cock flew up to the rafters. As they were tired from the long journey, they soon went to sleep.

When midnight was past, and the robbers saw from a distance that the light was no longer burning and that all seemed quiet, the chief said, "We ought not to have been scared by a false alarm." And he ordered one of the robbers to go and examine the house.

Finding all quiet, the messenger went into the kitchen to kindle a light. And taking the cat's glowing, fiery eyes for live coals, he held a match close to them so as to light it. But the cat would stand no nonsense—it flew at his face, spat, and scratched. He was terribly frightened and ran away.

He tried to get out the back door, but the hound, who was lying there, jumped up and bit his leg. As he ran across the pile of straw in front of the house, the ass gave him a good sound kick with his hind legs; while the cock, who had awakened at the uproar quite fresh and gay, cried out from his perch, "Cock-a-doodle-doo."

Thereupon the robber ran back as fast as he could to his chief and said, "There is a gruesome witch in the house who breathed on me and scratched me with her long fingers. Behind the door there stands a man with a knife, who stabbed me, while in the yard lies a black monster who hit me with a club. And upon the roof the judge is seated, and he called out, 'Bring the rogue here!' So I hurried away as fast as I could."

Thenceforward the robbers did not venture again to the house, which pleased the four Bremen musicians so much that they never wished to leave it again.

Set Sail for Treasure Island!

Treasure Island by Robert Louis Stevenson is one of the greatest adventure novels of all time. The story begins when a boy named Jim Hawkins discovers a treasure map while working at his mother's inn, the Admiral Benbow. Very soon Hawkins gains the help of a wealthy squire named Mr. Trelawney and an even-keeled doctor named Livesey. The three outfit a ship—the Hispaniola— hire a crew and captain, and prepare to set sail for Treasure Island. The chapters printed here, narrated by Hawkins, will give you a good idea of what adventure lies ahead if you read the whole book.

Powder and Arms

THE *Hispaniola* lay some way out, and we went under the figureheads and round the sterns of many other ships, and their cables sometimes grated underneath our keel, and sometimes swung above us. At last, however, we got alongside, and were met and saluted as we stepped aboard by the mate, Mr. Arrow, a brown old sailor, with earrings in his ears and a squint. He and the squire were very thick and friendly, but I soon observed that things were not the same between Mr. Trelawney and the captain.

This last was a sharp-looking man, who seemed angry with everything on board, and was soon to tell us why, for we had hardly got down into the cabin when a sailor followed us.

"Captain Smollett, sir, axing to speak with you," said he.

"I am always at the captain's orders. Show him in," said the squire.

The captain, who was close behind the messenger, entered at once, and shut the door behind him.

"Well, Captain Smollett, what have you to say? All well, I hope; all shipshape and seaworthy?"

"Well, sir," said the captain, "better speak plain, I believe, even at the risk of offense. I don't like this cruise; I don't like the men; and I don't like my officer. That's short and sweet."

"Perhaps, sir, you don't like the ship?" inquired the squire, very angry, as I could see.

"I can't speak as to that, sir, not having seen her tried," said the captain. "She seems a clever craft; more I can't say."

"Possibly, sir, you may not like your employer, either?" says the squire.

But here Doctor Livesey cut in.

"Stay a bit," said he, "stay a bit. No use of such questions as that but to produce ill-feeling. The captain has said too much or he has said too little, and I'm bound to say that I require an explanation of his words. You don't, you say, like this cruise. Now, why?"

"I was engaged, sir, on what we called sealed orders, to sail this ship for that gentleman where he should bid me," said the captain. "So far so good. But now I find that every man before the mast knows more than I do. I don't call that fair, now, do you?"

"No," said Doctor Livesey, "I don't."

"Next," said the captain, "I learn we are going after treasure—hear it from my own hands, mind you. Now, treasure is ticklish work; I don't like treasure voyages on any account; and I don't like them, above all, when they are secret, and when (begging your pardon, Mr. Trelawney) the secret has been told to the parrot."

"Silver's parrot?" asked the squire.

"It's a way of speaking," said the captain. "Blabbed, I mean. It's my belief neither of you gentlemen know what you are about; but I'll tell you my way of it—life or death, and a close run."

"That is all clear, and, I dare say, true enough," replied Doctor Livesey. "We take the risk; but we are not so ignorant as you believe us. Next, you say you don't like the crew. Are they not good seamen?"

"I don't like them, sir," returned Captain Smollett. "And I think I should have had the choosing of my own hands, if you go to that."

"Perhaps you should," replied the doctor. "My friend should, perhaps, have taken you along with him; but the slight, if there be one, was unintentional. And you don't like Mr. Arrow?"

"I don't, sir. I believe he's a good seaman; but he's too free with the crew to be a good officer. A mate should keep himself to himself—shouldn't drink with the men before the mast!"

"Do you mean he drinks?" cried the squire.

"No, sir," replied the captain; "only that he's too familiar."

"Well, now, and the short and long of it, captain?" asked the doctor. "Tell us what you want."

"Well, gentlemen, are you determined to go on this cruise?"

"Like iron," answered the squire.

"Very good," said the captain. "Then, as you've heard me very patiently, saying things that I could not prove, hear me a few words more. They are putting the powder and the arms in the forehold. Now, you have a good place under the cabin; why not put them there?—first point. Then you are bringing four of your own people with you, and they tell me some of them are to be berthed forward. Why not give them the berths beside the cabin?—second point."

"Any more?" asked Mr. Trelawney.

"One more," said the captain. "There's been too much blabbing already."

"Far too much," agreed the doctor.

"I'll tell you what I've heard myself," continued Captain Smollett; "that you have a map of an island; that there's crosses on the map to show where treasure is; and that the island lies—" And then he named the latitude and longitude exactly.

"I never told that," cried the squire, "to a soul!"

"The hands know it, sir," returned the captain.

"Livesey, that must have been you or Hawkins," cried the squire.

"It doesn't much matter who it was," replied the doctor. And I could see that neither he nor the captain paid much regard to Mr. Trelawney's protestations. Neither did I, to be sure, he was so loose a talker; yet in this case I believe he was really right, and that nobody had told the situation of the island.

292

"Well, gentlemen," continued the captain, "I don't know who had the map; but I make it a point, it shall be kept secret even from me and Mr. Arrow. Otherwise I would ask you to let me resign."

"I see," said the doctor. "You wish us to keep the matter dark, and to make a garrison of the stern part of the ship, manned with my friend's own people, and provided with all the arms and powder on board. In other words, you fear a mutiny."

"Sir," said Captain Smollett, "with no intention to take offense, I deny your right to put words into my mouth. No captain, sir, would be justified in going to sea at all if he had ground enough to say that. As for Mr. Arrow, I believe him thoroughly honest; some of the men are the same; all may be for what I know. But I am responsible for the ship's safety and the life of every man Jack aboard of her. I see things going, as I think, not quite right. And I ask you to take certain precautions, or let me resign my berth. And that's all."

"Captain Smollett," began the doctor, with a smile, "did you ever hear the fable of the mountain and the mouse? You'll excuse me, I dare say, but you remind me of that fable. When you came in here, I'll stake my wig you meant more than this."

"Doctor," said the captain, "you are smart. When I came in here I meant to get discharged. I had no thought that Mr. Trelawney would hear a word."

"No more I would," cried the squire. "Had Livesey not been here, I should have seen you to the deuce. As it is, I have heard you. I will do as you desire; but I think the worse of you."

"That's as you please, sir," said the captain. "You'll find I do my duty."

And with that he took his leave.

"Trelawney," said the doctor, "contrary to all my notions, I believe you have managed to get two honest men on board with you—that man and John Silver."

"Silver, if you like," cried the squire; "but as for that intolerable humbug, I declare I think his conduct unmanly, unsailorly, and downright un-English."

294

"Well," says the doctor, "we shall see."

When we came on deck, the men had begun already to take out the arms and powder, yo-ho-ing at their work, while the captain and Mr. Arrow stood by superintending.

The new arrangement was quite to my liking. The whole schooner had been overhauled; six berths had been made astern, out of what had been the afterpart of the main hold; and this set of cabins was only joined to the galley and forecastle by a sparred passage on the port side. It had been originally meant that the captain, Mr. Arrow, Hunter, Joyce, the doctor, and the squire, were to occupy these six berths. Now, Redruth and I were to get two of them, and Mr. Arrow and the captain were to sleep on deck in the companion, which had been enlarged on each side till you might almost have called it a round-house. Very low it was

still, of course; but there was room to swing two hammocks, and even the mate seemed pleased with the arrangement. Even he, perhaps, had been doubtful as to the crew, but that is only guess; for, as you shall hear, we had not long the benefit of his opinion.

We were all hard at work, changing the powder and the berths, when the last man or two, and Long John along with them, came off in a shore boat.

The cook came up the side like a monkey for cleverness, and, as soon as he saw what was doing, "So, ho, mates!" says he, "what's this?"

"We're a-changing of the powder, Jack," answers one.

"Why, by the powers," cried Long John, "if we do, we'll miss the morning tide!"

"My orders!" said the captain shortly. "You may go below, my man. Hands will want supper."

"Aye, aye, sir," answered the cook; and, touching his forelock, he disappeared at once in the direction of his galley.

"That's a good man, captain," said the doctor.

"Very likely," replied Captain Smollett. "Easy with that, men—easy," he ran on, to the fellows who were shifting the powder; and then suddenly observing me examining the swivel we carried amidships, a long brass nine—"Here, you ship's boy," he cried, "out o' that! Off with you to the cook and get some work."

And then, as I was hurrying off, I heard him say, quite loudly, to the doctor:

"I'll have no favorites on my ship."

I assure you I was quite of the squire's way of thinking, and hated the captain deeply.

The Voyage

ALL THAT night we were in a great bustle getting things stowed in their place, and boatfuls of the squire's friends, Mr. Blandly and the like, coming off to wish him a good voyage and a safe return. We never had a night at the Admiral Benbow when I had half the work; and I was dog-tired when, a little before dawn, the boatswain sounded his pipe, and the crew began to man the capstan bars. I might have been twice as weary, yet I would not have left the deck; all was so new and interesting to me—the brief commands, the shrill note of the whistle, the men bustling to their places in the glimmer of the ship's lanterns.

"Now, Barbecue, tip us a stave," cried one voice.

"The old one," cried another.

"Aye, aye, mates," said Long John, who was standing by, with his crutch under his arm, and at once broke out in the air and words I knew so well—

"Fifteen men on the Dead Man's Chest—"

And then the whole crew bore chorus:

"Yo-ho-ho, and a bottle of rum!"

And at the third "ho!" drove the bars before them with a will.

Even at that exciting moment it carried me back to the old Admiral Benbow in a second; and I seemed to hear the voice of the captain piping in the chorus.

But soon the anchor was short up; soon it was hanging dripping at the bows; soon the sails began to draw, and the land and shipping to flit by on either side; and before I could lie down to snatch an hour of slumber the *Hispaniola* had begun her voyage to the Isle of Treasure.

I am not going to relate that voyage in detail. It was fairly prosperous. The ship proved to be a good ship, the crew were capable seamen, and the captain thoroughly understood his business. But before we came the length of Treasure Island, two or three things had happened which require to be known.

Mr. Arrow, first of all, turned out even worse than the captain had feared. He had no command among the men, and people did what they pleased with him. But that was by no means the worst of it; for after a day or two at sea he began to appear on deck with hazy eye, red cheeks, stuttering tongue, and other marks of drunkenness. Time after time he was ordered below in disgrace. Sometimes he fell and cut himself; sometimes he lay all day long in his little bunk at one side of the companion; sometimes for a day or

two he would be almost sober and attend to his work at least passably.

In the meantime, we could never make out where he got the drink. That was the ship's mystery. Watch him as we pleased, we could do nothing to solve it; and when we asked him to his face, he would only laugh, if he were drunk, and if he were sober deny solemnly that he ever tasted anything but water.

He was not only useless as an officer, and a bad influence amongst the men, but it was plain that at this rate he must soon kill himself outright; so nobody was much surprised, nor very sorry, when one dark night, with a head sea, he disappeared entirely and was seen no more.

"Overboard!" said the captain. "Well, gentlemen, that saves the trouble of putting him in irons."

But there we were, without a mate; and it was necessary, of course, to advance one of the men. The boatswain, Job Anderson, was the likeliest man aboard, and, though he kept his old title, he served in a way as mate. Mr. Trelawney had followed the sea, and his knowledge made him very

299

useful, for he often took a watch himself in easy weather. And the coxswain, Israel Hands, was a careful, wily, old, experienced seaman, who could be trusted at a pinch with almost anything.

He was a great confidant of Long John Silver, and so the mention of his name leads me on to speak of our ship's cook, Barbecue, as the men called him.

Aboard ship he carried his crutch by a lanyard round his neck, to have both hands as free as possible. It was something to see him wedge the foot of the crutch against a bulkhead; and, propped against it, yielding to every movement of the ship, to get on with his cooking like someone safe ashore. Still more strange was it to see him in the heaviest of weather cross the deck. He had a line or two rigged up to help him across the widest spaces—Long John's earrings, they were called; and he would hand himself from one place to another, now using the crutch, now trailing it alongside by the lanyard, as quickly as another man could walk. Yet some of the men who had sailed with him before expressed their pity to see him so reduced.

"He's no common man, Barbecue," said the coxswain to me. "He had good schooling in his young days, and can speak like a book when so minded; and brave—a lion's nothing alongside of Long John! I seen him grapple four, and knock their heads together—him unarmed."

All the crew respected and even obeyed him. He had a way of talking to each, and doing everybody some particular service. To me he was unweariedly kind; and always glad to see me in the galley, which he kept as clean as a new pin; the dishes hanging up burnished and his parrot in a cage in one corner.

"Come away, Hawkins," he would say, "come and have a yarn with John. Nobody more welcome than yourself, my son. Sit you down and hear the news. Here's Cap'n Flint—I call my parrot Cap'n Flint, after the famous buccaneer —here's Cap'n Flint perdicting success to our v'yage. Wasn't you, cap'n?"

And the parrot would say, with great rapidity, "Pieces of eight! pieces of eight! pieces of eight!" till you wondered

300

that it was not out of breath, or till John threw his handker-
chief over the cage.

"Now, that bird," he would say, "is, maybe, two hundred
years old, Hawkins—they lives forever mostly; and if anybody's seen more wickedness, it must be the devil himself.
She's sailed with England, the great Cap'n England, the
pirate. She's been at Madagascar, and at Malabar, and Suri-
nam, and Providence, and Portobello. She was at the fish-
ing-up of the wrecked plate ships. It's there she learned
'Pieces of eight,' and little wonder; three hundred and fifty
thousand of 'em, Hawkins! She was at the boarding of the
Viceroy of the Indies out of Goa, she was; and to look at her
you would think she was a babby. But you smelt powder
—didn't you, cap'n?"

"Stand by to go about," the parrot would scream.

"Ah, she's a handsome craft, she is," the cook would say,
and give her sugar from his pocket, and then the bird
would peck at the bars and swear straight on, passing
belief for wickedness. "There," John would add, "you can't
touch pitch and not be mucked, lad. Here's this poor old
innocent bird o' mine swearing blue fire, and none the
wiser, you may lay to that. She would swear the same, in a
manner of speaking, before chaplain." And John would

touch his forelock with a solemn way he had, that made me
think he was the best of men.

In the meantime, squire and Captain Smollett were still
on pretty distant terms with one another. The squire made
no bones about the matter; he despised the captain. The
captain, on his part, never spoke but when he was spoken
to, and then sharp and short and dry, and not a word
wasted. He owned, when driven into a corner, that he
seemed to have been wrong about the crew, that some of
them was as brisk as he wanted to see, and all had behaved
fairly well. As for the ship, he had taken a downright fancy
to her. "She'll lie a point nearer the wind than a man has a
right to expect of his own married wife, sir. But," he would
add, "all I say is we're not home again, and I don't like the
cruise."

The squire, at this, would turn away and march up and
down the deck, chin in air.

"A trifle more of that man," he would say, "and I should
explode."

303

We had some heavy weather, which only proved the qualities of the *Hispaniola*. Every man on board seemed well content, and they must have been hard to please if they had been otherwise; for it is my belief there was never a ship's company so spoiled since Noah put to sea. Double grog was going on the least excuse; there was duff on odd days, as, for instance, if the squire heard it was any man's birthday; and always a barrel of apples standing broached in the waist, for anyone to help himself that had a fancy.

"Never knew good come of it yet," the captain said to Doctor Livesey. "Spoil foc's'le hands, make devils. That's my belief."

But good did come of the apple barrel, as you shall hear: for if it had not been for that, we should have had no note of warning, and might all have perished by the hand of treachery.

This was how it came about.

We had run up the trades to get the wind of the island we were after—I am not allowed to be more plain—and now we were running down for it with a bright lookout day and night. It was about the last day of our outward voyage, by the largest computation; sometime that night, or, at latest, before noon of the morrow, we should sight the Treasure Island. We were heading S.S.W., and had a steady breeze abeam and a quiet sea. The *Hispaniola* rolled steadily, dipping her bowsprit now and then with a whiff of spray. All was drawing alow and aloft; everyone was in the bravest spirits, because we were now so near an end of the first part of our adventure.

Now, just after sundown, when all my work was over, and I was on my way to my berth, it occurred to me that I should like an apple. I ran on deck. The watch was all forward looking out for the island. The man at the helm was watching the luff of the sail, and whistling away gently to himself; and that was the only sound excepting the swish of the sea against the bows and around the sides of the ship.

In I got bodily into the apple barrel, and found there was scarce an apple left; but, sitting down there in the dark,

304

what with the sound of the waters and the rocking movement of the ship, I had either fallen asleep, or was on the point of doing so, when a heavy man sat down with rather a clash close by. The barrel shook as he leaned his shoulders against it, and I was just about to jump up when the man began to speak. It was Silver's voice, and, before I had heard a dozen words, I would not have shown myself for all the world, but lay there, trembling and listening, in the extreme of fear and curiosity; for from these dozen words I understood that the lives of all the honest men aboard depended upon me alone.

What I Heard in the Apple Barrel

"NO, not I," said Silver. "Flint was cap'n; I was quartermaster, along of my timber leg. The same broadside I lost my leg, old Pew lost his headlights. It was a master surgeon, him that ampytated me—out of college and all—Latin by the bucket, and what not; but he was hanged like a dog, and sun-dried like the rest, at Corso Castle. That was Roberts's men, that was, and comed of changing names to their ships—*Royal Fortune* and so on. Now, what a ship was christened, so let her stay, I says. So it was with the *Cassandra*, as brought us all safe home from Malabar, after England took the *Viceroy of the Indies*; so it was with the old *Walrus*. Flint's old ship, as I've seen a-muck with the red blood and fit to sink with gold."

"Ah!" cried another voice, that of the youngest hand on board, and evidently full of admiration, "he was the flower of the flock, was Flint!"

"Davis was a man, too, by all accounts," said Silver. "I never sailed along of him; first with England, then with Flint, that's my story; and now here on my account, in a manner of speaking. I laid by nine hundred safe, from England, and two thousand after Flint. That ain't bad for a man before the mast—all safe in bank. 'Tain't earning now, it's saving does it, you may lay to that. Where's all England's men now? I dunno. Where's Flint's? Why, most on 'em aboard here, and glad to get the duff—been begging before that, some on 'em. Old Pew, as had lost his sight, and

might have thought shame, spends twelve hundred pound in a year, like a lord in Parliament. Where is he now? Well, he's dead now and under hatches; but for two year before that, shiver my timbers! the man was starving. He begged, and he stole, and he cut throats, and starved at that by the powers!"

"Well, it ain't much use, after all," said the young seaman.

" 'Tain't much use for fools, you may lay to it—that, not nothing," cried Silver. "But now, you look here; you're young, you are, but you're as smart as paint. I see that when I set my eyes on you, and I'll talk to you like a man."

You may imagine how I felt when I heard this abominable old rogue addressing another in the very same words of flattery as he had used to myself. I think, if I had been able, that I would have killed him through the barrel. Meantime, he ran on, little supposing he was overheard.

"Here it is about gentlemen of fortune. They lives rough, and they risk swinging, but they eat and drink like fighting-cocks, and when a cruise is done, why, it's hundreds of pounds instead of hundreds of farthings in their pockets. Now, the most goes for rum and a good fling, and to sea again in their shirts. But that's not the course I lay. I puts it all away, some here, some there, and none too much any-wheres, by reason of suspicion. I'm fifty, mark you; once back from this cruise, I set up gentleman in earnest. Time enough, too, says you. Ah, but I've lived easy in the mean-time; never denied myself o' nothing heart desires, and slep' soft and ate dainty all my days, but when at sea. And how did I begin? Before the mast, like you!"

"Well," said the other, "but all the other money's gone now, ain't it? You daren't show face in Bristol after this."

"Why, where might you suppose it was?" asked Silver, derisively.

"At Bristol, in banks and places," answered his companion.

"It were," said the cook, "it were when we weighed anchor. But my old missus has it all by now. And the 'Spy-glass' is sold, lease and goodwill and rigging; and the old girl's off to meet me. I would tell you where, for I trust you; but it 'ud make jealousy among the mates."

"And can you trust your missus?" asked the other.

"Gentlemen of fortune," returned the cook, "usually trusts little among themselves, and right they are, you may lay to it. But I have a way with me, I have. When a mate brings a slip on his cable—one as knows me, I mean—it won't be in the same world with old John. There was some that was feared of Pew, and some that was feared of Flint; but Flint his own self was feared of me. Feared he was, and proud. They was the roughest crew afloat, was Flint's; the devil himself would have been feared to go to sea with them. Well, now, I tell you, I'm not a boasting man, and you seen yourself how easy I keep company; but when I was quartermaster, *lambs* wasn't the word for Flint's old buc-caneers. Ah, you may be sure of yourself in old John's ship."

"Well, I tell you now," replied the lad, "I didn't half a

308

quarter like the job till I had this talk with you, John; but there's my hand on it now."

"And a brave lad you were, and smart, too," answered Silver, shaking hands so heartily that all the barrel shook, "and a finer figurehead for a gentleman of fortune I never clapped my eyes on."

By this time I had begun to understand the meaning of their terms. By a "gentleman of fortune" they plainly meant neither more nor less than a common pirate, and the little scene that I had overheard was the last act in the corruption of one of the honest hands—perhaps of the last one left aboard. But on this point I was soon to be relieved, for Silver giving a little whistle, a third man strolled up and sat down by the party.

"Dick's square," said Silver.

"Oh, I know'd Dick was square," returned the voice of the coxswain, Israel Hands. "He's no fool, is Dick." And he turned his quid and spat. "But, look here," he went on, "here's what I want to know, Barbecue: how long are we a-going to stand off and on like a blessed bumboat? I've had a-most enough o' Cap'n Smollett; he's hazed me long enough, by thunder! I want to go into that cabin, I do. I want their pickles and wines, and that."

309

"Israel," said Silver, "your head ain't much account, nor ever was. But you're able to hear, I reckon; leastways, your ears is big enough. Now, here's what I say: you'll berth forward, and you'll live hard, and you'll speak soft, and you'll keep sober, till I give the word; and you may lay to that, my son."

"Well, I don't say no, do I?" growled the coxswain. "What I say is, when? That's what I say."

"When! by the powers!" cries Silver. "Well now, if you want to know, I'll tell you when. The last moment I can manage; and that's when. Here's a first-rate seaman, Cap'n Smollett, sails the blessed ship for us. Here's this squire and doctor with a map and such—I don't know where it is, do I? No more do you, says you. Well, then, I mean this squire and doctor shall find the stuff, and help us to get it aboard, by the powers. Then we'll see. If I was sure of you all, sons of double Dutchmen, I'd have Cap'n Smollett navigate us halfway back again before I struck."

"Why, we're all seamen aboard here, I should think," said the lad Dick.

"We're all foc's'le hands, you mean," snapped Silver. "We can steer a course, but who's to set one? That's what all you gentlemen split on, first and last. If I had my way, I'd have Cap'n Smollett work us back into the trades at least; then we'd have no blessed miscalculations and a spoonful of water a day. But I know the sort you are. I'll finish with 'em at the island, as soon's the blunt's on board, and a pity it is. But you're never happy till you're drunk. Split my sides, I've a sick heart to sail with the likes of you!"

"Easy all, Long John," cried Israel. "Who's a-crossin' of you?"

"Why, how many tall ships, think ye, now, have I seen laid aboard? and how many brisk lads drying in the sun at Execution Dock?" cried Silver—"and all for this same hurry and hurry and hurry. You hear me? I seen a thing or two at sea, I have. If you would on'y lay your course, and a p'int to windward, you would ride in carriages, you would. But not you! I know you. You'll have your mouthful of rum tomorrow, and go hang."

"Everybody know'd you was kind of a chapling, John; but there's others as could hand and steer as well as you," said Israel. "They liked a bit o' fun, they did. They wasn't so high and dry, nohow, but took their fling, like jolly companions every one."

"So?" says Silver. "Well, and where are they now? Pew was that sort, and he died a beggarman. Flint was, and he died of rum at Savannah. Ah, they was a sweet crew, they was! on'y, where are they?"

"But," asked Dick, "when we do lay 'em athwart, what are we to do with 'em, anyhow?"

"There's the man for me!" cried the cook, admiringly. "That's what I call business. Well, what would you think? Put 'em ashore like maroons? That would have been England's way. Or cut 'em down like that much pork? That would have been Flint's or Billy Bones's."

"Billy was the man for that," said Israel. " 'Dead men don't bite,' says he. Well, he's dead now hisself; he knows the long and short on it now; and if ever a rough hand come to port, it was Billy."

"Right you are," said Silver, "rough and ready. But mark you here: I'm an easy man—I'm quite the gentleman, says you; but this time it's serious. Dooty is dooty, mates. I give my vote—death. When I'm in Parlyment, and riding in my coach, I don't want none of these sea-lawyers in the cabin a-coming home, unlooked for, like the devil at prayers. Wait is what I say; but when the time comes, why, let her rip!"

"John," cried the coxswain, "you're a man!"

"You'll say so, Israel, when you see," said Silver. "Only

one thing I claim—I claim Trelawney. I'll wring his calf's head off his body with these hands. Dick!" he added, breaking off, "you just jump up, like a sweet lad, and get me an apple, to wet my pipe like."

You may fancy the terror I was in! I should have leaped out and run for it if I had found the strength; but my limbs and heart alike misgave me. I heard Dick begin to rise, and then someone seemingly stopped him, and the voice of Hands exclaimed: "Oh, stow that! Don't you get sucking of that bilge, John. Let's have a go of the rum."

"Dick," said Silver, "I trust you. I've a gauge on the keg, mind. There's the key; you fill a pannikin and bring it up."

Terrified as I was, I could not help thinking to myself that this must have been how Mr. Arrow got the strong waters that destroyed him.

Dick was gone but a little while, and during his absence Israel spoke straight on in the cook's ear. It was but a word or two that I could catch, and yet gathered some important news; for, besides other scraps that tended to the same purpose, this whole clause was audible: "Not another man of them'll jine." Hence there were still faithful men on board.

When Dick returned, one after another of the trio took the pannikin and drank—one "To luck"; another with a "Here's to old Flint"; and Silver himself saying, in a kind of song, "Here's to ourselves, and hold your luff, plenty of prizes and plenty of duff."

Just then a sort of brightness fell upon me in the barrel, and, looking up, I found the moon had risen, and was silvering the mizzen-top and shining white on the luff of the fore-sail; and almost at the same time the voice of the lookout shouted, "Land-ho!"

Arithmetic

Carl Sandburg

Arithmetic is where numbers fly
  like pigeons in and out of your head.
Arithmetic tells you how many you lose or win
  if you know how many you had
  before you lost or won.
Arithmetic is seven eleven all good children
  go to heaven—or five six bundle of sticks.
Arithmetic is numbers you squeeze from your
  head to your hand to your pencil to your paper
  till you get the right answer . . .

If you have two animal crackers, one good and one bad,
    and you eat one and a striped zebra
    with streaks all over him eats the other,
    how many animal crackers will you have
    if somebody offers you five six seven and you say
    No no no and you say Nay nay nay
    and you say Nix nix nix?
If you ask your mother for one fried egg
    for breakfast and she gives you
    two fried eggs and you eat
    both of them, who is better in arithmetic,
    you or your mother?

Marilla Cuthbert Is Surprised

Marilla Cuthbert, her brother Matthew, and Anne Shirley are three unforgettable characters you will meet if you read L.M. Montgomery's Anne of Green Gables. *In Chapter 3 of the book, which is printed below, all of them are together for the first time. As the chapter begins, Marilla stands ready to meet the orphan boy she and her brother plan to adopt.*

MARILLA came briskly forward as Matthew opened the door. But when her eyes fell on the odd little figure in the stiff, ugly dress, with the long braids of red hair and the eager luminous eyes, she stopped short in amazement.

"Matthew Cuthbert, who's that?" she ejaculated. "Where is the boy?"

"There wasn't any boy," said Matthew wretchedly. "There was only *her.*"

He nodded at the child, remembering that he had never even asked her name.

"No boy! But there *must* have been a boy," insisted Marilla. "We sent word to Mrs. Spencer to bring a boy."

"Well, she didn't. She brought *her.* I asked the station-master. And I had to bring her home. She couldn't be left there, no matter where the mistake had come in."

"Well, this is a pretty piece of business!" ejaculated Marilla.

During this dialogue the child had remained silent, her eyes roving from one to the other, all the animation fading out of her face. Suddenly she seemed to grasp the full meaning of what had been said. Dropping her precious carpet-bag she sprang forward a step and clasped her hands.

"You don't want me!" she cried. "You don't want me because I'm not a boy! I might have expected it. Nobody ever did want me. I might have known it was all too beautiful to last. I might have known nobody really did want me. Oh, what shall I do? I'm going to burst into tears!"

Burst into tears she did. Sitting down on a chair by the table, flinging her arms out upon it, and burying her face in them, she proceeded to cry stormily. Marilla and Matthew looked at each other deprecatingly across the stove. Neither of them knew what to say or do. Finally Marilla stepped lamely into the breach.

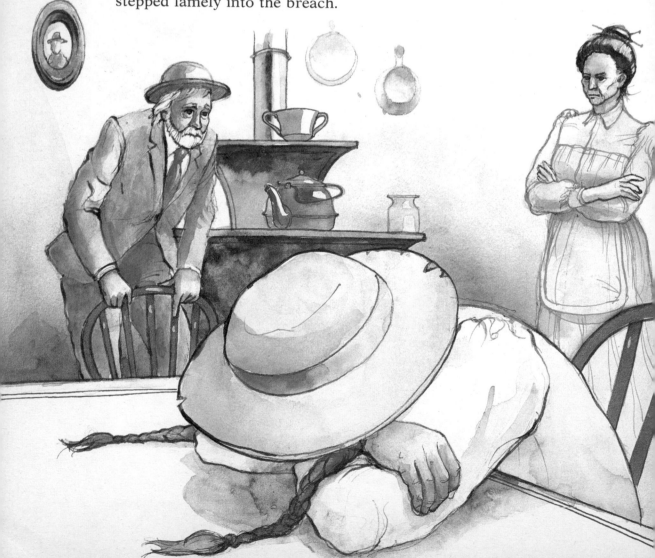

"Well, well, there's no need to cry so about it."

"Yes, there *is* need!" The child raised her head quickly, revealing a tear-stained face and trembling lips. "*You* would cry, too, if you were an orphan and had come to a place you thought was going to be home and found that they didn't want you because you weren't a boy. Oh, this is the most *tragical* thing that ever happened to me!"

Something like a reluctant smile, rather rusty from long disuse, mellowed Marilla's grim expression.

"Well, don't cry any more. We're not going to turn you out-of-doors tonight. You'll have to stay here until we investigate this affair. What's your name?"

The child hesitated for a moment.

"Will you please call me Cordelia?" she said eagerly.

"*Call* you Cordelia? Is that your name?"

"No-o-o, it's not exactly my name, but I would love to be called Cordelia. It's such a perfectly elegant name."

"I don't know what on earth you mean. If Cordelia isn't your name, what is?"

"Anne Shirley," reluctantly faltered forth the owner of that name, "but, oh, please do call me Cordelia. It can't matter much to you what you call me if I'm only going to be here a little while, can it? And Anne is such an unromantic name."

"Unromantic fiddlesticks!" said the unsympathetic Marilla. "Anne is a real good plain sensible name. You've no need to be ashamed of it."

"Oh, I'm not ashamed of it," explained Anne, "only I like Cordelia better. I've always imagined that my name was Cordelia—at least, I always have of late years. When I was young I used to imagine it was Geraldine, but I like Cordelia better now. But if you call me Anne please call me Anne spelled with an *e*."

"What difference does it make how it's spelled?" asked Marilla with another rusty smile as she picked up the teapot.

"Oh, it makes *such* a difference. It *looks* so much nicer.

When you hear a name pronounced can't you always see it in your mind, just as if it was printed out? I can; and A-n-n looks dreadful, but A-n-n-e looks so much more distinguished. If you'll only call me Anne spelled with an *e* I shall try to reconcile myself to not being called Cordelia."

"Very well, then, Anne spelled with an *e*, can you tell us how this mistake came to be made? We sent word to Mrs. Spencer to bring us a boy. Were there no boys at the asylum?"

"Oh, yes, there was an abundance of them. But Mrs. Spencer said *distinctly* that you wanted a girl about eleven years old. And the matron said she thought I would do. You don't know how delighted I was. I couldn't sleep all last night for joy. Oh," she added reproachfully, turning to Matthew, "why didn't you tell me at the station that you didn't want me and leave me there? If I hadn't seen the White Way of Delight and the Lake of Shining Waters it wouldn't be so hard."

"What on earth does she mean?" demanded Marilla, staring at Matthew.

"She—she's just referring to some conversation we had on the road," said Matthew hastily. "I'm going out to put the mare in, Marilla. Have tea ready when I come back."

"Did Mrs. Spencer bring anybody over besides you?" continued Marilla when Matthew had gone out.

"She brought Lily Jones for herself. Lily is only five years old and she is very beautiful. She has nut-brown hair. If I was very beautiful and had nut-brown hair would you keep me?"

"No. We want a boy to help Matthew on the farm. A girl would be of no use to us. Take off your hat. I'll lay it and your bag on the hall table."

Anne took off her hat meekly. Matthew came back presently and they sat down to supper. But Anne could not eat. In vain she nibbled at the bread and butter and pecked at the crab-apple preserve out of the little scalloped glass dish by her plate. She did not really make any headway at all.

321

"You're not eating anything," said Marilla sharply, eyeing her as if it were a serious shortcoming. Anne sighed.

"I can't. I'm in the depths of despair. Can you eat when you are in the depths of despair?"

"I've never been in the depths of despair, so I can't say," responded Marilla.

"Weren't you? Well, did you ever try to *imagine* you were in the depths of despair?"

"No, I didn't."

"Then I don't think you can understand what it's like. It's a very uncomfortable feeling indeed. When you try to eat a lump comes right up in your throat and you can't swallow anything, not even if it was a chocolate caramel. I had one chocolate caramel once two years ago and it was simply delicious. I've often dreamed since then that I had a lot of chocolate caramels, but I always wake up just when I'm going to eat them. I do hope you won't be offended because I can't eat. Everything is extremely nice, but still I cannot eat."

"I guess she's tired," said Matthew, who hadn't spoken since his return from the barn. "Best put her to bed, Marilla."

Marilla had been wondering where Anne should be put to bed. She had prepared a couch in the kitchen chamber for the desired and expected boy. But, although it was neat and clean, it did not seem quite the thing to put a girl there somehow. But the spare room was out of the question for such a stray waif, so there remained only the east gable room. Marilla lighted a candle and told Anne to follow her, which Anne spiritlessly did, taking her hat and carpet-bag from the hall table as she passed. The hall was fearsomely clean; the little gable chamber in which she presently found herself seemed still cleaner.

Marilla set the candle on a three-legged, three-cornered table and turned down the bedclothes.

"I suppose you have a nightgown?" she questioned.

Anne nodded.

"Yes, I have two. The matron of the asylum made them for me. They're fearfully skimpy. There is never enough to go around in an asylum, so things are always skimpy—at least in a poor asylum like ours. I hate skimpy night-dresses. But one can dream just as well in them as in lovely trailing ones, with frills around the neck, that's one consolation."

"Well, undress as quick as you can and go to bed. I'll come back in a few minutes for the candle. I daren't trust you to put it out yourself. You'd likely set the place on fire."

When Marilla had gone Anne looked around her wistfully. The whitewashed walls were so painfully bare and staring that she thought they must ache over their own bareness. The floor was bare, too, except for a round braided mat in the middle such as Anne had never seen before. In one corner was the bed, a high, old-fashioned one, with four dark, low-turned posts. In the other corner was the aforesaid three-cornered table adorned with a fat, red velvet pincushion hard enough to turn the point of the

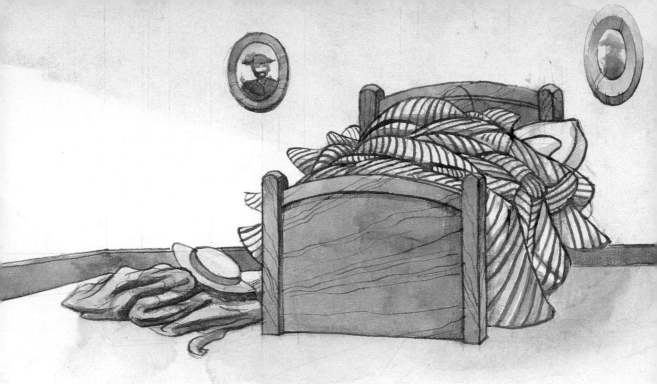

most adventurous pin. Above it hung a little six by eight mirror. Midway between table and bed was the window, with an icy white muslin frill over it, and opposite it was the wash-stand. The whole apartment was of a rigidity not to be described in words, but which sent a shiver to the very marrow of Anne's bones. With a sob she hastily discarded her garments, put on the skimpy nightgown and sprang into bed where she burrowed face downward into the pillow and pulled the clothes over her head. When Marilla came up for the light various skimpy articles of raiment scattered most untidily over the floor and a certain tempestuous appearance of the bed were the only indications of any presence save her own.

She deliberately picked up Anne's clothes, placed them neatly on a prim yellow chair, and then, taking up the candle, went over to the bed.

"Good night," she said, a little awkwardly, but not unkindly.

Anne's white face and big eyes appeared over the bedclothes with a startling suddenness.

"How can you call it a *good* night when you know it must be the very worst night I've ever had?" she said reproachfully.

Then she dived down into invisibility again.

Marilla went slowly down to the kitchen and proceeded to wash the supper dishes. Matthew was smoking—a sure sign of perturbation of mind. He seldom smoked, for Marilla set her face against it as a filthy habit; but at certain times and seasons he felt driven to it and then Marilla winked at the practice, realizing that a mere man must have some vent for his emotions.

"Well, this is a pretty kettle of fish," she said wrathfully. "This is what comes of sending word instead of going ourselves. Robert Spencer's folks have twisted that message somehow. One of us will have to drive over and see Mrs. Spencer tomorrow, that's certain. This girl will have to be sent back to the asylum."

"Yes, I suppose so," said Matthew reluctantly.

"You *suppose* so! Don't you know it?"

"Well now, she's a real nice little thing, Marilla. It's kind of a pity to send her back when she's so set on staying here."

"Matthew Cuthbert, you don't mean to say you think we ought to keep her!"

Marilla's astonishment could not have been greater if Matthew had expressed a predilection for standing on his head.

"Well now, no, I suppose not—not exactly," stammered Matthew, uncomfortably driven into a corner for his precise meaning. "I suppose—we could hardly be expected to keep her."

"I should say not. What good would she be to us?"

"We might be some good to her," said Matthew suddenly and unexpectedly.

"Matthew Cuthbert, I believe that child has bewitched you! I can see as plain as plain that you want to keep her."

"Well now, she's a real interesting little thing," persisted Matthew. "You should have heard her talk coming from the station."

"Oh, she can talk fast enough. I saw that at once. It's nothing in her favour, either. I don't like children who have so much to say. I don't want an orphan girl and if I did she isn't the style I'd pick out. There's something I don't understand about her. No, she's got to be despatched straightway back to where she came from."

"I could hire a French boy to help me," said Matthew, "and she'd be company for you."

"I'm not suffering for company," said Marilla shortly. "And I'm not going to keep her."

"Well now, it's just as you say, of course, Marilla," said Matthew rising and putting his pipe away. "I'm going to bed."

To bed went Matthew. And to bed, when she had put her dishes away, went Marilla, frowning most resolutely. And upstairs, in the east gable, a lonely, heart-hungry, friendless child cried herself to sleep.

The Little Match Girl

Hans Christian Andersen

IT WAS late on a bitterly cold New Year's Eve. The snow was falling. A poor little girl was wandering in the dark cold streets; she was bareheaded and barefoot. She had of course had slippers on when she left home, but they were not much good, for they were so huge. They had last been worn by her mother, and they fell off the poor little girl's feet when she was running across the street to avoid two carriages that were rolling rapidly by. One of the shoes could not be found at all, and the other was picked up by a boy who ran off with it, saying that it would do for a cradle when he had some children of his own.

So the poor little girl had to walk on with her little bare feet, which were red and blue with the cold. She carried a quantity of matches in her old apron, and held a packet of them in her hand.

Nobody had bought any of her during all the long day, and nobody had even given her a copper. The poor little creature was hungry and perishing with cold, and she looked the picture of misery.

The snowflakes fell on her long yellow hair, which curled so prettily round her face, but she paid no attention to that. Lights were shining from every window, and there was a most delicious odor of roast goose in the streets, for it was New Year's Eve. She could not forget that! She found a corner where one house projected a little beyond the next

328

one, and here she crouched, drawing up her feet under her,
but she was colder than ever. She did not dare to go home,
for she had not sold any matches and had not earned a single
penny. Her father would beat her, and besides it was almost
as cold at home as it was here. They had only the roof over
them, and the wind whistled through it although they
stuffed up the biggest cracks with rags and straw.

Her little hands were almost dead with cold. Oh, one little
match would do some good! If she only dared, she would
pull one out of the packet and strike it on the wall to warm
her fingers. She pulled out one. *R-r-sh-sh!* How it sputtered
and blazed! It burnt with a bright clear flame, just like a
little candle, when she held her hand round it.

Now the light seemed very strange to her! The little girl
fancied that she was sitting in front of a big stove with polished brass feet and handles. There was a splendid fire blaz-
ing in it and warming her so beautifully, but—what happened? Just as she was stretching out her feet to warm
them, the flame went out, the stove vanished—and she was
left sitting with the end of the burnt match in her hand.

She struck a new one. It burnt, it blazed up, and where the light fell upon the wall, it became transparent like gauze, and she could see right through it into the room.

The table was spread with a snowy cloth and pretty china. A roast goose stuffed with apples and prunes was steaming on it. And what was even better, the goose hopped from the dish with the carving knife sticking in his back and waddled across the floor. It came right up to the poor child, and then—the match went out and there was nothing to be seen but the thick black wall.

She lit another match. This time she was sitting under a lovely Christmas tree. It was much bigger and more beautifully decorated than the one she had seen when she peeped through the glass doors at the rich merchant's house on the last Christmas. Thousands of lighted candles gleamed under its branches. And colored pictures, such as she had seen in the shop windows, looked down at her. The little girl stretched out both her hands towards them—then out went the match. All the Christmas candles rose higher and higher, till she saw that they were only the twinkling stars. One of them fell and made a bright streak of light across the sky.

"Now someone is dying," thought the little girl, for her old grandmother, the only person who had ever been kind to her, used to say, "When a star falls, a soul is going up to God."

Now she struck another match against the wall, and this time it was her grandmother who appeared in the circle of flame. She saw her quite clearly and distinctly, looking so gentle and happy.

"Grandmother!" cried the little creature. "Oh, do take me with you. I know you will vanish when the match goes out. You will vanish like the warm stove, the delicious goose, and the beautiful Christmas tree!"

She hastily struck a whole bundle of matches, because she did so long to keep her grandmother with her. The light of the matches made it as bright as day. Grandmother had never before looked so big or so beautiful. She lifted the little girl up in her arms, and they soared in a halo of light and joy, far, far above the earth, where there was no more cold, no hunger, and no pain—for they were with God.

In the cold morning light the poor little girl sat there, in the corner between the houses, with rosy cheeks and a smile on her face—dead. Frozen to death on the last night of the old year. New Year's Day broke on the little body still sitting with the ends of the burnt-out matches in her hand.

"She must have tried to warm herself," they said. Nobody knew what beautiful visions she had seen, nor in what a halo she had entered with her grandmother upon the glories of the New Year.

Nonsense Verse

The common cormorant or shag
Lays eggs inside a paper bag.
The reason you will see no doubt
It is to keep the lightning out.
But what these unobservant birds
Have never noticed is that herds
Of wandering bears may come with buns
And steal the bags to hold the crumbs.

There was an old man from Peru
Who dreamed he was eating his shoe.
He woke in a fright
In the middle of the night
And found it was perfectly true.

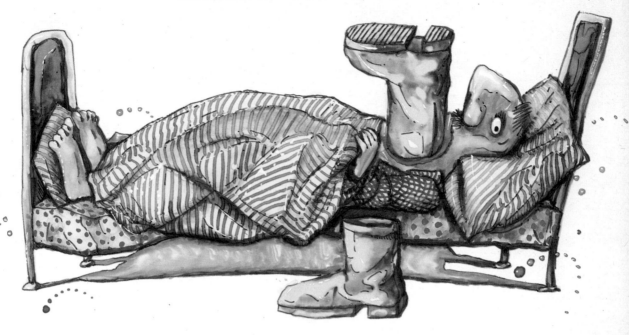

I eat my peas with honey,
I've done it all my life,
They do taste kind of funny,
But it keeps them on the knife.

Swift Things Are Beautiful

Elizabeth Coatsworth

Swift things are beautiful:
Swallows and deer,
And lightning that falls
Bright-veined and clear,
Rivers and meteors,
Wind in the wheat,
The strong-withered horse,
The runner's sure feet.

And slow things are beautiful:
The closing of day,
The pause of the wave
That curves downward to spray,
The ember that crumbles,
The opening flower,
And the ox that moves on
In the quiet of power.

The Raggedy Man

James Whitcomb Riley

O The Raggedy Man! He works fer Pa;
An' he's the goodest man ever you saw!
He comes to our house every day,
An' waters the horses, an' feeds 'em hay;
An' he opens the shed—an' we all ist laugh
When he drives out our little old wobblely calf;
An' nen—ef our hired girl says he can—
He milks the cow for 'Lizabuth Ann.—
  Aint he a' awful good Raggedy Man!
    Raggedy! Raggedy! Raggedy Man!

W'y The Raggedy Man—he's ist so good
He splits the kindlin' an' chops the wood;
An' nen he spades in our garden, too,
An' does most things 'at *boys* can't do!—
He climbed clean up on our big tree
An' shooked a' apple down fer me—
An' nother'n, too, fer 'Lizabuth Ann—
An' nother'n, too, for The Raggedy Man—
  Ain't he a' awful kind Raggedy Man?
    Raggedy! Raggedy! Raggedy Man!

An' The Raggedy Man, he knows most rhymes
An' tells 'em, ef I be good, sometimes:
Knows 'bout Giunt, an' Griffuns, an' Elves,
An' the Squidgicum-Squees 'at swallers themselves!
An', wite by the pump in our pasture-lot,
He showed me the hole 'at the Wunks is got,
'At lives 'way deep in the ground, an' can
Turn into me, er 'Lizabuth Ann!
  Ain't he a funny old Raggedy Man?
    Raggedy! Raggedy! Raggedy Man!

336

The Raggedy Man—one time when he
Wuz makin' a little bow-'n'-orry fer me,
Says "When *you're* big like your Pa is,
Air you go' to keep a fine store like his—
An' be a rich merchant—an' wear fine clothes?
Er what *air* you go' to be, goodness knows!"
An' nen he laughed at 'Lizabuth Ann,
An' I says, "'M go' to be a Raggedy Man!
  I'm ist go' to be a nice Raggedy Man!
    Raggedy! Raggedy! Raggedy Man!"

From Tiger to Anansi

This tale, featuring the remarkable West Indian character Anansi, comes from Philip M. Sherlock's book Anansi, the Spider Man: Jamaican Folk Tales.

ONCE upon a time and a long long time ago the Tiger was king of the forest.

At evening when all the animals sat together in a circle and talked and laughed together, Snake would ask,

"Who is the strongest of us all?"

"Tiger is strongest," cried the dog. "When Tiger whispers the trees listen. When Tiger is angry and cries out, the trees tremble."

"And who is the weakest of all?" asked Snake.

"Anansi," shouted dog, and they all laughed together. "Anansi the spider is weakest of all. When he whispers no one listens. When he shouts everyone laughs."

Now one day the weakest and strongest came face to face, Anansi and Tiger. They met in a clearing of the forest. The frogs hiding under the cool leaves saw them. The bright green parrots in the branches heard them.

When they met, Anansi bowed so low that his forehead touched the ground. Tiger did not greet him. Tiger just looked at Anansi.

"Good morning, Tiger," cried Anansi. "I have a favor to ask."

"And what is it, Anansi?" said Tiger.

"Tiger, we all know that you are strongest of us all. This is why we give your name to many things. We have Tiger lilies, and Tiger stories and Tiger moths and Tiger this and Tiger that. Everyone knows that I am weakest of all. This is

338

why nothing bears my name. Tiger, let something be called after the weakest one so that men may know my name too."

"Well," said Tiger, without so much as a glance toward Anansi, "what would you like to bear your name?"

"The stories," cried Anansi. "The stories that we tell in the forest at evening time when the sun goes down, the stories about Br'er Snake and Br'er Tacamah, Br'er Cow and Br'er Bird and all of us."

Now Tiger liked these stories and he meant to keep them as Tiger stories. He thought to himself, How stupid, how weak this Anansi is. I will play a trick on him so that all the animals will laugh at him. Tiger moved his tail slowly from side to side and said, "Very good, Anansi, very good. I will let the stories be named after you, if you do what I ask."

"Tiger, I will do what you ask."

"Yes, I am sure you will, I am sure you will," said Tiger, moving his tail slowly from side to side. "It is a little thing that I ask. Bring me Mr. Snake alive. Do you know Snake who lives down by the river, Mr. Anansi? Bring him to me alive and you can have the stories."

Tiger stopped speaking. He did not move his tail. He looked at Anansi and waited for him to speak. All the animals in the forest waited. Mr. Frog beneath the cool leaves, Mr. Parrot up in the tree, all watched Anansi. They were all ready to laugh at him.

"Tiger, I will do what you ask," said Anansi. At these words a great wave of laughter burst from the forest. The frogs and parrots laughed. Tiger laughed loudest of all, for how could feeble Anansi catch Snake alive?

Anansi went away. He heard the forest laughing at him from every side.

That was on Monday morning. Anansi sat before his house and thought of plan after plan. At last he hit upon one that could not fail. He would build a Calaban.

On Tuesday morning Anansi built a Calaban. He took a strong vine and made a noose. He hid the vine in the grass. Inside the noose he set some of the berries that Snake loved best. Then he waited. Soon Snake came up the path. He saw the berries and went toward them. He lay across the vine and ate the berries. Anansi pulled at the vine to tighten the noose, but Snake's body was too heavy. Anansi saw that the Calaban had failed.

Wednesday came. Anansi made a deep hole in the ground. He made the sides slippery with grease. In the bottom he put some of the bananas that Snake loved. Then he hid in the bush beside the road and waited.

Snake came crawling down the path toward the river. He was hungry and thirsty. He saw the bananas at the bottom of the hole. He saw that the sides of the hole were slippery. First he wrapped his tail tightly around the trunk of a tree, then he reached down into the hole and ate the bananas. When he was finished he pulled himself up by the tail and crawled away. Anansi had lost his bananas and he had lost Snake, too.

Thursday morning came. Anansi made a Fly Up. Inside the trap he put an egg. Snake came down the path. He was happy this morning, so happy that he lifted his head and a third of his long body from the ground. He just lowered his head, took up the egg in his mouth, and never even touched the trap. The Fly Up could not catch Snake.

What was Anansi to do? Friday morning came. He sat and thought all day. It was no use.

Now it was Saturday morning. This was the last day. Anansi went for a walk down by the river. He passed by the hole where Snake lived. There was Snake, his body hidden in the hole, his head resting on the ground at the entrance to the hole. It was early morning. Snake was watching the sun rise above the mountains.

"Good morning, Anansi," said Snake.

"Good morning, Snake," said Anansi.

"Anansi, I am very angry with you. You have been trying to catch me all week. You set a Fly Up to catch me. The day before you made a Slippery Hole for me. The day before that you made a Calaban. I have a good mind to kill you, Anansi."

"Ah, you are too clever, Snake," said Anansi. "You are much too clever. Yes, what you say is so. I tried to catch you, but I failed. Now I can never prove that you are the longest animal in the world, longer even than the bamboo tree."

"Of course I am the longest of all animals," cried Snake. "I am much longer than the bamboo tree."

"What, longer than that bamboo tree across there?" asked Anansi.

"Of course I am," said Snake. "Look and see." Snake came out of the hole and stretched himself out at full length.

"Yes, you are very, very long," said Anansi, "but the bamboo tree is very long, too. Now that I look at you and at the bamboo tree I must say that the bamboo tree seems longer. But it's hard to say because it is farther away."

"Well, bring it nearer," cried Snake. "Cut it down and put it beside me. You will soon see that I am much longer."

Anansi ran to the bamboo tree and cut it down. He placed it on the ground and cut off all its branches. Bush, bush, bush, bush! There it was, long and straight as a flagstaff.

"Now put it beside me," said Snake.

Anansi put the long bamboo tree down on the ground beside the Snake. Then he said:

"Snake, when I go up to see where your head is, you will crawl up. When I go down to see where your tail is, you will crawl down. In that way you will always seem to be longer than the bamboo tree, which really is longer than you are."

"Tie my tail, then!" said Snake. "Tie my tail! I know that I am longer than the bamboo, whatever you say."

Anansi tied Snake's tail to the end of the bamboo. Then he ran up to the other end.

"Stretch, Snake, stretch, and we will see who is longer."

A crowd of animals was gathering round. Here was something better than a race. "Stretch, Snake, stretch," they called.

Snake stretched as hard as he could. Anansi tied him around his middle so that he should not slip back. Now one

344

more try. Snake knew that if he stretched hard enough he would prove to be longer than the bamboo.

Anansi ran up to him. "Rest yourself for a little, Snake, and then stretch again. If you can stretch another six inches you will be longer than the bamboo. Try your hardest. Stretch so that you even have to shut your eyes. Ready?"

"Yes," said Snake. Then Snake made a mighty effort. He stretched so hard that he had to squeeze his eyes shut. "Hooray!" cried the animals. "You are winning, Snake. Just two inches more."

And at that moment Anansi tied Snake's head to the bamboo. There he was. At last he had caught Snake, all by himself.

The animals fell silent. Yes, there Snake was, all tied up, ready to be taken to Tiger. And feeble Anansi had done this. They could laugh at him no more.

And never again did Tiger dare to call these stories by his name. They were Anansi stories forever after, from that day to this.

Playing Pilgrims

Little Women by Louisa May Alcott is an old, old book. You will probably feel the oldness as you meet the little women—Meg, Jo, Beth, and Amy March—in the first chapter, printed below. Consider, as you read, that the "old feeling" comes not so much from the fact that the story takes place during the American Civil War as from the time-honoured values that brim on every page: faith, hope, charity. Many generations of readers have been drawn into the warm circle of the March family's goodness, and perhaps you will be, too.

"CHRISTMAS won't be Christmas without any presents," grumbled Jo, lying on the rug.

"It's so dreadful to be poor!" sighed Meg, looking down at her old dress.

"I don't think it's fair for some girls to have plenty of pretty things, and other girls nothing at all," added little Amy, with an injured sniff.

"We've got father and mother and each other," said Beth contentedly, from her corner.

The four young faces on which the firelight shone brightened at the cheerful words, but darkened again as Jo said sadly:

"We haven't got father, and shall not have him for a long time." She didn't say "perhaps never," but each silently added it, thinking of father far away, where the fighting was.

Nobody spoke for a minute; then Meg said in an altered tone:

"You know the reason mother proposed not having any presents this Christmas was because it is going to be a hard winter for every one; and she thinks we ought not to spend money for pleasure, when our men are suffering so in the army. We can't do much, but we can make our little sacrifices, and ought to do it gladly. But I am afraid I don't''; and Meg shook her head as she thought regretfully of all the pretty things she wanted.

"But I don't think the little we should spend would do any good. We've each got a dollar, and the army wouldn't be much helped by our giving that. I agree not to expect anything from mother or you, but I do want to buy Undine and Sintram for myself; I've wanted it *so* long," said Jo, who was a bookworm.

"I planned to spend mine on new music," said Beth, with a little sigh, which no one heard but the hearth-brush and kettle-holder.

"I shall get a nice box of Faber's drawing pencils; I really need them," said Amy decidedly.

"Mother didn't say anything about our money, and she won't wish us to give up everything. Let's each buy what we want, and have a little fun; I'm sure we work hard enough to earn it," cried Jo, examining the heels of her shoes in a gentlemanly manner.

"I know *I* do—teaching those tiresome children nearly all day, when I'm longing to enjoy myself at home," began Meg, in the complaining tone again.

"You don't have half such a hard time as I do," said Jo. "How would you like to be shut up for hours with a nervous, fussy old lady, who keeps you trotting, is never satisfied, and worries you till you're ready to fly out of the window or cry?"

"It's naughty to fret; but I do think washing dishes and keeping things tidy is the worst work in the world. It makes me cross; and my hands get so stiff, I can't practise well at all"; and Beth looked at her rough hands with a sigh that anyone could hear that time.

"I don't believe any of you suffer as I do," cried Amy; "for you don't have to go to school with impertinent girls, who plague you if you don't know your lessons, and laugh at your dresses, and label your father if he isn't rich, and insult you when your nose isn't nice."

"If you mean *libel*, I'd say so, and not talk about *labels*, as if papa was a pickle-bottle," advised Jo, laughing.

"I know what I mean, and you needn't be *statirical* about it. It's proper to use good words, and improve your *vocabilary*," returned Amy, with dignity.

"Don't peck at one another, children. Don't you wish we had the money papa lost when we were little, Jo? Dear me, how happy and good we'd be, if we had no worries!" said Meg, who could remember better times.

"You said the other day, you thought we were a deal happier than the King children, for they were fighting and fretting all the time, in spite of their money."

"So I did, Beth. Well, I think we are; for, though we do have to work, we make fun for ourselves, and are a pretty jolly set, as Jo would say."

"Jo does use such slang words," observed Amy, with a reproving look at the long figure stretched out on the rug. Jo immediately sat up, put her hands in her pockets, and began to whistle.

"Don't, Jo; it's so boyish."

"That's why I do it."

"I detest rude, unlady-like girls!"

"I hate affected, niminy-piminy chits."

" 'Birds in their little nests agree,' " sang Beth, the peace-maker, with such a funny face that both sharp voices softened to a laugh and the "pecking" ended for that time.

"Really, girls, you are both to be blamed," said Meg, beginning to lecture in her elder-sisterly fashion. "You are old enough to leave off boyish tricks, and to behave better, Josephine. It didn't matter so much when you were a little girl; but now you are so tall, and turn up your hair, you should remember that you are a young lady."

"I'm not! and if turning up my hair makes me one, I'll wear it in two tails till I'm twenty," cried Jo, pulling off her net and shaking down a chestnut mane. "I hate to think I've got to grow up and be Miss March, and wear long gowns, and look as prim as a China-aster. It's bad enough to be a girl, anyway, when I like boys' games and work and manners. I can't get over my disappointment in not being a boy, and it's worse than ever now, for I'm dying to go and fight with papa, and I can only stay at home and knit, like a poky old woman!" And Jo shook the blue army-sock till the needles rattled like castanets, and her ball bounded across the room.

"Poor Jo! It's too bad, but it can't be helped; so you must try to be contented with making your name boyish, and playing brother to us girls," said Beth, stroking the rough head at her knee with a hand that all the dish-washing and dusting in the world could not make ungentle in its touch.

"As for you, Amy," continued Meg, "you are altogether too particular and prim. Your airs are funny now, but you'll grow up an affected little goose if you don't take care. I like your nice manners and refined ways of speaking when you don't try to be elegant; but your absurd words are as bad as Jo's slang."

"If Jo is a tomboy and Amy a goose, what am I, please?" asked Beth, ready to share the lecture.

"You're a dear, and nothing else," answered Meg warmly; and no one contradicted her, for the "Mouse" was the pet of the family.

As young readers like to know "how people look," we will take this moment to give them a little sketch of the four sisters, who sat knitting away in the twilight, while the December snow fell quietly without, and the fire crackled cheerfully within. It was a comfortable old room, though the carpet was faded and the furniture very plain; for a good picture or two hung on the walls, books filled the recesses, chrysanthemums and Christmas roses bloomed in the windows, and a pleasant atmosphere of home-peace pervaded it.

Margaret, the eldest of the four, was sixteen, and very pretty, being plump and fair, with large eyes, plenty of soft, brown hair, a sweet mouth, and white hands, of which she was rather vain. Fifteen-year-old Jo was very tall, thin, and brown, and reminded one of a colt; for she never seemed to know what to do with her long limbs, which were very much in her way. She had a decided mouth, a comical nose, and sharp grey eyes, which appeared to see everything, and were by turns fierce, funny, or thoughtful. Her long, thick hair was her one beauty; but it was usually bundled into a net to be out of her way. Round shoulders had Jo, big hands and feet, a fly-away look to her clothes, and the uncomfortable appearance of a girl who was rapidly shooting up into

a woman, and didn't like it. Elizabeth—or Beth, as everyone called her—was a rosy, smooth-haired, bright-eyed girl
of thirteen, with a shy manner, a timid voice, and a peaceful
expression, which was seldom disturbed. Her father called
her "Little Tranquillity," and the name suited her excel-
lently; for she seemed to live in a happy world of her own,
only venturing out to meet the few whom she trusted and
loved. Amy, though the youngest, was a most important
person—in her own opinion at least. A regular snow maid-
en, with blue eyes and yellow hair curling on her shoulders;
pale and slender, and always carrying herself like a young
lady mindful of her manners. What the characters of the
four sisters were, we will leave to be found out.

The clock struck six; and, having swept up the hearth,
Beth put a pair of slippers down to warm. Somehow the
sight of the old shoes had a good effect upon the girls; for

mother was coming, and everyone brightened to welcome
her. Meg stopped lecturing, and lighted the lamp, Amy got
out of the easy-chair without being asked, and Jo forgot
how tired she was as she sat up to hold the slippers nearer
to the blaze.

"They are quite worn out; Marmee must have a new pair."

"I thought I'd get her some with my dollar," said Beth.

"No, I shall!" cried Amy.

"I'm the oldest," began Meg, but Jo cut in with a decided—

"I'm the man of the family now papa is away, and *I* shall provide the slippers, for he told me to take special care of mother while he was gone."

"I'll tell you what we'll do," said Beth; "let's each get her something for Christmas, and not get anything for ourselves."

"That's like you, dear! What will we get?" exclaimed Jo.

Everyone thought soberly for a minute; then Meg announced, as if the idea was suggested by the sight of her own pretty hands, "I shall give her a nice pair of gloves."

"Army shoes, best to be had," cried Jo.

"Some handkerchiefs, all hemmed," said Beth.

"I'll get a little bottle of cologne; she likes it, and it won't cost much, so I'll have some left to buy my pencils," added Amy.

"How will we give the things?" asked Meg.

"Put them on the table, and bring her in and see her open the bundles. Don't you remember how we used to do on our birthdays?" answered Jo.

"I used to be *so* frightened when it was my turn to sit in the big chair with the crown on, and see you all come marching round to give the presents, with a kiss. I liked the things and the kisses, but it was dreadful to have you sit looking at me while I opened the bundles," said Beth, who was toasting her face and the bread for tea, at the same time.

"Let Marmee think we are getting things for ourselves, and then surprise her. We must go shopping to-morrow afternoon, Meg; there is so much to do about the play for Christmas night," said Jo, marching up and down, with her hands behind her back and her nose in the air.

"I don't mean to act any more after this time; I'm getting

too old for such things," observed Meg, who was as much a child as ever about "dressing-up" frolics.

"You won't stop, I know, as long as you can trail round in a white gown with your hair down, and wear gold-paper jewelry. You are the best actress we've got, and there'll be an end of everything if you quit the boards," said Jo. "We ought to rehearse to-night. Come here, Amy, and do the fainting scene, for you are as stiff as a poker in that."

"I can't help it; I never saw anyone faint, and I don't choose to make myself all black and blue, tumbling flat as you do. If I can go down easily, I'll drop; if I can't, I shall fall into a chair and be graceful; I don't care if Hugo does come at me with a pistol," returned Amy, who was not gifted with dramatic power, but was chosen because she was small enough to be borne out shrieking by the villain of the piece.

"Do it this way; clasp your hands so, and stagger across the room, crying frantically, 'Roderigo! save me! save me!'" and away went Jo, with a melodramatic scream which was truly thrilling.

Amy followed, but she poked her hands out stiffly before her, and jerked herself along as if she went by machinery; and her "Ow!" was more suggestive of pins being run into her than of fear and anguish. Jo gave a despairing groan, and Meg laughed outright, while Beth let her bread burn as she watched the fun, with interest.

"It's no use! Do the best you can when the time comes, and if the audience laugh, don't blame me. Come on, Meg."

Then things went smoothly, for Don Pedro defied the world in a speech of two pages without a single break; Hagar, the witch, chanted an awful incantation over her kettleful of simmering toads, with weird effect; Roderigo rent his chains asunder manfully, and Hugo died in agonies of remorse and arsenic, with a wild "Ha! ha!"

"It's the best we've had yet," said Meg, as the dead villain sat up and rubbed his elbows.

"I don't see how you can write and act such splendid things, Jo. You're a regular Shakespeare!" exclaimed Beth,

who firmly believed that her sisters were gifted with wonderful genius in all things.

"Not quite," replied Jo modestly. "I do think 'The Witch's Curse, an Operatic Tragedy,' is rather a nice thing; but I'd like to try Macbeth, if we only had a trapdoor for Banquo. I always wanted to do the killing part. 'Is that a dagger that I see before me?'" muttered Jo, rolling her eyes and clutching at the air, as she had seen a famous tragedian do.

"No, it's the toasting-fork, with mother's shoe on it instead of the bread. Beth's stage-struck!" cried Meg, and the rehearsal ended in a general burst of laughter.

"Glad to find you so merry, my girls," said a cheery voice at the door, and actors and audience turned to welcome a tall, motherly lady, with a "can-I-help-you" look about her which was truly delightful. She was not elegantly dressed, but a noble-looking woman, and the girls thought the grey cloak and unfashionable bonnet covered the most splendid mother in the world.

"Well, dearies, how have you got on to-day? There was so much to do, getting the boxes ready to go to-morrow, that I didn't come home to dinner. Has anyone called, Beth? How is your cold, Meg? Jo, you look tired to death. Come and kiss me, baby."

While making these maternal inquiries, Mrs. March got her wet things off, her warm slippers on, and, sitting down

356

in the easy-chair, drew Amy to her lap, preparing to enjoy the happiest hour of her busy day. The girls flew about, trying to make things comfortable, each in her own way. Meg arranged the tea-table; Jo brought wood, and set chairs, dropping, overturning, and clattering everything she touched; Beth trotted to and fro between parlour and kitchen, quiet and busy; while Amy gave directions to everyone, as she sat with her hands folded.

As they gathered about the table, Mrs. March said, with a particularly happy face: "I've got a treat for you after supper."

A quick, bright smile went round like a streak of sunshine. Beth clapped her hands, regardless of the biscuit she held, and Jo tossed up her napkin, crying: "A letter! a letter! Three cheers for father!"

"Yes, a nice long letter. He is well, and thinks he shall get through the cold season better than we feared. He sends all sorts of loving wishes for Christmas, and an especial message to you girls," said Mrs. March, patting her pocket as if she had got a treasure there.

"Hurry and get done! Don't stop to quirk your little finger and simper over your plate, Amy," cried Jo, choking on her tea, and dropping her bread, butter side down, on the carpet, in her haste to get at the treat.

Beth ate no more, but crept away, to sit in her shadowy corner and brood over the delight to come, till the others were ready.

"I think it was so splendid in father to go as a chaplain when he was too old to be drafted, and not strong enough for a soldier," said Meg warmly.

"Don't I wish I could go as a drummer, a *vivan*—what's its name?—or a nurse, so I could be near him and help him," exclaimed Jo, with a groan.

"It must be very disagreeable to sleep in a tent, and eat all sorts of bad-tasting things, and drink out of a tin mug," sighed Amy.

"When will he come home, Marmee?" asked Beth, with a little quiver in her voice.

"Not for many months, dear, unless he is sick. He will

stay and do his work faithfully as long as he can, and we won't ask for him back a minute sooner than he can be spared. Now come and hear the letter."

They all drew to the fire, mother in the big chair with Beth at her feet, Meg and Amy perched on either arm of the chair, and Jo leaning on the back, where no one would see any sign of emotion if the letter should happen to be touching.

Very few letters were written in those hard times that were not touching, especially those which fathers sent home. In this one little was said of the hardships endured, the dangers faced, or the home-sickness conquered; it was a cheerful, hopeful letter, full of lively descriptions of camp life, marches, and military news; and only at the end did the writer's heart overflow with fatherly love and longing for the little girls at home.

" 'Give them all my dear love and a kiss. Tell them I think of them by day, pray for them by night, and find my best comfort in their affection at all times. A year seems very long to wait before I see them, but remind them that while we wait we may all work, so that these hard days need not be wasted. I know they will remember all I said to them, that they will be loving children to you, will do their duty faithfully, fight their bosom enemies bravely, and conquer themselves so beautifully, that when I come back to them I may be fonder and prouder than ever of my little women.' "

Everybody sniffed when they came to that part; Jo wasn't ashamed of the great tear that dropped off the end of her nose, and Amy never minded the rumpling of her curls as she hid her face on her mother's shoulder and sobbed out: "I *am* a selfish girl! but I'll truly try to be better, so he mayn't be disappointed in me by and by."

"We all will!" cried Meg. "I think too much of my looks, and hate to work, but won't anymore, if I can help it."

"I'll try and be what he loves to call me, 'a little woman,' and not be rough and wild; but do my duty here instead of wanting to be somewhere else," said Jo, thinking that keeping her temper at home was a much harder task than facing a rebel or two down South.

358

Beth said nothing, but wiped away her tears with the blue army-sock, and began to knit with all her might, losing no time in doing the duty that lay nearest her, while she resolved in her quiet little soul to be all that father hoped to find her when the year brought round the happy coming home.

Mrs. March broke the silence that followed Jo's words, by saying in her cheery voice: "Do you remember how you used to play Pilgrim's Progress when you were little

things? Nothing delighted you more than to have me tie my piece-bags on your backs for burdens, give you hats and sticks and rolls of paper, and let you travel through the house from the cellar, which was the City of Destruction, up, up, to the house-top, where you had all the lovely things you could collect to make a Celestial City."

"What fun it was, especially going by the lions, fighting Apollyon, and passing through the Valley where the hobgoblins were!" said Jo.

"I liked the place where the bundles fell off and tumbled downstairs," said Meg.

"My favorite part was when we came out on the flat roof where our flowers and arbours and pretty things were, and all stood and sung for joy up there in the sunshine," said Beth, smiling, as if that pleasant moment had come back to her.

"I don't remember much about it, except that I was afraid of the cellar and the dark entry, and always liked the cake and milk we had up at the top. If I wasn't too old for such things, I'd rather like to play it over again," said Amy, who began to talk of renouncing childish things at the mature age of twelve.

"We never are too old for this, my dear, because it is a play we are playing all the time in one way or another. Our burdens are here, our road is before us, and the longing for goodness and happiness is the guide that leads us through many troubles and mistakes to the peace which is a true Celestial City. Now, my little pilgrims, suppose you begin again, not in play, but in earnest, and see how far on you can get before father comes home."

"Really, mother? Where are our bundles?" asked Amy, who was a very literal young lady.

"Each of you told what your burden was just now, except Beth; I rather think she hasn't got any," said her mother.

"Yes, I have; mine is dishes and dusters, and envying girls with nice pianos, and being afraid of people."

Beth's bundle was such a funny one that everybody wanted to laugh; but nobody did, for it would have hurt her feelings very much.

360

"Let us do it," said Meg thoughtfully. "It is only another name for trying to be good, and the story may help us; for though we do want to be good, it's hard work, and we forget, and don't do our best."

"We were in the Slough of Despond to-night, and mother came and pulled us out as Help did in the book. We ought to have our roll of directions, like Christian. What shall we do about that?" asked Jo, delighted with the fancy which lent a little romance to the very dull task of doing her duty.

"Look under your pillows, Christmas morning, and you will find your guide-book," replied Mrs. March.

They talked over the new plan while old Hannah cleared the table; then out came the four little work-baskets, and the needles flew as the girls made sheets for Aunt March. It was uninteresting sewing, but to-night no one grumbled. They adopted Jo's plan of dividing the long seams into four parts, and calling the quarters Europe, Asia, Africa, and America, and in that way got on capitally, especially when they talked about the different countries as they stitched their way through them.

At nine they stopped work, and sang, as usual, before they went to bed. No one but Beth could get much music out of the old piano; but she had a way of softly touching

the yellow keys, and making a pleasant accompaniment to the simple songs they sang. Meg had a voice like a flute, and she and her mother led the little choir. Amy chirped like a cricket, and Jo wandered through the airs at her own sweet will, always coming out at the wrong place with a croak or a quaver that spoilt the most pensive tune. They had always done this from the time they could lisp

Crinkle, crinkle, 'ittle 'tar,

and it had become a household custom, for the mother was a born singer. The first sound in the morning was her voice, as she went about the house singing like a lark; and the last sound at night was the same cheery sound, for the girls never grew too old for that familiar lullaby.

Staver and His Wife Vassilissa

Here is an exciting Russian folktale that has but one fault—it should have been called "Vassilissa and Her Husband Staver." Read it and see if you don't agree. The tale comes from Hans Baumann's book Hero Legends of the World.

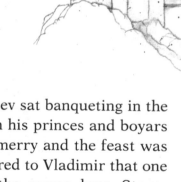

G RAND Duke Vladimir of Kiev sat banqueting in the great hall of his castle with his princes and boyars round him. Everyone was merry and the feast was already in full swing when it occurred to Vladimir that one of the boyars was not present, the young hero Staver Godinovitch. Immediately the Grand Duke sent a messenger to summon Staver to the merrymaking.

Presently Staver the boyar arrived on horseback. He dismounted and strode through the white stone palace, crossed himself, as was the custom, and bowed to left and right to greet those present. Everyone rose to receive him, even the Grand Duke himself and Staver saluted him with particular warmth. Then they all sat down again at the oaken tables and the banquet continued.

When the heroes had eaten and drunk their fill, they began to boast, and the loudest of the braggarts were the Grand Duke's men. Nowhere, they insisted, was there more gold, nowhere more silver, nowhere greater heaps of pearls than in the palace of Kiev.

364

This was too much for Staver. "Listen to those boasters," he murmured in his neighbour's ear. "Their mouths are big, but their heads are empty. They talk and talk of their city of Kiev, its gold, silver and pearls. But what is this stone box compared with my castle? Why, mine is so vast that it's better to ride on horseback through it rather than walk. All the rooms are oak-panelled and hung with beaver and sable. The steel door-handles and hinges are all gilded and the floors are made of pure silver. I have iron-bound coffers filled with silver and gold, to say nothing of pearls. And I have a treasure in my house that puts everything else in the shade, my wife, Vassilissa. There is no one to compare with her. Her face is as fair as the freshly fallen snow, she has brows of sable and a falcon's eyes. And she is not only a superb housekeeper. She also knows how to bend the bow and she excels in other manly arts. That's my wife Vassilissa for you!"

Staver had spoken to no one but his neighbour, yet many ears pricked as he uttered these words. And at once, tale-bearers brought the Grand Duke's notice to the way that Staver had boasted to his fellow guest.

Vladimir flushed with anger. In a voice loud enough for all to hear he said: "Princes and boyars, do you consider it right that someone humiliates me here in my own hall? This Staver Godinovitch is a windbag who insults me with his talk. Seize him and carry him down to the dungeons. Put him behind iron doors and wall up the cell with yellow sand, so that he can no longer offend my ears. Then ten of you ride to Staver's castle, seal it up, together with his treasure chests, and bring me the peerless Vassilissa! Bring her here to me, the Grand Duke Vladimir of Kiev!"

Staver was seized and thrown into prison. He was locked behind iron doors and yellow sand, while ten boyars rode off to seal up Staver's castle and to bring Vassilissa to Kiev.

But there was one boyar who was loyal to Staver and he galloped ahead of the others to tell Vassilissa what Vladimir had done to her husband Staver.

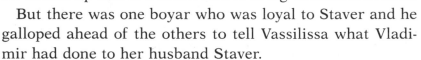

Then Vassilissa dressed herself in men's clothing and arranged her hair like a man's. She put on boots of green morocco leather and she armed herself with a goodly sword, a Tartar spear, a bow and a quiver that contained many arrows, all of which she had sharpened with her own hands. So Vassilissa became Vassili. She climbed into her Circassian saddle and with twelve of her men she set out for Kiev.

Half way there, she met Vladimir's envoys who had been ordered to take Vassilissa prisoner. They did not recognize her and one of them asked her: "Where have you come from, young man, and where are you riding?"

"We have come from the Khan of the Golden Hordes," Vassilissa answered, "to remind the Grand Duke Vladimir that he owes the Khan tribute for the last twelve years. We have orders to take many golden rings back to the Khan, two thousand for each year that is outstanding. And where are you riding?"

At this, the Grand Duke's messengers felt afraid, but at last their leader said: "We are going to Staver's castle, to seal it up and to carry his wife Vassilissa to the Grand Duke Vladimir."

"We have just passed Staver's castle. Vassilissa is not there. She has ridden away."

So Vladimir's envoys turned back and returned to Kiev at the gallop to report to the Grand Duke. The latter listened to them with bad grace, and his young wife Apraksiya, too, was greatly out of humour. And when Vassilissa and her attendants came riding up, everyone took her for the ambassador sent by the Khan of the Golden Hordes. The Grand Duke himself conducted her into the great hall and there he offered her hospitality.

Apraksiya, however, had scrutinized the new arrivals very closely. She led Vladimir away and beneath the portico she said to him softly: "Listen to me, Vladimir. These are no envoys from the Golden Hordes, they have not been sent by the Tartar Khan. Their leader is not a man but Staver's young wife. She sails across the courtyard as a duck swims, and when she sits down, she keeps her knees together."

368

At this, the Grand Duke recovered his high spirits. He
invited all the nobles to a banquet and the merrymaking
grew louder than ever. Vassilissa and her attendants were
also among the guests. When they had feasted enough,
Vladimir said secretly to Apraksiya: "Now I shall put to the
test this young man whom the Tartar Khan has sent to me.
He shall measure himself at wrestling against my finest
champions."

At the table sat seven very famous champions: Ilya Muro-
metz, Alyosha Popovitch, Kungur and Suchan, Samson, and
Chapil's two sons. And no less than five other heroes were
also present. The champions challenged Vassilissa to single
combat and she declared herself ready to wrestle with
them all. They went out into the courtyard, where they
lined up in a row.

The first man stepped forth and Vassilissa hit him on the
head so hard that he had to be carried from the courtyard.
The second had seven of his ribs broken by a single blow of
her fist. The third had three of his vertebrae dislocated,
and he had to crawl away on all fours. The rest took to their
heels.

Vladimir spat, so great was his rage. When he was alone again with Apraksiya, he said to her. "Your hair may be long, but you haven't much brain. And you say the Khan's envoy is not a man! Why, my court has never seen a hero with such strength."

"Look at her properly," retorted Apraksiya. "Isn't her face as white as freshly fallen snow? Are not her brows like sable? Has she not the bright eyes of the falcon, just as Staver boasted? She is Vassilissa I tell you. You are all blind."

"Very well," said Vladimir. "I shall submit this ambassador to another trial. He shall show us if he can shoot arrows better than my champions."

In an open meadow outside the palace, Vladimir's heroes shot their arrows at an oak tree. Each time it was hit, the oak swayed, as if it had been caught in a gust of wind. But when Vassilissa shot her arrow, the bowstring sang, and the mighty oak was felled to the ground, shattered into fragments no bigger than knifehandles.

The heroes were dumbfounded.

Vladimir spat for the second time, and he shouted resentfully to Apraksiya: "Look at that oak tree now! I'm not sorry for the tree but for the arrow! We've never seen such an archer here before, and you still believe it's a woman! Now I shall challenge the envoy myself and see if he is also supreme at chess."

He sat down with Vassilissa at an oak chess table and they played with chessmen carved from maplewood. Vassilissa won the first game, then the second and also the third. She laughed, for Vladimir had played for high stakes. Then she pushed the chessboard aside and said to the Grand Duke: "Now let's get down to business. I did not come here to feast with you, nor yet to while away the time playing chess. And the duels with your champions bore me to death. What about the tribute you owe? You have not paid it for twelve whole years. I demand two thousand gold rings for every year. Produce them here and now! The Khan of the Golden Hordes refuses to wait any longer."

Then Vladimir began to whine: "Times are bad you know. Few merchants still come to Kiev to trade, and there is little collected in taxes. Even fur-trapping brings no profit these days. How can I pay?" Then he winked an eye slyly and said in jest: "Why don't you take me and Apraksiya instead of the tribute?"

"What use are you to the Khan of the Golden Hordes? If you have no golden rings, I must take him something that will give him pleasure."

"But what would please him?" asked Vladimir.

"Have you no one who plays the gusla?"

"Yes, indeed. I have the finest gusla player in the land," said Vladimir promptly, for he suddenly remembered that Staver was a most accomplished gusla player. "He is Staver, the young boyar, and he plays the gusla better than anyone else. You may take him as a present to the Tartar Khan."

Vladimir had the yellow sand shovelled away, the iron doors of the dungeon were opened and Staver was led into the great hall. The Grand Duke handed him a gusla and placed him opposite Vassilissa, saying: "Now play for the Khan's ambassador, and then you can return with him to the Golden Hordes. I hope that that will please you."

Staver said nothing but started to play at once. First he played the Great Song of Tsargrad, then he played all the dances and the other pieces that he knew, until Vassilissa said: "He is a good player and I like him better than any tribute, and better than you and your Grand Duchess Apraksiya. I'll take him with me."

Then Vladimir's cares fell from him, and as Vassilissa and Staver rode away together with their attendants, the Grand Duke cried out joyfully: "The Khan of the Golden Hordes is welcome to that fellow Staver! My gold rings are saved. Come, my heroes! We have good reason to celebrate!"

The Devil's Trick

A Jewish folktale by Isaac Bashevis Singer.

THE SNOW had been falling for three days and three nights. Houses were snowed in and window-panes covered with frost flowers. The wind whistled in the chimneys. Gusts of snow somersaulted in the cold air.

The devil's wife rode on her hoop, with a broom in one hand and a rope in the other. Before her ran a white goat with a black beard and twisted horns. Behind her strode the devil with his cobweb face, holes instead of eyes, hair to his shoulders, and legs as long as stilts.

In a one-room hut, with a low ceiling and soot-covered walls, sat David, a poor boy with a pale face and black eyes. He was alone with his baby brother on the first night of Hanukkah. His father had gone to the village to buy corn, but three days had passed and he had not returned home. David's mother had gone to look for her husband, and she too had not come back.

The baby slept in his cradle. In the Hanukkah lamp flickered the first candle, which David himself had lit.

David was so worried he could not stay home any longer. He put on his padded coat and his cap with earlaps, made sure that the baby was covered, and went out to look for his parents.

That was what the devil had been waiting for. He immediately whipped up the storm. Black clouds covered the sky. David could hardly see in the thick darkness. The frost burned his face. The snow fell dry and heavy as salt. The wind caught David by his coattails and tried to lift him up off the ground. He was surrounded by laughter, as if from a thousand imps.

David realized the goblins were after him. He tried to turn back and go home, but he could not find his way. The snow and darkness swallowed *everything*. It became clear to him that the devils must have caught his parents. Would they get him also? But heaven and earth have vowed that

374

the devil may never succeed completely in his tricks. No matter how shrewd the devil is, he will always make a mistake, especially on Hanukkah.

The powers of evil had managed to hide the stars, but they could not extinguish the single Hanukkah candle. David saw its light and ran toward it. The devil ran after him. The devil's wife followed on her hoop, yelling and waving her broom, trying to lasso him with her rope. David ran even more quickly than they, and reached the hut just ahead of the devil. As David opened the door the devil tried to get in with him. David managed to slam the door behind him. In the rush and struggle the devil's tail got stuck in the door.

"Give me back my tail," the devil screamed.

And David replied, "Give me back my father and mother."

The devil swore that he knew nothing about them, but David did not let himself be fooled.

"You kidnapped them, cursed Devil," David said. He picked up a sharp ax and told the devil that he would cut off his tail.

"Have pity on me. I have only one tail," the devil cried. And to his wife he said, "Go quickly to the cave behind the black mountains and bring back the man and woman we led astray."

His wife sped away on her hoop and soon brought the couple back. David's father sat on the hoop holding on to the witch by her hair; his mother came riding on the white goat, its black beard clasped tightly in her hands.

"Your mother and father are here. Give me my tail," said the devil.

David looked through the keyhole and saw his parents were really there. He wanted to open the door at once and let them in, but he was not yet ready to free the devil.

He rushed over to the window, took the Hanukkah candle, and singed the devil's tail. "Now, Devil, you will always remember," he cried, "Hanukkah is no time for making trouble."

Then at last he opened the door. The devil licked his singed tail and ran off with his wife to the land where no people walk, no cattle tread, where the sky is copper and the earth is iron.

A Visit from St. Nicholas

Clement Clarke Moore

'Twas the night before Christmas, when all through the
  house
Not a creature was stirring, not even a mouse;
The stockings were hung by the chimney with care,
In hopes that St. Nicholas soon would be there;
The children were nestled all snug in their beds;
While visions of sugar-plums danced in their heads;
And mamma in her 'kerchief, and I in my cap,
Had just settled our brains for a long winter's nap—
When out on the lawn there arose such a clatter,
I sprang from my bed to see what was the matter.
Away to the window I flew like a flash,
Tore open the shutters, and threw up the sash.
The moon, on the breast of the new-fallen snow,
Gave the luster of midday to objects below;
When, what to my wondering eyes should appear,
But a miniature sleigh and eight tiny reindeer,
With a little old driver, so lively and quick,
I knew in a moment it must be St. Nick.

More rapid than eagles his coursers they came,
And he whistled, and shouted, and called them by name:
"Now, *Dasher!* now, *Dancer!* now, *Prancer* and *Vixen!*
On, *Comet!* on, *Cupid!* on, *Donder* and *Blitzen!*
To the top of the porch! to the top of the wall!
Now dash away! dash away! dash away all!"
As dry leaves that before the wild hurricane fly,
When they meet with an obstacle, mount to the sky;
So up to the house-top the coursers they flew
With the sleigh full of toys, and St. Nicholas too.

And then, in a twinkling, I heard on the roof
The prancing and pawing of each little hoof—
As I drew in my head, and was turning around,
Down the chimney St. Nicholas came with a bound.
He was dressed all in fur, from his head to his foot,
And his clothes were all tarnished with ashes and soot;
A bundle of toys he had flung on his back,
And he looked like a pedlar just opening his pack.

His eyes—how they twinkled; his dimples, how merry!
His cheeks were like roses, his nose like a cherry!
His droll little mouth was drawn up like a bow,
And the beard of his chin was as white as the snow;
The stump of a pipe he held tight in his teeth,
And the smoke it encircled his head like a wreath;
He had a broad face and a little round belly
That shook, when he laughed, like a bowl full of jelly.
He was chubby and plump, a right jolly old elf,
And I laughed when I saw him, in spite of myself;
A wink of his eye and a twist of his head
Soon gave me to know I had nothing to dread;
He spoke not a word, but went straight to his work,
And filled all the stockings; then turned with a jerk,
And laying his finger aside of his nose,
And giving a nod, up the chimney he rose;
He sprang to his sleigh, to his team gave a whistle,
And away they all flew like the down of a thistle.
But I heard him exclaim, ere he drove out of sight,
"Happy Christmas to all, and to all a good night!"

All Things Bright and Beautiful

Cecil Frances Alexander

All things bright and beautiful,
All creatures great and small,
All things wise and wonderful,
The Lord God made them all.

Each little flower that opens,
Each little bird that sings,
He made their glowing colors,
He made their tiny wings.

The purple-headed mountain,
The river running by,
The sunset, and the morning,
That brightens up the sky;

The cold wind in the winter,
  The pleasant summer sun,
The ripe fruits in the garden,
  He made them every one.

He gave us eyes to see them,
  And lips that we might tell,
How great is God Almighty,
  Who has made all things well.

Index

Acknowledgements

Care has been taken to trace ownership of copyright material contained in this book. The publishers will gladly receive any information that will enable them to rectify any reference or credit line in subsequent editions.

"All Things Bright and Beautiful" (Cecil Frances Alexander) (page 380). From *The Random House Book of Poetry for Children*, published by Random House, Inc.

"Alligator Pie" (Dennis Lee) (page 267). "Alligator Pie" © copyright 1974 by Dennis Lee. Reprinted by permission of Macmillan of Canada, A Division of Canada Publishing Corporation.

"Belling the Cat" (Aesop) (page 121). From *The Fables of Aesop* by Joseph Jacobs, published by Macmillan & Co. Ltd., London.

"The Carefree Miller" (Edith Fowke) (page 76). From *Folktales of French Canada*. Courtesy of NC Press Limited.

"The Cat and the Pain-killer" (Mark Twain) (page 233). From *The Adventures of Tom Sawyer*, published by Harper & Row Publishers, Inc.

"The Charge of the Light Brigade" (Alfred, Lord Tennyson) (page 262). Reprinted from *A Treasury of the World's Best-Loved Poems*. Copyright © 1961 by Crown Publishers, Inc. Used by permission of Crown Publishers, Inc.

"The Devil's Trick" (Isaac Bashevis Singer) (page 374). From *Zlateh the Goat and Other Stories* by Isaac Bashevis Singer. Text copyright © 1966 by Isaac Bashevis Singer. Reprinted by permission of Harper & Row, Publishers, Inc.

"Dreams" (Langston Hughes) (page 249). Copyright 1932 by Alfred A. Knopf Inc. and renewed in 1960 by Langston Hughes. Reprinted from *The Dream Keeper and Other Poems* by Langston Hughes, by permission of the publisher. Reprinted by permission of Harold Ober Associates Incorporated.

"Eeyore Loses a Tail and Pooh Finds One" (A.A. Milne) (page 241). From *Winnie-the-Pooh* by A.A. Milne. Used by permission of The Canadian Publishers, McClelland and Stewart Limited, Toronto; E.P. Dutton; and Associated Book Publishers (U.K.) Ltd. Credit for reprinting of the text is also due to Methuen Children's Books. Illustrations by E.H. Shepard copyright under the Berne Convention, reproduced by permission of Curtis Brown Ltd., London, and E.P. Dutton.

"The Elephant and His Son" (Arnold Lobel) (page 198). From *Fables* by Arnold Lobel, illustrated by the author. Copyright © 1980 by Arnold Lobel. Reprinted by permission of Harper & Row, Publishers, Inc., and Jonathan Cape Ltd.

"The Elephant's Child" (Rudyard Kipling) (page 3). From *Just So Stories*. Reprinted by permission of The National Trust and Macmillan, London Ltd.

"From Tiger to Anansi" (Philip M. Sherlock) (page 338). From *Anansi, The Spider Man* by Philip M. Sherlock (Thomas Y. Crowell). Copyright 1954 by Philip Sherlock. Reprinted by permission of Harper & Row, Publishers, Inc., and Macmillan, London and Basingstoke.

"The General's Horse" (Robert Davis) (page 251). Copyright 1939, 1948 by Robert Davis. Reprinted from *Padre Porko* by permission of Holiday House and McIntosh and Otis Inc.

"The Highwayman" (Alfred Noyes) (page 154). Reprinted from *A Treasury of the World's Best-Loved Poems*. Copyright © 1961 by Crown Publishers, Inc. Used by permission of Crown Publishers, Inc.

"How Glooskap Found the Summer" (Charles Godfrey Leland) (page 185). From *The Algonquin Legends of New England*, published by Houghton Mifflin Company.

"If you talk to animals . . ." (Chief Dan George) (page 50). Reprinted by permission of Hancock House Publishers Ltd., 19313 Zero Avenue, Surrey, B.C., Canada V3S 5J9.

"Introduction to Songs of Innocence" (William Blake) (page 240). Reprinted from *A Treasury of the World's Best-Loved Poems*. Copyright © 1961 by Crown Publishers, Inc. Used by permission of Crown Publishers, Inc.

"The Little Match Girl" (Hans Christian Andersen) (page 328). Reprinted by permission of J.M. Dent & Sons Ltd Publishers.

"Lochinvar" (Sir Walter Scott) (page 40). Reprinted from *A Treasury of the World's Best-Loved Poems*. Copyright © 1961 by Crown Publishers, Inc. Used by permission of Crown Publishers, Inc.

"The Man from Snowy River" (A.B. Paterson) (page 42). From *The Collected Verse of A.B. Paterson*. Reprinted with the permission of Angus & Robertson Publishers, Sydney, Australia, on behalf of the copyright owner. © Retusa Pty Ltd.

"Marilla Cuthbert Is Surprised" (L.M. Montgomery) (page 316). From *Anne of Green Gables* by L.M. Montgomery. With permission of Farrar, Straus and Giroux and the heirs of Lucy Maud Montgomery.

"Miraculous Hind, The" (Elizabeth Cleaver) (page 164). Reprinted by permission of Frank J. Mrazik and Rosita Mrazik Terbocz.

"Mother to Son" (Langston Hughes) (page 248). Copyright 1926 by Alfred A. Knopf Inc. and renewed in 1954 by Langston Hughes. Reprinted from *Selected Poems of Langston Hughes*, by Langston Hughes, by permission of the publisher.

"Mutt Makes His Mark" (Farley Mowat) (page 190). Reprinted by permission of Farley Mowat.

"The Origin of Stories" (Elizabeth Clark) (page 106). Reprinted by permission of American Indian Fund of the Association of American Indians.

"The Owl and the Pussy-Cat" (Edward Lear) (page 182). Reprinted from *A Treasury of the World's Best-Loved Poems*. Copyright © 1961 by Crown Publishers, Inc. Used by permission of Crown Publishers, Inc.

"Playing Pilgrims" (Louisa May Alcott) (page 347). From *Little Women* by Louisa May Alcott, published by Little, Brown and Company, Publishers.

"Rebecca" (Hilaire Belloc) (page 84). Reprinted by permission of Alfred A. Knopf, Inc., and Gerald Duckworth & Co. Ltd.

"The Shepherd's Boy" (Aesop) (page 120). From *The Fables of Aesop* by Joseph Jacobs, published by Macmillan & Co. Ltd., London.

"Song of the Witches" (William Shakespeare) (page 266). From *The Random House Book of Poetry for Children*, published by Random House, Inc.

"Staver and His Wife Vassilissa" (Hans Baumann) (page 364). From *Hero Legends of the World*. Reprinted by permission of J.M. Dent & Sons Ltd Publishers and Hans Baumann.

"Stopping by Woods on a Snowy Evening" (Robert Frost) (page 229). From *The Poetry of Robert Frost* edited by Edward Connery Lathem. Copyright 1923, © 1969 by Holt, Rinehart and Winston. Copyright 1951 by Robert Frost. Reprinted by permission of Henry Holt and Company and Jonathan Cape Ltd. Acknowledgement is also due to The Estate of Robert Frost.

"Swift Things Are Beautiful" (Elizabeth Coatsworth) (page 334). Reprinted with permission of Macmillan Publishing Company from *Away Goes Sally* by Elizabeth Coatsworth. Copyright 1934 by Macmillan Publishing Company, renewed 1962 by Elizabeth Coatsworth Beston.

"Two of Everything" (Alice Ritchie) (page 98). From *The Treasure of Li Po* by Alice Ritchie. Reproduced by permission of The Bodley Head and Harcourt Brace Jovanovich, Inc.

"The Ugly Duckling" (Hans Christian Andersen) (page 168). From *The Golden Treasury of Children's Literature*, published by Western Publishing Company, Inc., Racine, Wisconsin.

"The Village Blacksmith" (Henry Wadsworth Longfellow) (page 82). Reprinted from *A Treasury of the World's Best-Loved Poems*. Copyright © 1961 by Crown Publishers, Inc. Used by permission of Crown Publishers, Inc.

"The Wizard" (Jack Prelutsky) (page 162). From *Nightmares* by Jack Prelutsky. Copyright © 1976 by Jack Prelutsky. By permission of Greenwillow Books (A Division of William Morrow & Company).

"The Woman Who Flummoxed the Fairies" (Sorche Nic Leodhas) (page 87). From *Heather and Broom* by Sorche Nic Leodhas. Copyright © 1960 by Leclaire G. Alger. Reprinted by permission of Henry Holt and Company, Inc., and McIntosh and Otis, Inc.

The Illustrators

VictoR GAD

"Aladdin and the Wonderful Lamp"; "Alligator Pie"; "Arithmetic"; "A Mad Tea-Party"; "Nonsense Verse"; "The Owl and the Pussy-Cat"; "Rebecca"; "Song of the Witches"; "The Wizard"

Colin Gillies

"Dreams"; "The Little Match Girl"; "Mother to Son"; "The Raggedy Man"; "Introduction to Songs of Innocence"; "A Visit from St. Nicholas"; "Young Black Beauty"

Emma Hesse

"All Things Bright and Beautiful"; "Hansel and Grethel"; "The Man from Snowy River"; "Snow-White and the Seven Dwarfs"; "Stopping by Woods on a Snowy Evening"; "Swift Things Are Beautiful"

Robert Johannsen

"The Bremen Town Musicians"; "From Tiger to Anansi"; "The General's Horse"; "If you talk to animals . . ."; "Marilla Cuthbert Is Surprised"; "Playing Pilgrims"; "Staver and His Wife Vassilissa"; "The Ugly Duckling"

Peter Kovalic

"Belling the Cat"; "The Dog and His Shadow"; "The Goose with the Golden Eggs"; "The Grasshopper and the Ants"; "The Hare and the Tortoise"; "A Lion and a Mouse"; "Lochinvar"; "The Miller, His Son, and the Ass"; "The Miraculous Hind"; "Rapunzel"; "The Shepherd's Boy"; "The Town Mouse and the Country Mouse"; "A Wolf in Sheep's Clothing"

Arnold Lobel

"The Elephant and His Son"

Sharon Matthews

"The Brave Little Tailor"; "The Elephant's Child"; "How Glooskap Found the Summer"; "The Origin of Stories"; "The Woman Who Flummoxed the Fairies"

Paul McCusker

"The Cat and the Pain-killer"; "The Highwayman"; "Mutt Makes His Mark"; "The Riverbank"; "The Train Dogs"; "The Village Blacksmith"

E. H. Shepard

"Eeyore Loses a Tail and Pooh Finds One"

Henry Van Der Linde

"Baucis and Philemon"; "The Carefree Miller"; "The Charge of the Light Brigade"; "Proserpine"; "Set Sail for Treasure Island!"; "Two of Everything"